A near future novel

MOPPERS

ANONYMOUS

JON BEST

It is not reasonable that those who gamble with men's lives
should not stake their own.

-    H. G. Wells

CONTENTS:

1

QUARANTINE

L EON SWITCHED THE RADIO off for now, favouring the heavy drumming of the rain against the windshield. It consumed him, and briefly he forgot the world and its problems. Despite whirring down the country lane at high speed, he felt he could almost curl up in his cocoon of rain and thought and drift peacefully to sleep.

A road sign pulled Leon from his dreamy haze. He squinted, barely making out the distorted rectangle through the bursting droplets against his window. Recognising it as his turn, he screeched the removals van sharp to the left, skidded across both lanes, and fought the sodden tarmac for control of the wheels. Leon's electric engine whined in protest as he corrected and barely avoided being swatted from the street by an oncoming truck.

Leon pulled to the side, heart racing, and took a moment to calm himself. He let warm thoughts of whisky, radio waves, and his armchair surround him. He only noticed the approaching figure when it stepped into the headlights, and the shock set his heart racing again. The figure wore full protective gear of a sort Leon had never seen before, and it had a strange instrument hanging from its waist. The thing that caught Leon's attention, however, was the firearm in one hand, its barrel glowing a cool blue. A speaker on the figure's suit clicked alive and broadcast a voice.

"This area is under quarantine. Stay in your vehicle and turn back immediately."

Leon sat, confused. He glanced through the downpour and saw one house, barely a silhouette, covered in foam. He had previously seen the foam in the news, where he watched the government systematically foam his parents' old suburb. It was the only protective measure against the outbreak of a mysterious and supposedly deadly parasite.

More trucks like the one Leon had just passed were parked at all angles, barricading the road. A flash came from between them. Then another. He couldn't hear much through the rain, but he didn't doubt that the flashes belonged to gunshots.

The figure's speaker blared once more. "There is a detour through Highway 7. Remove yourself from this area immediately. It is for your own safety. I will not ask you again."

The figure twitched a finger and the firearm barrel darkened, turning a muddy red.

Leon pulled himself from his shock and clicked his van into reverse. He flew backwards down the road, only turning completely around once the foamed house was well out of sight. He switched on the radio, hoping to catch a broadcast about what was going on, but found nothing but pop songs and infomercials. As he sped towards Highway 7, he began calculating just how much longer the trip would now take him. He shook his head with disappointment, knowing it was going to be yet another long night on the road.

Leon adjusted the station and cranked up the volume to distract himself from the thought of an outbreak so close to the city. He could at least try to enjoy the detour. The much-disliked Discussions FM had already given way to its follow-up program, and DJ T's soothing beats soon worked their magic on Leon's stirring mind.

"Thanks to the Pepper Corns for that explo-zastic taste of the new rock that's here to shock. And now to bring this baby back to the ground with a smooth blend of melodies that will melt in your ear holes. This is DJ T, and you're listening to Ocean Air, the cooling waves that guide you home."

Like always, the radio seemed to do the trick. Leon felt as if no time at all had passed as he bumped into the customer's driveway. The customer, of course, felt differently. She was leaning against the wall of the open garage, just out of the rain, and looked as if she'd been waiting there for quite a while.

"What time do you call this?" she croaked between cigarette puffs.

Leon reluctantly climbed out of the van, re-tuning his focus from DJ T to real life. He grabbed a rain jacket from behind his seat and popped the lock for the back hatch in one practised motion. He began dropping boxes into the garage, one after another, as quickly as he could. Almost as an afterthought, he looked back at the woman and asked, "Hear anything about the roadblock back there?"

The woman flicked her cigarette into the damp earth. "Ah, roadblock, was it? I wondered when you would give me your excuse."

Leon was ready to tell the story but decided he would rather just finish the delivery sooner and get himself home. The woman sucked her teeth and disappeared into the house. With the finalising click of the lock on the hatch, Leon climbed from damp earth to driver's seat. He turned on the radio once more.

Melting back, Leon felt the first smile of the day reach his lips. He was fighting the urge to close his eyes as he pulled back onto the highway with his whining engine. DJ T's music grew over him like a fresh blanket made even warmer by the cold rain still hammering outside. Leon flew onwards into the darkness, looking forward even more to that whisky he'd promised himself.

2

DJ. T

STEPPING INTO A DARK hall, Leon dropped his keys on a side table and kicked off his shoes. He stumbled through a doorway and flicked on the light. He stood there for a moment and looked across his room. There wasn't a lot to see, but when he thought about it, he didn't know what else he needed. A large rug covered most of the otherwise bare floorboards. A desk and a bookshelf in the corner. Two armchairs, though only one had the concave shape of regular use. Opposite the chairs was a rather impressive speaker system—the one thing Leon was really proud of—accompanied by a tall radio, a phone, and a shelf of different alcohols.

He dropped his wet clothes into a pile by the door and slipped into the warm dressing gown that was draped over the back of the spare armchair. He poured himself a glass, switched on the radio, and reached for the phone. It rang just as he picked it up.

"Oh, hello?"

"Leon! Hey, man. I was wondering if I would get to speak to you today. Some damn rock band is sponsoring our channel, so after every few good songs, I gotta play one o' theirs. Was hoping for any reason not to have to actually *listen* to it."

Leon slumped in his chair, swigged his whisky, and told DJ T all about how bad his day had been. He never asked why DJ T listened. All he knew was that DJ T was the only person in the world who really knew that Leon existed, and even if it were only for a few minutes between songs, Leon looked forward to coming home and having someone to talk to.

"So the roadblock was out east by the wheat belt?" DJ T asked.

"It seemed like more than just a roadblock, but yeah, it was out that way."

"Hmmm. Seems strange that nothing has been announced. Yet another cover-up operation, no doubt."

Leon shrugged, though it did no good over the phone. "They were foaming down a house and everything. Reminded me of the zones from the news."

"Foaming? Really? Well I hope for everybody's sake they got it under control. I know some people out that way; guess I should make a few phone calls."

Leon sat in silence. He hadn't really thought about what was going on, just about how inconvenient the whole thing had been for his delivery.

DJ T pulled the conversation back. "You listen to any of that Discussions *for Morons* today?" he said with a snort. He was always coming up with alternative meanings for what the FM stood for. If there was uneasiness in DJ T's voice, Leon hadn't noticed, and he went gladly along with the subject change.

"I do my best not to. I did catch a whiff of it, though; that was enough, believe me."

They chortled together at the other radio presenter's expense. It was the only real thing the two of them had in common.

DJ T heard the rattle of ice cubes over the line. "You drinking again, man?"

"Nah… I mean yeah, just some water. Why?"

"Water? Hah! How stupid you think I am? You gotta watch it. You're gettin' the taste, man. Once you got it, ain't easy givin' it up."

"Sorry, *Mother*. Pshhh, give me a break, DJ. It calms me down."

"Hey, hey now. It ain't 'DJ'—it's 'DJ *T.*' If you just be calling me DJ, how am I supposed to know you ain't talking to any other dude with a vinyl?"

Leon decided not to point out the stupidity of this comment and instead let loose an irritated breath, making sure DJ T heard it.

"Secondly, what you mean it calms you down? That's what my music's for, ain't it?"

Leon knew he had a point there and considered putting down the glass; he didn't do it, though. There weren't that many things he looked forward to nowadays, so why should he deny himself the ones that did? Instead, he quietly refilled his glass and let DJ T ramble on about the rock band that was still using up his airtime. He didn't like them, and Leon couldn't blame him. It was the wrong program to be playing such music. After another few songs, DJ T came back on the line, and Leon—through his encroaching haze—managed to partially pay attention.

"You know, you're not alone, man. There's a group of people…"

"Ah, not another bloody support group, DJ. You know I don't have time for that."

"I've told you, it's DJ *T.* And this ain't just another support group. You gotta trust me. This place is something else. I don't just hand their info out to anyone. Plus, being honest, you'd be doing me a huge favour if you head over."

"You the ambassador of some secret club now?" Leon managed a huff.

DJ T didn't often get angry, but if Leon were a little more conscious, he might have noticed an underlying tone of frustration in his voice.

"Just trust me. I've already told them you're going. Don't let me down…"

DJ T's music lulled Leon, swaddling him in the trance of calm and stillness. As the night crawled on, he played his most relaxing tunes yet. He whispered a name across the phone line, but Leon was too busy counting sheep to respond. DJ T disconnected the call.

3

SUNRISE

A BUZZER RAISED LEON from the grips of sleep. Squirming in the armchair, he swiped away the last of the sleeping dust and stretched before heading to the adjacent room. His grogginess wouldn't last forever, and he knew it, so he pushed through the blurry-eyed stumble in the hopes that his hangover would give up and leave if he ignored it for long enough.

His removals uniform was still damp and crumpled in a corner, so without time for a proper wash, he hung it crudely by the curtain-drawn window. After slipping into a generic T-shirt and jeans, Leon headed outside.

His hazy mind told him he'd locked the front door behind him last night, so whether he actually had or not wasn't much of a bother. He shimmied past the removals van, which took up most of the width of the driveway, and stepped onto the footpath. Something squeezed into his thoughts, and for a second, he stopped, glanced back at the van, and let a few mumbled profanities pass his lips. In his rush to get home last night, he'd forgotten to take the van back to the yard, which meant that it wouldn't have been loaded overnight and that he was in for yet another extended day of work. Not wanting to miss the whole point of waking up this early, however, he made a mental note to deal with it later.

The top of his road opened into a T junction where the traffic had already reached a dizzying blur. Leon took a couple of minutes to listen to the whining electric engines flowing mostly towards the city, and he pitied every single driver that passed. They were so busy rushing back and forth that they were about to miss the best thing that would happen today.

Leon headed uphill. He stepped away from the main road and onto a side street, partially because of the noise but mostly because it was the longer route. He didn't want the morning walk to end so soon, as it meant another day's work would almost be upon him. He slowed and eyed the dark of the sky giving way to an orange glow. He was a bit later than usual, but not so late as to miss the second half of the sunrise.

He neared the peak of the hill, and as he walked, the entire city unfolded beneath him. The sun was high enough to start reflecting golden balls of light from any surface it hit.

Leon had refrained from activating his contact lenses so far, as he didn't like the way their UV tint distorted the colours.

In the wash of light, it seemed as if the city, and those who resided there, were being purged of all wrongdoing. The filthy inhabitants of the filthy streets were being given a second chance for the millionth time. Leon often wondered if this was why he enjoyed coming up here as much as he did. He felt that whoever he'd let down was reaching out to him now with forgiveness, and for that brief moment, he was completely at peace with himself. The moment never lasted long enough, and already the sun was losing its warm glow and becoming harsh and bright. The phrase "blink and you will miss it" came to Leon's mind, and to his surprise, he felt his insides grinding. This wasn't about people accidentally blinking and missing it; this was about people blatantly refusing to take the few seconds out of their schedules to actually look. That is why they missed it. It was no accident—it was neglect. And those people, so busy working their fingers to the bone or playing games with other people's money, would never realise what was most important in life.

Leon's mind rant stopped as he spotted a scanner-craft floating high above the city, just beneath cloud level. It was moving, ever so slowly, with its beams licking the buildings below. It was searching for someone. Leon tried to guess what the person might have done to warrant having scanners sent after them. He pictured a man on the run, hiding out in empty apartments, peering over ledges, and feeling his bowels loosen as a beam washed over his location.

A crunch of leaves behind Leon made his heart jump. It was a sound he rarely heard so close to the city. The trees Leon was used to seeing—if any at all—were a sort of plastic and didn't drop their leaves. He looked back.

The sight of a retreating figure, her curled shining hair caught in the wind, doused Leon's lingering bitterness. He felt something in his chest. Only a subtle thing, but it was definitely there. For as long as he could remember, he had been the only person to watch the sunrise. This spot had always been his, and he wasn't sure what to make of sharing it with another. Naturally, his thoughts were defensive, but he also felt a sense of pride that maybe he had led the way for another lost soul in this ever-growing city. The woman slid down the hill and turned out of sight.

He wondered what the woman had thought when she saw him there. He turned back to the view and saw the sun shine through the haze. What once looked like a golden city of promise now looked like any other smoggy sky over a pile of bricks, concrete, and machinery. With the sunrise well and truly finished, he tapped his temples to activate his contact lenses, which darkened the view. As he did so, he heard a vibration and pulled an old phone from his jacket pocket. The screen showed a phone number he really didn't want to answer right now. He sighed.

"It's Leon."

"What's wrong with you? It's not a hard job. Take the van, drop stuff off, and bring the van back. I get a late phone call with a customer complaint, yet again, and I wake up this morning to see my van still missing. Listen, I know you seem to find life difficult, and I've tried helping you, but I can't keep this up. Bring me the van back, we'll square the money, and then you're done. Think you can manage that?"

Leon huffed. "I'm sorry, Deano. There was a roadblock, and—"

"Look, I don't want to hear it. Just be decent enough to return the van this morning, would you? Don't keep me waiting all day."

The phone clicked. Leon stared down at his handset. He wasn't completely surprised by the call, but that didn't mean he was prepared for it. Still feeling too murky to make any decisions on the matter, he put the phone back into his pocket, tightened the jacket around his shoulders, and walked down towards the grime of the city.

4

SELF HELP

PULLING HIS COAT CLOSE, Leon fought off the wind one step at a time. He had returned the van and used most of his payment to restock his liquor cabinet. The rest of the day passed in a slow, self-defeating blur until the setting sun beckoned him into the brisk air of a cool evening. With his head still reeling from losing his job and the cocktails that followed, Leon decided to go for a walk in the outside air. He thought the light rain might refresh him and was disappointed when its gentle pattering turned into a blunt assault as the breeze grew into a gale. Even so, walks on evenings like this did make him feel alive. What he was doing with that life, and what it would amount to, was anybody's guess. Sometimes Leon felt these thoughts calming and therapeutic, though tonight, they seemed to ignite an anxiety deep in his chest. He increased his pace, hoping to find something, anything, that would give him direction. He pulled a small flask from his jacket pocket and took a swig, feeling the liquid burn his throat but soothe his nerves.

There was a *crunch* beneath his shoe, and he looked down to see the back half of a cockroach splattered across the pavement. He felt bad. This little creature was also just out for a stroll, taking in the town, before a misplaced step so suddenly ruined his night. Leon's compassion quickly evaporated, however, as the remains of the roach twitched alive and continued to crawl across the pavement slab, spilling a trail of guts and eggs as it went. A now intentionally placed step finished the job with one last *crunch*. With open disgust, Leon continued his stumbling through the streets. He devoured the sights and smells and navigated the crowds like a drunken sailor. He hummed to the tune of whining engines and near-empty beggars' tins. He scoffed at suits and talked to the traffic. All the while, thoughts of that cockroach scuttled through his mind—thoughts that told him he was no better than the crushed bug whose entrails still clung desperately to the bottom of his shoe.

The rain intensified, and like many others in the street before him, Leon began searching for a dry place to wait it out. The shop fronts were already filled with people huddling beneath awnings and doorways and arches. Somewhere further down the street, a group of silhouettes stood in a strange arrangement on the footpath as a slow-moving scanner-craft, hidden in the darkness above the city, sheltered them from part of the downpour. Not wanting to get cosy with either group, Leon spotted a blinking "open" sign and headed over. He pushed his way through a few people at the entrance and stumbled into a hall, which was much grander-looking than he had expected. The tiled floor was slippery, and spattered black footprints made their way to one of the last doorways on the right. Not wanting to hang out with the huddled figures behind him, Leon followed the marks to the doorway, listening for any clues as to what was happening inside.

As he approached, a pimple-faced youth skulked into the hall and bowed his head. He looked up at Leon and managed a smile. "Hi."

Unsure of the youth's intentions, Leon nodded at him.

"You can have my seat. No one cares about me anyway. I knew this would be a waste of time." He walked past Leon and out towards the street exit.

Confused but now intensely curious, Leon poked his head around the doorway and saw a few small clusters of people standing around tables of food and drink and one large group sat in a semicircle at the back. One member was stood at the head of the semicircle, talking to the rest about something he obviously found emotional. The others were just staring and maybe nodding occasionally.

Leon casually walked up to the closest group and reached straight for a slice of cake. The group continued its whispered conversation, not paying any attention. Only after Leon reached for a second slice did one man look over, gold tooth glinting. "Yo, friend. I don't believe we've met. Been here before?" He extended a hand to Leon, who took it confidently.

"Second time, actually, but I tend to keep my head down. My name's Sam," Leon lied.

The man's smile grew, and the others of the group stepped away to continue their conversation at the end of the table. "Well, it's nice to meet ya, Sam. My name's Tyrone. So what are ya? Labourer? Road sweep?" Tyrone let Leon's hand go slowly, feeling for calloused skin as he did so. He pursed his lips and nodded to himself, as if he had already answered his own question.

"I'm a delivery man."

"Ah yes, we've had a few of those in the past."

A man hobbled over, shook hands with Tyrone, and growled at him with what was left of his throat. One side of his body was badly damaged by what looked like a chemical-burn incident. There was no way a normal fire would have left such a mess. He nodded at Leon, then hobbled away.

Tyrone leaned in close to Leon and lowered his voice. "He's from a generation of vat cleaners. Been attending *MA* for twelve years."

As Leon tried to keep his composure at the sight of the man, Tyrone examined him. His smile faded and was replaced by something else. "Well, you got plenty of folks around here. Feel free to mingle. After all, that's what we are all about." Tyrone pointed over to one group in the far corner. "Just watch yourself with the exterminators. They tend to get a little too much exposure to their own bug spray, if you know what I'm sayin'. These guys here are into some sort of philosophy, always talking about the *powers that be* and whatnot. Those down at the horseshoe are the ones experiencing a rough patch in their lives at the moment. You take turns and talk about it and help each other out. Maybe you would like to start there."

There was something familiar about the way Tyrone spoke, but not wanting to raise any more suspicion around himself, Leon took the opportunity to slip away and headed for the semicircle. As the young man at the entrance had mentioned, there was a spare seat, and Leon sat quietly, not wanting to interrupt the girl whose turn it was to pour her heart out to the group.

The girl held a broom in both hands and was demonstrating a twist-flick technique. She had witnessed someone using it at a restaurant to quickly disperse larger chunks of food under the counters instead of properly sweeping them up. Suddenly panicked that the group might think she also swept this way, she went on to explain that it wasn't at all how *she* did business, then demonstrated her own technique. Most people just stared, mouths agape, and if their eyes weren't following the rocking motion of the broom handle, Leon would have thought they were all asleep. It was only when the girl retrieved the mop that a lanky man from the group pushed his thick-framed glasses high upon his nose and jumped to his feet.

"And what an excellent job you do, Grace. Really, I speak from personal experience. I ate there myself last week and, wouldn't you know, the floor was immaculate!" The man rushed to the girl's side and tried to sit her down while still chattering away about how little dust or dirt he'd seen.

The girl with the broom shed a tear and fell heavily to her seat. "Do you really mean it? I didn't think anyone had noticed."

The man nodded fiercely in reply and snatched the mop. He wasn't about to let that snivelling girl try to outdo his own mopping technique! Without introduction, he began faux-mopping the carpet, humming a tune to the movement of his arms and twists of his wrists. Almost instantly, the crowd started guffawing and nudging each other's shoulders with a *here he goes again!*

"Get out, you bloody show-off!" One man laughed, waving a dismissing hand. The mopping man added a quick manoeuvre into his dance and the mop flicked towards the heckler's face. He finished this off with a spin before going back to mopping the carpet at an increasing pace. This made one or two burst into hysterics. "Legend! Absolute legend!" cried a woman, slapping her knee. The whole display ended with jazz-hands before the man slumped back into his chair and high-fived his admiring fans. Trying to stay undercover, Leon got in on the action and threw a few high-fives to the people around him, including the mopping man himself.

One of the younger members of the group darted off to fetch the man some water. Only after he drained the glass did the others calm down. The man looked over at Leon once quiet had been restored. "Fresh meat, huh? Welcome to Moppers Anonymous. I'm Roger. Friend's call me King Neptune, but you can opt out of using a name if you like. I've been mopping floors down at city hall since I was old enough to work." Cool as a cat, he flicked the mop over to Leon and smirked. "Now let's see what you've got."

Leon reached for the mop handle too slowly and it slipped, clattering to the ground. A sudden lull fell over the room as everyone looked at Leon. As he bent to pick it up, someone nearby snorted. Others tutted and whispered.

King Neptune stepped to Leon's side. "Hey now, is this how we treat a fellow brother in arms?"

The scoffing subsided, and once King Neptune felt he had enough attention aimed back at him, he kicked his foot out and jerked it up, letting the mop roll up his leg, before he spun it around his knee and caught it firmly in one hand. He flashed his teeth again. *A smile that makes you hate a man*, Leon thought.

King Neptune went back to showing off to his fan group, so Leon walked back to the cake table. As absurd as this meeting seemed, he could see why the others attended. It was a place for the people that didn't belong anywhere else, and although he hated to admit it, Leon was one of those people. Despite the embarrassing situation he just found himself in and the glowing he felt in his cheeks, he couldn't help but smile. He felt better having had a genuine laugh, and he also felt better knowing that he wasn't as far gone as these sad souls.

Leon thought back to his previous conversation with DJ T. There'd been talk of a support group—a relatively unknown group that DJ T was sure could help Leon. Then he realised that Moppers Anonymous was the group DJ T had mentioned the night before. This was the place.

Leon felt his cheeks glow red again, this time with a different sort of embarrassment. Was this how his friend viewed him? Removing the flask from his coat pocket, Leon took a quick pull and let the drink burn his mouth. He breathed in deep and held his breath. The drum of his heart was loud but slowing. One more mouthful from his flask.

"Sam. Hey, man. I'm sorry to say that this is an alcohol-free organisation." Tyrone looked down meaningfully at the flask in Leon's hand. Leon stood for a moment, considering walking out there and then, but couldn't bring himself to step away from the free cake just yet. He tucked the flask back into his coat. Tyrone nodded. "I appreciate it. Look, maybe this isn't quite your style. There's another member I would like you to meet. He's in the lounge."

Leon made to respond, but Tyrone spoke over him. "I think I understand you, Sam. This guy may just be able to offer what you're looking for." He headed over to a side door, removing a seemingly unnecessary number of keys from his back pocket. He flicked through them for a second, turned the lock, and waved Leon inside. Leon took a few cautious steps and peeked around the doorframe. The lounge was small but looked comfortable enough. There were four armchairs, three of which were empty. The entire room seemed to exist purely for its one occupant—an almost giant of a man sat facing the corner, mohawk shimmering from the log fire nearby. Leon made to step back, but a forceful push sent him stumbling into the lounge, where he landed face-first on a rug. The door swung shut and latched behind him.

The man in the room stood and stretched slowly, as if he were unfolding. He turned to Leon, lit a cigar, and took a long, slow drag. His good eye looked almost as cold and hard as his mechanical one, which buzzed quietly as it focused its vision. His sleeves were rolled up above his elbows, the stitching taut against his biceps. His thick belt had pockets sewn in, which held small packets of what looked like more cigars, and Leon didn't doubt that the stubble on the man's jaw was enough to light them.

On the table beside the man's armchair was an open file, and after the cigar smoke had cleared and the man was satisfied, he looked down at some documents. A thick finger followed a few lines of text, and he nodded and mumbled to himself. "Right. Leon. Removals van driver. Nine point three..." He flicked over a page, read something else, and let free a throaty chuckle. "Good, good." He took another drag of the cigar and looked back at Leon, who was now standing atop shaking legs.

"How do you know my name?" Leon asked.

The man ignored the question. "Okay, kid. Here's the deal. I need a driver. A *good* driver, and you've been recommended. Whatever the removals are paying you, consider it tripled, but I need an answer right away. You interested?"

"Well..." Leon looked around the room once more, giving himself time to slow his thoughts. "I suppose I am in the market for a new job."

The man laughed. "Perfect."

He tossed some car keys at Leon, whose hand lashed out and caught them instinctively. The man nodded again. "There's a vintage guzzler out back. If I'm impressed, then you're hired. If not, well..." The man considered his words. Leon's mind flashed back to the ass end of the cockroach, and he grimaced.

"Yeah, you seem to get the gist," the man growled. "So are you ready?"

5

TRIAL BY TYRE

THE MYSTERIOUS MAN exited to the lane. He watched Leon intently but said nothing since the lounge. Leon pictured a retro-style hot rod waiting in the laneway—something old, noisy, and mostly just for show. What he found was much, much more than that. This petrol's body was low, sleek, and mysterious. It sported quad exhausts and mirrored windows, and when Leon clicked the key's remote, the doors hissed and lifted.

Leon's jaw dropped. "Butterfly doors?"

Without a word, the man folded his arms, still examining Leon. Leon stumbled towards the car, doing his best not to grin like a child, and climbed in. He waited for the man to jump into the passenger's seat before he roared the engine to life. Leon was unable to contain his excitement any longer, and his foot found the floor and the car tore backwards. The next few minutes passed in a cocktail of octane combustion and adrenaline.

Screeching to a halt, Leon tilted his head sideways, smirking at the passenger. They eyed each other cautiously. The passenger took a long drag on his cigar and blew a deep blue cloud into the tight gap between them. Leon heard the lens over his left eye quietly buzzing and refocusing as the smoke swirled. Only once the air cleared did a grin split his face.

"You keep drivin' like that, kid, and we could make some *real* money."

Leon took the passenger's hand and gave it a firm shake before returning to the steering wheel. Once more, the world around him faded. Once more it was just him and the growl of the engine.

6

WHOS THE BOSS?

L EON CONTINUED TOWARDS the sign, its green tinge caressing the stagnant shadows with each flicker. He folded his directions and tore the paper into a few small pieces before scattering them down the closest drain, as per the mysterious employer's instructions.

Reaching what looked like the end of the alley, Leon looked up at the sign, which read "Pizza Open," and wondered if he had found the right place. A driveway wrapped around the building and led to a small car park on the other side. Next to where he stood, out of sight from the main road, was a door.

He tried the handle cautiously, and at his touch, the door swung wide and a thick cloud of cigar smoke escaped. Leon turned away, coughing. As the smoke thinned, a figure appeared in the doorway. Blinking the sting from his eyes, Leon watched the figure bow his head slightly as he stepped outside, his mohawk brushing the doorframe.

Leon froze but kept his eyes fixed on the towering man before him, whom he recognised from Moppers Anonymous the night before. They stood in the alley and faced each other.

The mohawked giant took a drag of the stubby cigar clamped between his teeth, as seemed to be his habit, and watched the newcomer carefully. As before, he only smiled once the air had cleared. "Howdy, kid."

The man gripped Leon's shoulder and pulled him inside, slamming the door with his free hand. A thick bolt fell across it. Any greeting on the man's face had already made way for a serious gaze.

"Toilets there, storeroom here, kitchen through there—it's off limits—chiller room just here." He showed Leon each door in turn as they marched down the passageway towards the front of the building.

"Here's your keys, there's your car, and here's where the pizzas come through." He slammed his hand down on a silver unit with a large opening at the front.

"Always take the payment first. No money, no drop-off. Don't tamper with the delivery or the payments. Don't mix the deliveries up. Don't hang about after the transaction is done. We don't run on friendly, smiley service here; we run on reliability and speed. Got that?"

Leon nodded, quite liking the idea of not having to talk to his customers.

The boss told him of a satchel under the driver's seat, but before he could elaborate on the contents, a buzz sounded and a heat-wrapped bag appeared in the chute. The display on top indicated that the contents were currently ninety-eight per cent purity at sixty-four degrees. The boss grabbed the bag and handed it to Leon.

"Whatever you need should be in the satchel. Tuck the rest back under your seat. Never take it out of the car. I can't afford to keep replacing lost gear."

Leon nodded, then exited the blue cloud of the shop and stepped into the grime of the car park and the smells that came with it. Before him sat the car from the previous night; the only difference was that the license plates had been removed. For a moment, he wondered if this really was the car his boss had meant for him to drive. It looked far too expensive to lend to an employee. He scanned the car park, but in the dim light coming from the window behind him, he saw nothing but empty bays. The boss exploded from the shop door.

"Get movin', kid!"

Leon poked his elbow in the direction of the car. "There's no plates. Should I be..." He trailed off as the boss's head met the boss's palm. "Yeah. No plates. So what?"

"I don't want to get a ticket."

"Why do you think you're drivin' a petrol? See a cop, put ya foot down. Anythin' else?"

Leon frowned but said nothing as he watched the boss disappear into his familiar cloud. Leon tried the zapper on his keychain and the doors hissed open, heated fur seats inviting him inside. He smiled, remembering how powerful he felt in this motor car and wondering how he could ever go back to using standard vehicles after working here.

With a deep rumble, the engine rocked the frame of the car alive, and Leon idled there, attuning himself to the sound and the feel. It was only now, compared to the combustion engine's growl filling his ears, that he properly noticed the high-pitch whine of the electric vehicles gliding down the road behind him. He smirked at the slowness of the headlights crossing his mirrors and wondered how many of those drivers had even *seen* the type of car he was sitting at the wheel of.

A burst of static pulled Leon from his reverie. The hairs on his neck stood at attention as the sound filled the car. The static came again, this time accompanied by a vibration and a speck of light. He looked down to see that it was coming from the satchel the boss had mentioned. He opened it. Inside was a navigation system displaying a whole bunch of dots, the brightest of which was moving very fast.

The static formed into a voice. "Yo, Cookie, is that you? Cookie, where you been, man?"

The device must have switched itself on when the engine started. Leon placed it in a small holder on the dash and saw that his destination was already written at the top of the screen.

"Is something goin' on down there? Cookie?"

"Hi," was all Leon managed. He wasn't even sure if the other person would hear him properly.

"Oh, shit! Something *is* going on! Who the hell is this?"

"I'm Leon, the new guy. Just about to…"

"Ahh, so you're the rookie replacing Cookie, huh? 'Bout time someone did. He won't be happy knowing you're using his comms, though, man. His rep is in your hands. Don't disappoint!"

Leon's excitement took a back seat for a moment. This job wasn't about toying with past-world cars; it was big business. The boss's words from the night before were beginning to sink in.

The comms on the dashboard lit up once more. "Name's Xiao Qing Long, by the way, but everyone just calls me Voice. Boss has quite a reputation in this city, so I wouldn't expect problems—but if you find yourself in a spot, man, just holler. I won't be too far away. Good luck, Leon."

With shoulders relaxing once more, Leon sank back into the fur, smoothed the steering wheel, and backed out of the parking bay. With a gear shift and his foot to the floor, he merged into the heavy flow of traffic, cutting left and right between the vehicles whirring and whining around him.

7

SKIPPED A BEAT

THE LAST ARROW ON THE navigation screen pointed left, and with a hard pull on the steering wheel, the car leaned and caught the force with its suspension, gliding around the bend. Leon muted the radio and peered out into the night. He had slowed right down, trying to make out the dim numbers on each letterbox. Some had rusted away, some were only faint scratches, and some numbers were plain missing.

Six, twelve, sixteen…

By counting driveways from the last number he could see, he managed to guess which house was the one he was looking for. It stood right at the end of the cul-de-sac, so he rolled from the road and straight up the curb. With the engine still running, Leon hopped out, dragging the pizza bag with him, and strolled up the front lawn.

Ding dong.

Waiting by the door, Leon felt a slight chill on the breeze, whenever it bothered to blow his way. His skin raised, and he pulled the bag of pizzas closer to his chest, the warmth filling the front of his open jacket. He rang the bell again, but after another gust of chilled air, he decided to wait in the car until he saw the front door open. A sound poked at him from inside the house as he climbed back into the warmth of the car, but the front door remained closed. He turned the radio back on and sat, bobbing his head to the music and tooting the car horn in hopes that the customer might hear.

After another long minute of waiting, Leon remembered the satchel, pulled it from under his seat, and absentmindedly flicked through the contents. Cookie had left his driver's license in one of the pockets, so Leon placed it in the coin holder to hand to Boss later. Beside the license was a gas-go coupon for twenty-five per cent off the next full tank refuelled on the go. The slogan on the back shimmered slightly and Leon flipped the coupon over and read it: "When you *can't* afford to stop but you *can* afford not to." He dug around in the satchel some more. In the larger back pocket were some glasses and a crumpled cigarette. Leon flicked the specs onto his face, expecting his vision to blur, but nothing happened. The lenses seemed to be plain glass.

Leon hit the cigarette lighter on the car's console and lit up. Cigarette in mouth and glasses on nose, he climbed out of the car, balancing pizzas in hand, and made his way back to the door. Something stopped him from trying the bell, however: a shimmer across the bottom of his vision.

He blinked hard, looking around him, hoping it was only a moth or something flying past his headlights. He heard or saw nothing, though, and turned back to the doorway, taking another shallow drag of the cigarette. As he exhaled, the shimmer appeared again, and this time he made out a cluster of lines forming a familiar shape: the shape of a human being. It was lying down. As Leon looked through another cloud of exhaled smoke, the lines looked as if they were coming from inside the building, like they were glowing through the door.

Leon raised his specs and saw nothing more than a cloud of cigarette smoke. He puffed another cloud, closer to the door, and let the specs fall back over his eyes. The lines were the human's veins and arteries. They glowed gently now, and the pulse was noticeably slowing.

Leon tossed the cigarette aside, then stepped up and faced the door, noticing it was slightly ajar. Dread churned in his stomach, and without thinking about it, he decided to enter the house. He ducked slightly, not knowing why, and moved his hand slowly to the door handle. He pushed the door lightly and it creaked at the hinge. Risking a glance inside, he confirmed what he saw. In a bloody heap just in front of him was a dying man, face-down, with multiple holes in his back. Despite the man's blood-covered uniform, he was undoubtedly a police officer. But there was also something that Leon's heartbeat specs hadn't revealed: there was a second figure standing over the dying man, and her piercing eyes stared straight into Leon's.

8

COUGH MEDICINE

A FLYING CHAIR CAUGHT LEON in the chest, launching him backwards and out of the doorway. He landed in a flower bed on the front lawn and rolled to his feet, then dove through the window of the passenger's seat, leaving the pizza bag behind. The front door of the house was blown from its hinges as the woman jolted onto the front lawn, head twitching left and right, before she focused on Leon.

Leon's car was down the drive and clumping onto the road with a mighty roar. The house's security system awoke, screaming sirens and machine-gun fire. Leon spun the wheel and the car turned almost a perfect one-eighty before drifting down the street in a stream of burning rubber and exhaust fumes.

"Voice? Voice, man! I need your help."

The comms lit up immediately. "En route, Broseph. What's the problem?"

"First delivery. The glasses. There was a person. Front door was open so I looked in. There's this woman and… and a dead man. A dead cop. Something strange about this woman. Uh, she moved so quickly. She chased me from the house. I think she's after me. Last thing I saw was her driving out of the garage. Well, *through* the garage, actually. Set all the alarms off."

"She moved fast? Like, what do you mean?"

"Sort of… jolty, I guess. I dunno."

"What about the glasses?"

"From the satchel. They showed me his heartbeat, but not hers."

"Hmm, only one reason for that I can think of. It seems you've made a hell of a first impression."

"Who is it?"

"Never mind. Hey, listen. Just keep driving. I've got your position. I will come to you. Whatever you do, don't go back to the shop. Keep your eyes forward and your foot down. This chick isn't going to be far behind."

Leon made to reply but a spray of fence posts and solar lamps interrupted him. The pursuing vehicle burst from between two houses and slid into the side of Leon's car, forcing him across the divider line and into oncoming traffic as the glasses flew off his face. Leon turned to correct his course but overcompensated, bumping back over the line and up the curb and ripping through a hedge on one of the front lawns. Able to hear the other vehicle's engine whirring behind him, he dropped two gears and pulled back onto the road.

The gap between the two cars grew slowly, and with a little bit of swerving, Leon thought he'd get away. Then something penetrated his back tyres. He risked a glance behind him and saw that the pursuing vehicle had a broken window and the driver had somehow thrown shards of glass and pierced one of Leon's back tyres.

Leon leaned forwards in his chair, willing the car to move faster, but he could feel the back end slowing him down as the front wheels struggled to drag it along.

"Dammit, Voice, she's gonna catch up. Where are you?"

"My screen says I'm just ahead, but I can't see… Oh, there you are." Ahead of Voice, a plume of black smoke rose above the traffic where the pursuer rammed into the back of Leon, causing him to skid in a zigzag, tyres churning with the force. Voice ripped up his handbrake and let his car screech sideways towards Leon, who *just* drove past before Voice closed the gap between him and the pursuer. The pursuer slammed hard into the side of Voice as another car slammed into his other side. Another vehicle joined the pile-up. Then another.

Leon checked his mirror, and the sight of the crash forced his gut to flip.

"Voice? Voice!" The line was dead. Not even the hopeful sound of static came through his comms. Voice's car had been completely crushed.

Leon scanned the road quickly, trying to keep control of his shaking body, and only when he saw that no one had made it through the pile-up did he head back to the shop.

9

LOCKDOWN

LEON SLID INTO THE FAMILIAR blue haze, where Boss stood waiting, slightly agitated.

"Voice just went offline. Know anything about that?"

Leon tried hard to swallow the lump in his throat. His reply sounded more like a cough. "Crash." He paused. "A huge pile-up. He was trying to help me. Someone was chasing me."

Boss's face burned red, and he punched the wall beside him, splitting a tile.

"Motherfucker!" he growled to himself, then seemed to try taking a few deep breaths before giving up. He growled and punched the tiles again, cutting his finger on the glaze. "He knows how much these goddamn stunts of his costs me!" In search for someone to blame, Boss's eyes fell on Leon, who spoke quickly as his own anger ignited.

"Cost? I've just told you that Voice was crushed right in front of me!"

Leon flinched as Boss bellowed, but instead of the string of insults he expected, it was a laugh. A deep, loud laugh, which instantly reduced Leon to the nervous new kid he was. His shoulders ached from their sudden retraction, and he felt like a cornered animal pinned between a wall and a madman. It took a few seconds for Boss's next words to even register in his petrified brain.

"Voice is fine, kid. Jesus Christ..." He broke off into laughter once again. "He just gets bored sometimes. Wants to show off, does something stupid. Then I've gotta pay for the damn clean-up crew." His bloody hand struck the wall once more, but this time it was more to make a statement than out of anger.

"Who was after you, anyway? Probably those environmentalists again..." Apparently uninterested in Leon's response, Boss turned towards the kitchen.

"I don't know who it was. She had jolty movements, and Voice seemed to think she was bad news. It looked like she had just killed a cop. Should we call the police?"

Boss stopped dead in his tracks. He turned slowly, shoulders hunched, and stared at Leon. In one swift motion, he withdrew his cigar, launched himself against the front wall, and collected Leon in the process. He held him by the scruff and up against the tiles.

"Did she follow you here?" Spittle leapt onto Leon's face, but he made no move to wipe it. He watched Boss patiently. When he felt it safe to open his mouth, he started from the beginning, explaining what he had seen and what happened after. Only once the story was finished did Boss think to relax his grip on Leon, who immediately slipped out of Boss's reach.

Boss didn't lash out, though. In fact, something else replaced the anger in his face. He darted to the window and stole a glance before running into the kitchen. He re-emerged with what looked like a TV remote, hooked it into a wall socket, and set to work on a series of buttons and switches behind the counter.

"Now, I don't have a clue who sent her after *you*, but I don't need her finding *me*. This place is going on lockdown. Since you've destroyed my eyes on the streets, I need you to replace Voice for the time being. I've got some calls to make."

Boss shoved Leon towards the back entrance and half pushed, half threw him into the alley. In one long string and with barely a noticeable pause, he reeled off instructions to Leon, who was still straightening his shirt. "You gotta get Voice's comms back, kid, before anyone else goes snooping around the wreck. And get the pizza stack from the house while you're at it. If you find anything at all, be sure to report it to me. I will contact you in a couple of hours via the comms. Be sure to be somewhere safe by then."

Without warning, shutters came down across the doors and windows, making Leon jump at the slam. He stood there for a moment, staring dumbfounded at where Boss had been, and tried to process the information spat at him. A thousand thoughts crossed his mind, and he fought the urge to go bolting down the alley in the opposite direction of where Voice had crashed. He stood there for a long while, his rational mind fighting with his moral compass. It was clear that Boss really needed his help here, but just going home and forgetting about everything definitely felt like the smarter choice.

Leon remembered his small, almost empty home and his beloved whisky cabinet. He thought about how long he might keep it after the bills started piling up. He needed to decide whether he would give up on everything, including himself, or take Tyrone's recommendation, stay with the Pizza Boss, and see how it ended. He looked down at himself absently and only noticed then that his finger was still through the loop of the car keys. This told him all he needed to know. He nodded to himself and jogged around the alley, back towards the front of the shop. Maybe he would help Boss. Maybe he wouldn't. Either way, he knew he shouldn't just leave such a noticeable car parked in plain view. If that woman was looking for him, it would lead her straight here.

Leon replaced the shredded wheel with the spare from the boot and rolled the car out of the car park. He pulled down a side road and took off at speed, away from the pizza shop and away from Voice. The tune coming through the speakers took hold of him as he flew down another side road, headed for anywhere away from prying eyes.

10

THE RUNNER

MARBLES WAS GOOD AT THIS JOB. That didn't mean he liked it. The joviality and false smiles seemed to play games with his mind, but when the customers were happy, the manager was happy, and if the manager was happy, then his hourly rate went up. That was how Marbles did business, anyway. Whether the manager was aware of it or not was of no concern to him.

"Yes, sir?"

"Cappuccino to go."

"Certainly. And you, ma'am?"

"Flat white, six sugars."

"Uh, okay. Yep, coming right up."

One hand clicked buttons while the other collected money. By lunchtime, Marbles had sweated out most of his energy, so he headed to the back of the store, scribbled his name on the roster, and docked himself a fifteen-minute break. No, make that a thirty-minute break, as he was feeling peckish and wanted enough time to enjoy a few slices of pizza.

He was half-tempted to join the customers up on the balcony, but that probably would have broken a few policies, so he settled on staying in the car park, tucked behind an astro-tree. Producing a doggy bag from the back pocket of his trousers, Marbles slowly nibbled at his lunch, enjoying the buzz washing forwards from the back of his brain. He didn't really care who saw him, but in the interest of the Coffee Stop, he did his best to conceal his actions so as not to look unprofessional. He did a good job at keeping a casual look about him, too, and it was only when he started heading back inside that he heard the enraged growls behind him.

"Hey! What have you got there? Excuse me. I'm talking to you…"

Marbles turned to see a bloated man with a manager's badge storming towards the door, his arms waving. Marbles's ridiculous grin stopped him in his tracks. The manager replaced his anger with confusion. "Who the hell are you?"

Marbles glanced back at the till and thought about the six hours of work that he had yet to pay himself for. He tried to think of something that would let him back into the shop one more time. "I'm with the Agency. Just here to…"

"I didn't call the Agency. I've got all my staff members on duty today." The manager thrust his keys repeatedly in Marbles's direction, a little too close for comfort. "What are you up to?" The manager glanced through the window and saw everything running smoothly but didn't like the fact that an unknown person was in his shop and impersonating a staff member. His eyes narrowed as he examined Marbles, whose own bloodshot eyes had started to twitch.

Marbles hated the days he didn't get paid. He should have taken the money in advance. It was these amateur mistakes that made his job so difficult. He had to focus more. For now, though, it seemed like he needed to cut his losses and flee the scene. If he was lucky, the manager wouldn't be able to identify him to the Agency, who still had some of his details on file. If he kept making these damn mistakes, someone would eventually piece it together, putting him fast out of a job—or worse.

Marbles ran as shouts followed him down the road. He wasn't sure if the manager would give chase by car, so he ducked down alleys when he could, avoided main roads, and turned his shirt inside out to hide the logo and the iconic Coffee Stop colour.

He took the most complicated route he could find, doing his best the whole time to drown out the teasing voice in his head. It never had anything new to say anyway—just the same string of hindsight remarks that never did anybody any good. All he wanted now was to be at home with a fresh Portofino pizza and to feel his troubles drown in the musical waves of his favourite radio show, hosted by DJ T.

11

ALLEY CATS

A FIGURE CAUGHT THE WOMAN'S EYE. She stood in the harsh midday sun, watching him string together rolls, leaps, and sideways darts. He crossed a rooftop, climbed down a ladder, and sprinted through an alley and into the next street along. As she glanced down the street, past the acrobatic figure, she saw nothing but a leaf of trash caught in a gust of air. Whoever was following this figure had long since been left in the dust. Pushing back a golden lock of hair, the woman removed a cigarette from behind an ear and stepped out from the shadows. She walked as fast as she could while still looking casual, hoping to reach the end of the alley and once again observe the running figure.

Swatting a wolf whistle with a shake of her hips, the golden-haired woman kept her gaze forwards. She had no time to waste on the advances of the men around her, as every second meant more distance between her and the man she wanted.

Marbles slumped against a ring fence and wiped the sweat from his brow. He took another quick bite from his doggy-bagged pizza, then clambered back to his feet. He was hoping to have a proper rest, but something didn't quite feel right to him. He was almost certain that the owner of the Coffee Stop was no longer chasing him, yet he couldn't shake the feeling that someone was still on his tail. He looked back the way he had come and spotted a golden glow at the entrance to the alley. He stared for a while, trying to make out what it was, and then his eyes focused and his stomach dropped. It was a girl from his block whom he had been seeing around a lot recently. Feeling embarrassed at being covered in sweat and gasping for breath, Marbles turned the corner and took off down the street, not wanting her to see him this way.

The golden-haired woman stopped walking as the figure she was approaching turned the last corner and ran from her sight. With her feet cramped inside these heels, there was no way she could catch him, and taking them off and running after him was a good way to get noticed.

She took a long, thoughtful drag of her cigarette, scratched uncomfortably around her underwear-length shorts, and turned back the way she'd come. Upon turning, a man whom she hadn't heard approaching skidded to a halt, his face creasing with disgust as he eyeballed the woman up close.

The woman flexed her muscles and straightened her back as she glared down at the man, the intentions of whom were clearly unsavoury. He'd obviously mistaken her height as a trick of the high heels, but after being this close, he realised that actually, no, this woman was just bloody huge. As they stared each other down, footsteps hurried up behind her, but she held the man's gaze and took another drag.

"No… don't!" was all the man managed to yell before his partner, who was meant to snatch the woman's handbag from behind, instead caught her balled fist with his face. She turned and let out a mocking laugh, enjoying the confusion behind the man's exploded nose. He put out a hand and took a step back, opening his mouth to speak. Before he could make a sound, her solid knee found its way between his legs, sending the man hunching over and collapsing to the ground.

Her fingers searched her purse for the comforting handle of a snub-nose pistol, meaning to pull it on the first guy, only to find that he'd already taken off down the street. This brought a grin to her square jaw, but in that moment, the bag snatcher had clambered to his feet and charged up his right hook. She turned back and jerked to the left. His fist grazed the side of her face, shattering her UV lenses and revealing a hard-glaring eye. The man recoiled, holding his abraded hand in agony. Then, showing his arrogance, he kicked his leg out at her shins with one last pathetic attempt. Goldilocks pulled out her pistol and levelled it at the man's head.

"That's enough of your bullshit," she growled in her most intimidating voice. "Stop jerkin' me around and get outta my way!"

To her surprise, the man still hesitated slightly before fleeing in the direction of his partner, and she had to force herself not to gun him down just on principle. If the first guy hadn't run away, she would have considered it more seriously, but she didn't want to give them any more reason to come looking for her. For now, though, she was safe enough to leave this part of town without hassle. It seemed unlikely they would be in a hurry to tell anyone about how they'd had their asses handed to them by a back-alley girl.

Replacing her pistol, she headed the more public way back to her small family carrier on wheels—barely considered a vehicle. She cringed as the engine whined into action, then pulled onto the main road leading out of the area.

12

STALK THE STALKER

MARBLES VAULTED ONE MORE fence and rounded the last corner before his house. He quietly enjoyed the chase as much as the work, but after the third day of having to flee the job, he was beginning to wonder when he'd see his next paycheque. Tomorrow he would have a flick through his collection and dig out another coffee uniform. Coffee stores paid above average for entry-level work and he didn't mind it much, either. Bar work had always been another job he was good at, but he just wasn't too keen on the hours.

Marbles reached for his keys as he approached his door, but he didn't remove them. Instead of turning into his driveway, he continued past and headed further up the street. He could feel the weight of *her* eyes again and didn't want her catching a glimpse of his empty entrance hall at the end of a vehicle-less driveway.

Trying to stay subtle, he scratched the back of his neck and peered down the street. All he saw through encroaching darkness was houses, a row of parked vehicles, and the occasional plastic tree. Thinking that maybe his hunch was wrong, he slowed in anticipation of turning back but hesitated at the sight of movement up ahead. A small vehicle pulled out of a parking bay, flicked on its headlights, and drove past. Nothing suspicious. Probably a family heading out for a meal or maybe going to pick someone up from an after-school sporting event. Despite any number of plausible explanations, Marbles could have sworn that he never heard the engine click to *on*, as if the engine had been idling since he turned the corner, passengers just sitting quietly and with no lights on. *Watching him?*

The strange sensation left with the car, so Marbles turned and headed for home. He already felt how cold it would be inside. Today had been the hottest in a while, but the occasional hot day wasn't long enough to drive away the settled cold of winter. The doggy bag was already out of his pocket before he set foot through the door, but to his dismay, it was empty. Withdrawal came fast as his hands began to shake. Without any money to buy another slice, Marbles accepted the fact that he was going to be in for a long and restless night. *Home sweet home.*

Marbles poured himself a glass of water, stumbled into the bedroom, and slumped onto the foam mattress. He tried to stay distracted by switching on some of DJ T's smooth beats. He tapped his ear and turned his R-chip to sleep mode. The implant sent music directly to his brain whilst keeping tabs on cerebral activity. As Marbles drifted away, the R-chip's volume lowered until it detected that he was properly asleep, when it would power itself down completely.

Marbles rose to the rattling of an alarm clock, and with an aching head, he slumped over to the wardrobe. He donned his best-looking coffee uniform and promised himself that today would be a good day. Before heading to work, he would take a detour past the golden-haired woman's street and see if he could bump into her by chance and hopefully strike up a conversation. Once his hair seemed sufficiently brushed and he'd ingested enough coffee to feel mostly awake, he set off towards the front door.

Finally, after she had waited all night, a front door opened and a young man emerged. It took a while for the woman to realise that this was the same young man she'd been watching. Unlike the other times she had seen him, he looked quite normal and in control. She wondered if it were an attempt at a disguise. She watched him walk casually onto the footpath and head towards the end of the road. He caught the travellator down through the underpass, where a vehicle couldn't follow him. *Damn, he's good,* she thought.

Not wanting to have sat there all night for nothing, the golden-haired woman clicked on the engine and flew around the block, unlit cigarette forgotten between her fingers. She took the ramp down from the main road on the other side and sat, watching the exit of the underpass. The man failed to emerge.

Cursing, she set off down the adjacent street, peering through the morning darkness and searching for the mysterious man that had once again lost her as easily as if it were rehearsed.

She sped off again, one golden lock flailing against the stream of air entering the open window. This guy had known to duck through the underpass, so what else had he prepared to stop her from following him? The woman's gut churned as she speculated on different possibilities. Maybe he had stayed in the underpass, where he waited for her to go off in search of him. Then he more than likely double backed and could now be well on his way to wherever he wanted, free from the eyes that he somehow always seemed to sense. *This guy really is good.*

A yawn escaped her as she pulled the box on wheels into a U-turn and headed down a different road, towards her hideout home. Since she was so tired, she had forgotten about certain considerations, but at least now she knew where he lived. She could find him later—after a much-needed sleep.

That was if he didn't find *her* first, as she had failed to consider that maybe he'd been keeping tabs on her just as well as she had been on him. Sitting in the car now, however, she realised just how careless she had been.

As she pulled into a parking bay, her eyes focused on the silhouette at the other end of the street. So far, she couldn't make out who it was, but it wasn't hard for her to guess. Her fears were confirmed as the shadow of a man turned onto the property of her hideout, stood for a while, and stared at the door. He was looking all around, most likely checking for cameras. He seemed nervous, and the woman wondered what exactly he was hiding from. She wondered just how dangerous this man could be, as who else but a dangerous man would require such a set of skills?

Despite everything, she couldn't help but be impressed. This was definitely the guy for the job. Feeling confident that she'd been exposed a while ago now, she felt no need to commit to this ridiculous disguise; Boss removed his golden wig and scratched at his flattened mohawk, which had grown incredibly itchy over the last few hours. He smirked at the figure, head nodding. He considered how to approach the man without causing him to flee. If the man started running, there was no way Boss could catch him. That was the whole point, after all—the entire reason why Boss needed him at the pizza shop.

For now, though, he felt too tired to devise a proper plan. After a decent sleep, he would find a way to win over this mysterious trouble-dodger. *Decent* being the figurative word here, as it now seemed he would be sleeping in his box of a car.

13

WHAT AM I PAYING YOU FOR?

WIPING THE DROOL FROM his chin, Boss let his shirt fall from over his face, then looked around for what had woken him. It was his navs. Boss instantly thought of Voice and jumped to the front seat excitedly, slumber still tugging at him. After tapping the front of his screen, however, he discovered that it wasn't Voice at all. Of course it couldn't be, as he'd only checked on Voice's progress a few hours ago. Voice still had a few days until full recovery. The car that had just popped onto the grid was an unknown, but its owner was apparently "Cookie." *Leon must have switched the comms to a different vehicle. Smart.*

He watched the dot near his location and stepped out of his box once he heard a whine down the street. He put on his angriest face and stared the car down, doing his best to hide how happy he was to see a staff member, even if it was just the new guy. Boss didn't recognise the car, which pulled into a bay across the street, though when the door opened, Leon emerged. His mouth was open, ready to deliver an explanation, but before he made a sound, Boss jumped down his throat.

"Where the hell have you been!?" He felt steam escaping his ears and nose.

"Three days I've been out of business, waiting for you to contact me. Three fuckin' days!"

Leon stared at Boss, his face showing something Boss couldn't quite interpret. After a few seconds of staring, Leon burst into laughter, making no effort to conceal it. Boss felt legitimate rage this time, until he remembered that his topless body was still sporting the hot pants from his earlier disguise. He appreciated that it probably was quite a hilarious sight, and as rage turned to embarrassment, he managed to replace the lid on the verbal outburst that was brewing inside him. He chose instead to settle for a simple "fuck you" and a beckoning wave of the arm.

Leon, shoulders still bouncing uncontrollably, crossed the road and hopped into the passenger's seat of Boss's car. Without saying a word, they entered the main highway, heading towards the city centre. Leon looked around the cramped vehicle, a smile still on his face. "So I see you've been through a few changes since I've been gone."

"Don't get smart with me, kid. If you had followed my damn instructions, I wouldn't have needed to go undercover. Not only did you force me to wear this crap, but you stole my car, too!"

"No, no, I just moved it, so—"

"Yeah, I thought as much. The only reason you're still here is that you used your brains and quite possibly kept the shop from being discovered. I could still get some use out of you. Don't think I'm gonna forget about your little disappearing act, though. Two wrongs don't do a… make it okay to… you know. Just, next time I tell you to do somethin', don't leave me in lockdown for three days!" He reinforced this last point with a wave of the finger. The car's speed increased sharply as Boss released some of his anger through the accelerator.

Boss removed a cigar from the glovebox. Once he lit it, he filled the box-on-wheels with smoke in a single exhale. After a long and awkward period of time, Boss broke the silence. "In a few days, Voice will be ready to go. When he's back, I want the business up and running, same as usual. There's something I want sorted beforehand, so help me out here. Tell me everything you remember about that night."

Leon's face turned grim. "Well, I've seen that woman since. She must have been tracking your motor car somehow. I spent two days trying to lose her trail. She's damn fast! I'm afraid to tell you that I had to use a gas-go on a few occasions. Petrol was draining like there was a hole in the tank."

Boss punched the steering wheel and made a noise to himself, thinking about how much that cost him. This whole ordeal had been nothing but a black hole for his cash. He gritted his teeth. "I don't know what shit you've gotten us into. I think this woman may have been a tier of surrogate machine. Was there anything else?"

"Well, once I gained enough ground, I ditched the car. Luckily, it didn't seem like she was after *me*, only the car itself. Once the car stopped, she also stopped. I watched her for a while, but she was just circling."

"Don't call it a *she*. I think it's an *it*. And I think *it* was probably on autopilot."

He faced Leon, who looked terrified. "Please tell me you didn't leave anything in the car. The comms could lead it straight back to me…"

"Relax, I brought the comms with me. How do you think I found you?"

Just as Boss had thought. He did relax, though only a few of his hundreds of tensed muscles. "Wallet? Anything with ID or an address…"

"All in my pocket. I'd only been on one delivery, remember? Didn't exactly have long to move in. There's nothing in that car except empty seats."

Boss lifted his accusatory finger again, ready to add something, but Leon cut him off.

"Empty on top and beneath. I removed the whole satchel, since that was where you kept the nifty gadgets. I didn't know what I would need."

"Gadgets? You didn't waste much time, did ya, kid? You found the glasses?"

"The cigarettes, the glasses. Could sort of see things pulsing on the other side of the wall."

"And you saw the woman? Any part of her?"

"No, only the cop's weak heartbeat."

"Shit, Voice may have been right to worry. Definitely sounds like a surrogate machine. The Neuro-tier surrogate can move almost as fast as the controller's brain can think, which explains the quick, jerky motions. My guess is that the guy in control gave up at some point during your two-day escape and set the Neuro to continue chasing the car automatically while he slept or ate or whatever. It would explain how it didn't know to follow *you* once you left the car behind. I suppose it's only a matter of time before the controller returns to his console and finds the car sitting there in front of him. It will be no stretch from there to expect him to search it for clues of its owner."

"There's nothing there. I'm sure of it. Unless you had something in the boot."

This time Boss loosened most of his other muscles, as he remembered clearing the car out completely in preparation for Leon. His stomach remained tense and his head still hurt, though, and he didn't expect either of those things to ease off any time soon.

"For now, let's hope you're right. But we can't risk just leaving the car there. I'm gonna need it back. I can't afford any part of that vehicle even pointing gently in my direction. Plus, it was expensive." An idea plucked at the corner of Boss's mouth. "I think I've got the man for the job, but I'm gonna need your help, kid."

He looked down at Leon, but although Boss kept his features stern, he couldn't keep the worry from his human eye.

Leon squirmed uncomfortably in his chair. "Actually, Boss, I was sort of hoping that once I returned the keys I could turn my back on all of this. Not that interested in getting run off the road by machines while delivering pizzas. Know what I mean?" As he spoke, his face creased in anticipation of receiving either a wave of abuse or maybe a stray fist. Boss just focused on the traffic.

"There's somethin' I've gotta tell ya, kid. It isn't always just pizzas we're deliverin'."

Leon snorted. *"No shit."*

"This Neuro represents the invisible enemy that I'm at war with every day. They don't stop. It's *us* who need to stop *them*."

"And who are *they*, exactly?"

"Oh man, where do I start?" Boss scratched his head again. He realised that his evasiveness wasn't helping win Leon over one bit. He levelled his voice and acted as matter of fact as he could. "Look. I hired you because you had skills that we needed on the team. You've already proven you're worth a damn by surviving the last few days with a bloody Neuro on your ass. I'm just askin' one more favour. In return, you get a nice fat paycheque and get sent on your way. Just a local gig, nowhere near any Neuros or delivery shops or nothin'."

"If it's so simple, why aren't you doing it?"

"Ah, well unfortunately my disguise has been compromised. I'm afraid that if I approach this guy, he might think the worst of my intentions and run before I can pass on my message. All I ask is that you talk to him for me. Deliver the message."

"Which is?"

"That I want him to come for a job trial. ASAP. Say whatever you need. Convince him somehow. I need him on the team."

"Surely there are plenty of other drivers you could choose from?"

Boss smiled. "The last thing I need is another damn driver costin' me more than he's earnin'. Oh no. This guy ain't no driver, kid. He's a runner."

14

FAST FOOD FAST CASH

"**N**OW I THINK IT'S TIME for the master of rhyme! The next tune's so sweet you'll be on your feet in a heartbeat. That's right, I'm talking 'Pumpin' Smoke' by Warm Coffee."

Marbles kicked back, feet up on the plastic bags. The makeshift cushions around him weren't as comfortable as he was used to, but this was his best available option. He pulled his foot back as it slipped off the smooth surface. Then he replaced it with force, digging a better foothold into the bag of frozen chips with his heel. The harsh movement made something slide out of place behind him, and the corner of a box poked into his back. *This isn't working.*

He tapped his earlobe and willed the volume of his R-chip lower as he heard a set of footsteps approaching. With more energy than he had shown during the entire day of work, Marbles jumped from the pile of boxes and bags, picked one up, and made it seem as if he were organising them in some way. He continued his flurry, even when the footsteps stopped behind him, pretending he hadn't even realised someone was there. After a solid minute, the person coughed, and Marbles turned, practising his best "surprised" reaction. "Oh, I didn't realise—"

"Save it. I saw you lying down. We have cameras, you know."

Marbles stared back, not knowing how to respond. He wasn't used to being caught like this, and he was trying to work out if he should stick to his story and try to fast-talk his way out of the situation or just admit defeat. If he really had been seen through the cameras, then the latter was the only real choice. Feeling his face glowing redder by the second, he dropped the bag of chips and briskly walked straight out the front door. It was getting late, anyway, and Marbles wasn't a fan of working overtime.

Removing a small wad from his pocket, Marbles flicked through the notes, reminding himself why he worked such long days in the first place. He was glad to have taken payment in advance this time, as the last few jobs had all ended with him having to leave rather quickly and empty-handed.

He tucked the notes back into his pocket and heard a yell following him down the pathway. *Here we go again.*

"Hey! Hey you! Give that back!"

Marbles increased his pace.

"I saw you take that from the till. I've just watched the footage."

"I'm making it easier for the manager. I take care of my pay so he doesn't have to worry about it."

"I know it don't work like that, pal. Hand it over." The man increased his pace, too. He was jogging now and had a certain look about him that Marbles had seen before.

Marbles turned and ran. With the same ease as every time before, he sprung himself up a drain pipe and hopped from one roof to another. He slid down the edge of a ladder, hopped a fence, and rolled out into a main street, joining a stream of people who were also heading home from work.

Marbles wasn't that impressed at the pay rate for someone who had to go through so much effort each day. If only he knew to whom he should address a formal complaint. For now, though, he just had to worry about normalizing his breathing. He couldn't blend in if he were the only panting maniac. Marbles flicked his ear and asked the R-chip to turn the volume back up, and even over the bustling and chaos of the vehicles and people all around him, DJ T's music wove strands of calm through him. He saw an alley coming up on the left but decided against taking it. Just ahead of him was a fast-bus stop. If he could just board a fast-bus, this whole part of town, as well as the warehouse worker, would be far behind him in a matter of minutes.

As Marbles removed the notes from his pocket to purchase a ticket, they leapt from his grip and sprawled themselves across the pavement ahead of him. Something heavy had bashed him from behind. Dazed, Marbles fell straight onto his face. He tried to shake away the dizziness, but something held his flattened nose to the ground. He caught glimpses of his money being whipped away by shuffling feet or desperate hands.

Something metallic burned his neck.

"You have been placed under citizen's arrest. You have two weeks to turn yourself in to a police station. If you refuse, you will remain branded, you may be considered a fugitive, greater fines may apply, and you may be pursued by the full force of the law. You have the right to—oof!"

Marbles had heard enough and took pleasure in his left hook, catching the man's jaw as he rolled free and stumbled to his feet. He managed to snatch up a single note that still swirled in the wind, then turned back towards the nearby alley. A quick glance downwards revealed an almost useless amount in his hand, but he pocketed it anyway and jumped a barbed wire fence. This time, Marbles ran for a good thirty minutes, making sure to place as much distance as possible between him and the man from the warehouse. He also found that extra oxygen and adrenaline was the best cure for his dizziness; the man had taken him down hard.

Feeling he was far enough out of reach, Marbles ducked into a nook and waited for the sun to lower itself a bit further, making sure to take no chances this time. He felt his neck and a sharp pain leapt through him as his fingers bumped over the still tender skin. Almost as an afterthought, he reached to his nose and felt that it was swollen and slightly out of place.

Once the sun had completely set, he stepped out from where he'd been hiding. Marbles smirked at the averted gazes of the people around him. It was as if they were too scared to even acknowledge his existence. His nose must have been more grotesque than it felt, and mixed with the fact that he just emerged from a dark corner down an alley, he wasn't surprised when people ahead of him crossed the street. In fact, he preferred it this way. Although he felt that the situation was just a big misunderstanding, it was still embarrassing being publically branded and having to hand yourself in. He quickened his pace, wanting to reach the violently flashing POLICE sign before his lingering shadow cloak wore off. At the base of the blue and white chequered steps, he was approached by a figure that he hadn't noticed before and who must have been standing somewhere to the side of the station. By his appearance, Marbles realised that this man, too, was exploiting the shadow-cloak effect. The man fit the profile of someone people subconsciously steered clear of and whose direction people certainly didn't glance in. A long dark coat covered his body and scraped the floor. His cap covered his eyes, and his scarf was pulled up to his nose, muffling his voice.

"Nasty mark you got there, friend. Probably holds, what, five, maybe six minutes?"

Marbles wasn't overly familiar with the workings of the citizen's arrest brander, as he had been branded only once before, as a child. A shopkeeper had caught him slipping a pack of sweets up his sleeve, and he planted a mark right across Marbles's face. Needless to say, Marbles went straight down the station and got it removed, cashing it in for a "juvenile's warning slip." That was after the cops had watched the last few minutes of his memory leading up to the branding, which was all stored in the mark burned upon the skin.

"Uh, I wouldn't know," Marbles sputtered, feeling a little uneasy about the stranger talking to him.

The stranger smiled, eyes surprisingly warm. "Yeah, that's how they get you, you see? You hand yourself in, admitting guilt, assuming you've been caught, but really, you don't know what evidence they have against you. I mean, have you any idea what they will see on that mark o' yours?"

It was a fair question, and despite the bad feeling in his gut, Marbles couldn't help but consider it.

"Now that you mention it, I don't really know why I'm here. Was all a misunderstanding…"

The stranger waved a dismissing hand. "You needn't explain yourself to me, friend. That's not my business. My business is extracting information from marks like yours, for clients such as yourself. That way, you know exactly what you're handing over to the police *before* you do it. If there's anything unexpected saved in that little barcode of yours, at least you have the choice to leave it unread." He finished this sentence with a wink. He turned his head slightly, revealing a mark on his neck, which had been tattooed in. "Had this baby for twelve years! No one's come looking. No warrants out for my arrest. It's all scare tactics. They're busy enough without worrying about looking for guys with nothing but a little *suspicion* around them. If I had handed this in, I would be in a much worse place right now, let me tell you." He chuckled slightly, and Marbles, suddenly afraid of what the stranger might have done to earn that mark, felt his gut churn again. They watched each other for a little while before the stranger shrugged. "Eh, whatever. Up to you, friend. But I'd say that peace of mind is worth the small fee. Here's my card, but the number will have changed by tomorrow afternoon, so be sure to call me before then if you're interested." He turned to leave.

"Wait, um… okay. I'll do it. Out of curiosity if nothing else, what's the charge?"

The stranger turned and studied Marbles's face. His eyes seemed to pierce Marbles's skin as he assessed his new client.

"Hard for me to give you an exact figure right now, as it varies depending on the crime and the client's situation." His eyes faded as he noticed the rips, the sweat patches, and the undersized shirt of a low-paid warehouse worker. "Usually, warehouse getup suggests around one thousand dollars starting fee. Looking at the state of yours, however, I wouldn't be surprised if even that was too much of a stretch."

Marbles opened his wallet to confirm the stranger's theory. He laughed a raspy laugh into his scarf.

"Worse than I thought. Five bucks? Jesus. Well, I'm a man of solutions. Since I've already invested time into you and you've shown interest in what we offer, it would be stupid for me to turn you away now. Know what this is?" He opened a pouch around his waist to reveal a small disposable drive with a faint orange glow inside. Marbles nodded.

"Perfect!" He slapped Marbles on the shoulder and simultaneously dropped the drive into his pocket. They started walking together towards the stranger's hideout, voices kept low. "So let's get this under way. Send us five hundred in crypto bits and then destroy that drive. Payment due in, let's say, one week? You manage that?"

Marbles nodded again, thinking of his horde of crypto bits he'd never had the opportunity to actually spend. The stranger slapped his shoulder again and gave a hand signal to another shrouded figure down the way. "That guy'll take care of ya, friend. Good luck."

15

CRACKERS

MARBLES SLID UP TO THE LAST cloaked figure in a chain of people sending him in different directions. He flashed the back of his neck and could see the figure's eyes widen behind his night goggles. He quickly motioned Marbles to cover it back up and glanced around, checking if the street was clear. No one in sight. The figure tapped away at something hidden in a power box before clunking the cover back in place. He nodded and, without letting his eyes leave Marbles, pushed the door behind him ajar. The second Marbles had his feet through the doorway, the figure slammed it shut, jolting a young lady awake who'd been snoring at a desk. She wiped dust from her eyes and readjusted a couple of the studs in her face. A piece of gum found its way to the front of her mouth in the form of a bubble. She raised an eyebrow, looking Marbles up and down, who was nervously glued to the spot. She seemed to find some humour in his awkward stance.

"Alright, let's see it."

Marbles hesitated, blushing, then felt stupid when he realised what she meant. He leaned forwards and lowered his collar, revealing a blistering burn on his neck. The woman snorted. "Took it like a bitch, eh? Man, that's bad. Wanna see?"

Marbles nodded slowly as the woman rummaged through a box behind her, searching for a mirror. Through her top's thin material and occasional rips, he noticed at least five half-burned marks on her back and shoulder blades. They were prominent, but not in the same way as his. Where his was red and blistered, hers were smooth and black. Almost artistic. She turned back and read the look on Marbles's face. He made to speak but still couldn't find any words.

"Yeah, I had them tattooed. Once the blisters die down, I kinda like the look of 'em, you know?"

He didn't know.

"They heal quickly, especially if you actually *defend* yourself." She gave Marbles a look, which he didn't know how to interpret. "The only thing in these babies is a short clip of me smackin' my attacker. Never let 'em burn in more than a few seconds, ya see."

She held the mirror behind him and he looked at the screen, seeing the almost barcode-looking scar on his neck. It looked like it held at least five minutes, according to the young woman, who still hadn't quite shaken the laughter from her voice.

The thought of cracking into the police property on his neck put Marbles on edge, but at least the slightly insane young lady before him seemed to have done it before. Probably quite a few times, judging by the number on her body. Maybe it wasn't such a big deal. Truth was, with Marbles's job, he was used to a whole range of situations. By accepting the stranger's offer, he knew he'd signed over his life to another and couldn't do anything now except ride it out.

The young lady prodded at Marbles's barcode for a while with a series of various instruments, all of which were hooked up to this computer or that machine. Finally, she said something that dragged him out of his thoughts.

"Ah, I wondered when they were going to update. Looks like you got hit with the new and shiny 3.6 model. Lucky boy! Gonna take a few hours, I'm afraid. When I finish this scan, you can head down the hall. There's a TV. I'll call ya back when I'm done. What payment was discussed?" Before waiting for a response, she took a guess. "Two thousand bucks?"

"Five hundred…"

"You're shittin' me!"

Marbles kept his head pressed down and fumbled around in a pocket, then retrieved a small disposable flash drive.

"Ah, I see. Yeah, we're getting low on the old cryptos. If there's gonna be a problem with payment, best let me know now. I'm about to get started."

Marbles let out a sigh. "Well, I guess it's a bit late for me to just walk away?"

The woman jumped back in her chair, shocked. "The little pussy cat found his voice, eh? Damn right it's too late to pull out. Wastin' everyone's time. You'd still owe us at least half, or more, if you've got it. Trust me, you don't want to be shaken down for cash. Our guy is nice and thorough."

Suddenly Marbles wished he hadn't asked. Not that there was any money for them to find, but they were criminals, after all, and he didn't want to give them any excuse to get physical. The young lady sensed the change in atmosphere.

"Hey, chill, man. We do this all the time. You got nothin' to worry about. Okay, the scan's done. Hold this on your neck or it will bruise up nice. Now go entertain yourself. I'll call ya later." She finished the last sentence with a wink.

Not feeling any more confident, Marbles thanked the tattooed girl and stood to leave. She chuckled like a child stealing ice cream, and Marbles couldn't tell if she was mocking him.

"Thank me later. I've not done anythin' yet."

Marbles left the main room and followed the hall to the end. There were many doors, but few were open, and only one held the blue tinge of a screen. Entering the TV room was somehow even more unpleasant than he anticipated. Yes, there was a small box of a TV, balanced against the wall and atop what Marbles presumed would be a tripod, if only it still had all three of its legs. There was a bunk bed against each wall, except for the one, which housed the door and TV. The two bunks at the sides overlapped the one across the back, and the remaining floor space was around one meter squared. On the bottom bunk ahead of Marbles were three occupants sat shoulder to shoulder and watching what sounded like a football match, though all Marbles could see was static. Snores resonated from somewhere above, vibrating all of the bunks and the TV, restoring its picture temporarily. The slick-haired man in the middle glanced up briefly before setting his eyes back on the screen, and that was it.

Confident the men in the room wouldn't even notice his presence, Marbles considered just dropping himself down onto a bunk and trying to nap. Then he imagined a few hours of trying to sleep with static flicking his face and the snoring shaking his ears. He backed out of the room, doing his best not to break the line of sight between the men and the screen beside the door.

Exploring the hall a little more, Marbles poked his head into some of the other open doors, but they only seemed to lead to dark, empty rooms. A stairwell beside him spiralled upwards, and Marbles followed it round as it led to another hall almost identical to the one below. A few more closed doors before he came to one that was wedged slightly open, a warm breeze flowing out from inside. Marbles stopped short, listening to the raspy voice on the other side of the door. He tried to put a face to each voice he heard, imagining their roles in the gang. Mr. Raspy sounded like a grunge smoker with the way he coughed often and struggled to form words—probably a devoted client working for the addiction. There was also Deep and Booming, the intimidator. Quiet and Hard—the leader—and the normal-sounding guy. Marbles thought about this one for a moment. Although his voice carried some form of authority, from what Marbles had seen of it so far, he didn't sound like he belonged in this hideout.

"… nothing to worry about. It's a completely untraceable server," said the normal voice.

Marbles stepped back towards the steps as he heard the heavy slap of what was more than likely a wad of cash hitting the table. Then the claps of hands being shaken. The deal was done, and they would soon be out of the room. Marbles shuffled down the steps as fast as possible and ducked into the TV room, his back to the stairs. He tried to act as casually as possible, despite the adrenaline pumping his veins awake. Suppressing his instinct to flee was proving more difficult than he imagined. Footsteps were close behind him, but amidst the group's small talk, no one seemed to notice Marbles.

Once the group was halfway down the hall, Marbles stole a quick glance. Raspy was still struggling to keep the wad of cash concealed in his pocket. A man in a plain but expensive-looking dark suit ignored his struggles and clinked shiny boots along the floorboards. He gestured curtly at the tattooed girl, who buzzed the door unlocked, and in that moment, the light from the hall reflected off the badge pinned to his shoulder. The sigil of the Federal Agency burned brightly, and Marbles could see it long after the shadows of the street had consumed the rest of the man. *Interesting.*

After a couple of hours of doing laps through the empty hallway, Marbles heard the tattooed girl calling him. Glad the wait was over, he headed back to the first room and stood awkwardly by the desk, grinning.

The tattooed girl raised an eyebrow. "Um. Please take a seat," she said, putting on her most ladylike voice.

Marbles shuffled over and slumped himself into the chair, a giggle from Ink and Studs causing Marbles's cheeks to glow.

"Comfy?"

She didn't wait for a reply and turned on the TV behind her. This one had all three of its legs but was no bigger than the one in the other room.

"Seven minutes twenty!" She grinned. "Did you pass out or somethin'?"

"I just presumed I was caught. Didn't think to run," answered Marbles honestly.

"Funny you should say that, 'cos you don't seem to have a problem with runnin'. First few minutes o' this clip is you runnin' your ass off. Pretty cool, actually." She bounced around excitedly in her seat.

Marbles gave a single nod at the compliment, not wanting to show how happy it made him feel. He looked over at the static on the screen, and understanding his want, the tattooed girl jumped into gear.

She tapped away at a keyboard for a second, pressed a few buttons, and plugged in the screen. It flashed a few images too quickly for Marbles to interpret, then showed a rooftop. The skyline was blurred, but Marbles recognised it. He'd been there earlier today. The rooftop rushed away, and the camera looked down at a body, which was leaping across a gap between buildings. It was Marbles's body. His jaw dropped as he sat there and watched a memory of his play out on the screen in front of him. It wasn't perfect, flickering here and there, blurry around the edges, but there was no mistaking it was him. Watching it back like this, he couldn't help but agree with how cool it looked.

Like an action sequence in a movie. Marbles suddenly felt insecure about the tattooed girl watching one if his memories. It was like she was inside his head and poking around. His thoughts no longer felt safe. The screen flickered again as he jumped towards a drain pipe.

"What's making the screen flick like that?" "We call them blips." She paused and rewound the video in slow motion. "Sometimes, if you are focused on one thing, your brain forgets the details around it, so there's like a hole in the video. Sometimes, it's your brain prodding at other memories to help work whatever it needs to do. Look." She stopped the playback on one of the blips, and over the top of the frame of him jumping for a drain pipe was another image, this one of a green pipe. There was a hand reaching up from below and a bright light at the top of the screen. "Recognise that image?"

Marbles nodded. "That was the first time I climbed a drain pipe. There's the hand of the guy chasing me." He pointed to the arm at the bottom of the frame. "Right, so your brain draws details from that to help calculate the strength you're gonna need and stuff, I guess."

"That's scary."

She laughed. "Yep. That's why we don't hand 'em in. Fingerprints were one thing, but this is madness. I don't believe anyone should have this sort of information on us. What they gonna use it for? Blackmail, that's what."

Marbles glanced back at the screen as she resumed the video.

"That said, I didn't see anythin' incriminatin' in here. You might be alright to hand it in and get it removed without as much as a fine."

She skipped the last few minutes of Marbles running and continued from where Marbles tripped and dropped money all over the street.

"You steal that?"

Marbles ignored the question, still blown away by the fact his memories were playing out on a TV screen. The video ended in static after Marbles caught the arrester in the face with a balled fist.

"Oh, there it is! Better late than never!" The girl continued to tease Marbles about his not putting up a fight, but Marbles was distracted by one of the details he didn't know he remembered.

"Can you replay that last bit?"

"When you clock the guy? Want it on disk?"

"No, just play it back, slowly."

She did so, and Marbles shuffled towards the screen, examining the face of the arrester—or at least the pixelated blob where the face should be. "Why can't I see him?"

"Gotta protect the goody two-shoes, I guess. It's a built-in precaution. Each zapper encrypts its owner's face."

"Protect him from who, though, if only the police are supposed to see this?"

The girl shifted in her seat and tongued a cheek stud. After a few long seconds, she shrugged dramatically. "Beats me. I didn't make the thing. I just crack it."

Fair enough. Marbles didn't need to see the face anyway. He made out the guy's suit jacket, which definitely wasn't the uniform of the warehouse. This wasn't the same guy. He wondered who else could have chased him down. Surely no one had followed him across the rooftops. Why else would someone have arrested him if it wasn't the guy from the warehouse?

"You okay?" The girl had switched to poking at an eyebrow ring. "I wouldn't worry. The guy who arrested you will file a statement. Statement's then cross-referenced with the video. Nothing in this video matches anything criminal, 'less the guy also happens to own the property you technically trespassed on during your 'fitness regimen.'" She winked. "Yeah, the running looks suspicious, but it's hard evidence they need, and they ain't got it. Seriously, do you want it on disk? 'Cos if not, then we're done here." She slapped her desk and rolled her chair back to the computer, then switched off the video and disconnected the leads. Her forgotten gum was regurgitated on demand.

"So the arrester must have seen me running and nabbed me on the off chance, hoping that if I'd done something I'd turn myself in and provide whatever they needed to incriminate myself?"

The girl shrugged. "Wouldn't be the first time."

"Well, then that's everything." Marbles stood and thanked the young girl again, who gave him a toothy grin.

"Come back any time." She kissed the air, purely to watch his cheeks flare up, just as before. He turned rigidly and hurried to the door, walking straight into it when the handle didn't turn and the door failed to open. Then a buzzer sounded and he tried again. He made to speak, but feeling too embarrassed, he decided to just swing the door open and step outside, another giggle following him into the street. He stopped on the pavement and looked around. The weather had changed while he was inside, and a chilly breeze ruffled his coat.

"You need somethin'?" It was the guard at the door, who Marbles hadn't realised was standing uncomfortably close. He glared down at Marbles, arms crossed.

"Uh, no, I was just…"

"Then get movin'."

Marbles recognised the voice. It was the intimidator, Mr. Deep and Booming from upstairs. Happy to have identified him correctly, Marbles sensed his smirk was aggravating the doorman, so he stepped away fast. As he marched down the footpath, hopping over the cracks, a raindrop struck his neck. Another. Within a few seconds, the sky opened its floodgates. Marbles pulled his jacket around him to no effect. Once the cold settled in, he knew it would take all night to warm himself up again. Glancing at doorways around him, he wondered if it would be worth huddling up under an overhang and hoping the rain would stop or if he should just take the walk and deal with it. As if in answer to his question, a horn sounded over cheap speakers up ahead as an electro-car pulled into a parking bay.

The driver leaned out of his window. "Hey! Marbles, right?" In his lap was a fresh pizza. "Warm yourself up, man. Hop in. I will explain on the way."

"On the way to where?"

"Back to yours. I can give you a lift. Storm's only gonna get worse."

Through the dark, Marbles couldn't see who was talking, and he didn't recognise the car. "Who are you?"

Thunder clapped overhead. Some shuffling in the shadows.

"C'mon, let me shut my window or we're both gonna freeze. Get out of the rain. I will explain everything."

Marbles didn't like this situation. Cars made him nervous. He didn't like being closed in, unable to run if he needed to. But he knew the mysterious driver was right; he wouldn't make it back home in this storm without nearly freezing to death. Unable to believe how many risks he'd taken today, he ran to the side of the car and hopped in the passenger's side door. At least he could reach the car's controls from here—if he needed to.

The driver wasted no time and tore quickly away, leaving the gang hideout behind in a cloud of steam.

"So what's this about?" started Marbles.

The driver glanced up at his mirror, handed Marbles the pizza box, and managed a "juzza sec" before the vehicle was on two wheels, screeching around a corner. This continued for another few turns. The driver pulled onto a main road and joined a steady stream of traffic. "Sorry, this part of town gives me the creeps." He then glanced at Marbles and couldn't help but let out a mocking snort. Marbles was squashed back into his seat, holding onto the door and dash for dear life. "You don't drive much, huh?"

Marbles gulped down a slice of pizza for comfort. "Only when I have to. Which is never. So no, I guess I don't. Please slow down." He let out a quick breath and realised how pathetic he seemed. He laughed nervously, and the driver joined in. The traffic lights ahead turned amber and the driver pushed the electro-car to its limits once more. As they sped through the lights, a large sign flashed "Double demerit week. Please drive legally."

"Okay, that should give us enough distance. It will be a smooth ride from here." The driver switched on the radio. Marbles loosened up at the sound of DJ T and nodded his approval. The driver extended his hand to Marbles. "The name's Leon."

16

HAPPY FAMILY

BY THE TIME LEON HAD driven Marbles back to a familiar part of town, Marbles had relaxed. He was glad Leon had kept his word about it being a smooth ride. Driving seemed to be second nature to Leon, and Marbles couldn't help but be impressed at the ease with which he manoeuvred the vehicle.

"I can see why this *Boss* guy made you his driver," Marbles said, and Leon glanced back at him.

"Well, not for much longer, actually. In fact, trying to convince you to join is my last assignment."

"You got another job lined up?"

"It's a bit more complicated than that. Truth is, the money's good, but it's not without some risks. I'm just not sure I'm completely suited to it."

Marbles felt empathetic. "I know how it is. Just trying to earn a few bucks while constantly having to look over your shoulder. Worried the manager might fire your ass over having too long a break or for taking your pay in advance."

Leon looked quizzically at Marbles. "I don't know of anywhere that would let you take your pay in advance, to be honest…"

"Well if *they* paid me, then *I* wouldn't have to take it for myself," Marbles said with a look that suggested everything should now make sense.

"Uh… what is it you do exactly? If you don't mind me asking."

"I do a bit of everything, really. This and that. I used to distribute uniforms at a temping agency. Now I work for myself. Whatever I feel like doing, I go and do it. Help people out, ya know? Relieve some stress for the rest of the staff, share the workload. Only problem is that sometimes the managers get greedy and refuse to pay me. If I put the hours in, I don't think a paycheque is too much to ask."

Leon shook his head. "Well, you get paid with this job—and a good amount, too."

Marbles's eyes narrowed suspiciously as Leon took a turn that Marbles had not mentioned. It seemed that Leon already knew where the house was. He decided not to let on that he had noticed. "So tell me more about this job, anyway. You need me to retrieve something?"

"That's right. There's a car a few hours south of here. I can take you most of the way, but I believe someone could still be looking for me, so I can't get too close. You just need to pop in, grab the car, drive back. Cool?"

"But I hate driving. Do you really need me, specifically?"

"The car's been left for a while. There was another person looking for it. No doubt they've found it by now and could still be hanging around. We need someone to sneak in, on foot, and apparently that's what you're good at. Some of those uniforms you mentioned may come in handy, too."

Marbles huffed. "I don't know how good I really am. Went and got myself caught earlier today, didn't I?" He showed the mark on his neck to Leon, a hook of guilt snagging in his chest. He'd almost forgotten about the mark until just then.

A concerned look crossed Leon's brow. "That what you were doin' in Grey Town? Getting your neck scanned?"

Marbles nodded stupidly, surprised that Leon had heard of the procedure before.

"Whew, okay. That's actually a relief. I was worried about who I was dealing with when I picked you up from there.

You should steer clear of that part of town if you can help it. They're dangerous people, man."

Marbles shifted uncomfortably in his seat. He'd already given much thought to the risks involved in dealing with the mark-crackers and felt idiotic for taking those risks for the sake of his own curiosity. He didn't appreciate Leon telling him once again how reckless he had been.

"Were they the ones who busted your nose?"

Marbles shook his head, poking absently at the crusted blood on his face. "Nah, this is from before." He stewed in his thoughts for the rest of the drive.

Marbles led Leon into his apartment. Boss materialised from down the street and slid towards the door, then rapped on the thick wood. Marbles's eyes lit up for a split second. "Oh… I thought you were someone else…" His mood deflated as the flow of golden locks turned out to be a tease of his imagination.

"Expecting someone?" Boss asked.

"No."

"Good." Boss saw this as the end of the conversation and stepped inside, pushing past Marbles and entering the hall.

"Marbles, this is Boss. Boss, Marbles," blurted Leon in an attempt to make Marbles feel at ease with this giant, unknown intruder.

"Yeah, yeah," Boss mumbled as he entered the kitchen and began devouring large handfuls of Coco-Corn Crunch Cereal Flakes.

Leon had glanced quickly around the room, quite liking the minimalist style and expansive sound system. He took mental notes on the setup so he could duplicate it at his own place. Catching sight of Boss's back end hanging out of the cupboard, Leon yanked him clear and shut the door. They headed to the lounge, where Marbles was slumped in his deep sofa, radio on. He shut his eyes and curled up slightly. Boss looked over to Leon, who stood there and bobbed his head to the music. He was enjoying the tune and didn't mind taking a moment for him and Marbles to soak it up, if it was what the situation called for. When he looked back at Boss, Boss just sighed, irritated.

"Alright. Here's the deal… What the hell happened to your face? Anyway, we need the car. You've got the best chance of gettin' it back. Either that or we let the cops know about your trip to Grey Town this evenin'. I hear they've got their own little corner for people who deal with those mark-crackers—or anyone who works against the CCD for that matter." Boss had been referring to the Crowd Control Division, a government section that commissioned the barcode-burners.

Both Marbles and Leon looked up at this, each as insulted as the other. Leon made to defend Marbles, and Boss levelled his finger in his face, as he had done before. "Don't you say nothin'! I gave you one job, and now I've gotta come down here and do it for ya!"

Leon shook his head and spoke to Marbles. "Don't worry, man. He always says that sort of stuff. We're not going to the cops. And you will do fine, anyway. You get an earpiece, and I can guide you the whole way. Plus, once you get the car, you're basically home free. It's petrol, so just slam your foot down and—"

"I can't drive petrol." Marbles turned up the radio slightly and started rocking. "I can't drive petrol," he repeated, seemingly on the brink of a panic attack.

Boss expanded with rage. "It's the same as electric!"

Leon stepped between them before things got any more out of control. He spoke over Boss's rant.

"You can get us in, though, right? Find a path, lead the way. I can drive us out."

Boss was pacing the room, mumbling and shouting and cursing, waving his finger all over the place as if it meant something. "Perfect. Both of ya… Who needs quick and quiet? Should pack my own bags, too. Maybe tell the neighbours." He kicked out at the desk, which shook violently with the force. A belt of static escaped the speakers. "Get a whole team. Moonwalk right on in."

Leon shimmied closer to Marbles, who was staring at the ground and breathing fast and heavy.

"Hey, you need to calm down. You're a natural at this, right? That's why Boss chose you." He gave Marbles a slap on the shoulder, not knowing how to act in this situation.

Marbles reached for his neck, poking the tender mark. "I didn't do anything wrong. Was a misunderstanding…"

"Forget that for now. At the moment, all we need is that car."

Boss huffed the last of his steam and stopped in the centre of the room, hands on hips as he glared down. Leon gave him a short nod. It seemed that Marbles was regaining some control. He turned DJ T down to a quiet hum, and finally, he spoke.

"Do we have a plan?"

Boss nodded, still frowning, but the anger was falling away. He pulled a map from his back pocket, which already had a few markings scrawled across it, and slammed it onto the table next to the radio. Marbles leaned over for a glance but Boss caught him with one of his stares. It wasn't his usual angry stare, though. As fast as it came, the anger left, and a scheming grin found its way to his prickly chin. "First, let's see some of those uniforms of yours."

17

CAR. PARK.

BOSS RELUCTANTLY FLIPPED the screen of his navs to life and, beneath heavy eyelids, plotted a route for Leon and Marbles on a digital map. "There's an alleyway coming up on your right."

The trio had spent most of the night planning and most of the following day travelling, which didn't afford much time for sleep. Boss had given up arguing with Marbles about listening more and having fewer nervous breakdowns so the whole situation could move along more quickly. He was finally realising that his short temper didn't always help progress a situation. With the aid of an open vodka bottle snatched from Marbles's lounge, he did his best to stay calm whilst cramped in the back of his operations van.

A few words managed to push through the van's crackly speakers. It was Leon's voice. "Alley's blocked."

Boss growled and slammed down a fist, almost collapsing the foldout desk. A few seconds into his outburst, he realised he wasn't holding down the radio transmit button, and he felt stupid when he had to repeat himself, feigning the rage in his voice this time. "Having me as part of the plan was *not* part of the plan! I can't see if the alley's blocked. I'm working off of a nav-grid here. It's all just lines and boxes."

"Relax, Boss. We're doing fine so far," Leon whispered.

"You've only just left the bloody van!"

"Slow and steady…"

Boss let out a huff, really trying, though with no real success, to file his anger away for later. His jaw stayed clenched. "Seen anythin' yet?"

"Just a few people about, minding their own business. Streets are mostly empty."

Leon was crammed into a small trolley with a shelf of industrial road-sweep cleaning products balanced above him. He could only see through an eye slit that he'd dug for himself last minute. The vibrations were causing his vision to blur, but even through that, he could see the streets were basically empty. Only one more figure up ahead now. A slender woman's figure. She seemed to be hanging around, no real direction in her movement.

"Marbles, see that one ahead?"

Marbles, who was pushing the trolley, lifted his head and peered at the figure from underneath the cap over his eyes. His arms stiffened and the trolley veered off to the side and dropped off the footpath in a crash. Marbles continued in the direction as if he were meant to bump down the curb. He tapped the back of his cap, loosening the auto-adjust clip and allowing heat to escape his sweating head.

Leon peered through his eye slit again and saw that they'd caught the woman's attention. She was possibly moving towards them, but it was hard for him to tell.

"Heading this way, Marbles, but slowly. Maybe just a drunk stumbling about? Or she's trying to keep her movements slow to cover the jerkiness."

Another crash as Marbles rammed the trolley onto the footpath on the other side. The trash compartment that Leon was folded into felt suddenly hot, as he too felt sweat beads build up all over him. *This has bad idea written all over it. What the hell am I doing?*

"All good, Marbles. She's paying hardly any attention. Just keep us rolling along." Leon tried to sound calmer than he felt.

Boss chirped into the static. "Take a left. Dead end, so it should be free of people. Good time to switch to rooftops."

The trolley rattled over a drain cover, sending a rod of pain through Leon's cramped leg. He clenched his jaw to contain a yelp. The turn-off wasn't far ahead. He estimated the arrival time and counted it down in his mind as Marbles shuffled onwards.

Boss's nervous voice found Leon's ear. "How's the scout?"

"Can't see her at the moment." The vibrations of the trolley increased, and Leon took another look at the street. "Slow down, Marbles."

He didn't.

"Marbles?"

"She's coming this way," Marbles hissed in response.

"Keep calm. You're just a road-track cleaner, heading home, remember?"

Marbles gulped. He knew he wouldn't pull it off. He was far too nervous, and it showed. He kept his pace and took another glance down the road. The woman's eyes were fixed, and she was stumbling straight towards him. If he kept this pace, he would make the corner before she reached him.

"Boss, after the corner, where to?"

"Number seven, on the right. Has side access. Should be hidden enough."

"*Should* be?"

"We're not exactly swimming in options here, kid!"

Another burning pain as Marbles dropped the trolley down another curb and turned the corner without daring to check how close the woman was. He rapped his knuckles on the container and Leon burst out, kicking the trolley down the road so its rattling might mask the sound of their running. Marbles boosted Leon onto number seven's side roof. In an awkward motion, Leon rolled atop and extended his own arm for Marbles. They scrambled away from the ledge as fast as they could before hopping down a level and hiding behind a top-storey bedroom.

"Think she saw us?" Marbles whispered loudly over the sound of his own heart racing to keep up with them.

"Nothing's appeared on my screen," stated Boss, "though that only mean's she's beneath the speed threshold. I can see your trolley still rolling, though… Oh, shit."

The trolley faded from Boss's screen as it slammed into the side of a parked electro-car at the end of the cul-de-sac. An alarm screamed to life and a machine gun mounted above the owner's front door emptied an entire magazine into the trolley.

"*Goddammit!* Those alarms are so loud and unnecessary!" yelled Boss. "Also, a mark just popped onto my radar. No points for guessing what it might be."

Leon turned to Marbles, who was rocking slightly and staring at the floor.

"No time for that, Marbles. This is supposed to be the part you are good at."

Marbles tried to shake the doubt from his mind. He took a few deep breaths and climbed to his wobbly feet.

"Right," he said, and in that moment, he finally accepted his role in this mission. "You better keep up then."

And with that, he leapt from the roof, clamping his hands around a grime-covered pipe and sliding down into a fenced-off yard at the back of a housing estate. He looked back at Leon, who'd skidded to a halt on the edge of the roof and looked in horror at the pipe. "How the hell?"

Marbles looked around him in a flurry, grabbing the only thing nearby that seemed to have a use. He launched the hedge snips over the fence and Leon caught them with confusion.

"Cut the cable by the gutter. There. It's holding the scaffold." Marbles pointed out a painter's platform.

Leon kicked the handle of the snips and the cable crushed between the blunt blades, fraying and splitting under the pressure. A fail-safe activated and the platform began to screech slowly down the tracks on the side of the building. Leon leapt for the platform, slammed into it, and dislodged the last-resort break pad. The whole thing crashed down, leaving Leon dazed but no longer stuck on the roof.

"What're you guys doin'? She's headin' straight for ya!"

Leon climbed to his feet and glanced at Marbles through the yard's fence, which separated them. Marbles nodded and they both started running. Leon stuck to pathways around the yards, and Marbles sprung up drain pipes and back across rooftops. The woman was running straight down the alley between them and catching up—fast.

"How… is… she…" Marbles was blurting out between gasps for air.

"Shut the hell up and keep runnin'!" screamed Boss as he watched the three dots on his screen coming closer together. He started slapping the side of the screen on his nav-grid. "*Shit, shit, shit, shit.* Come on, Leon. Get back on the damn rooftops!"

There was no chance he would make it in time, and each of them knew it. Marbles felt guilt in his guts. This was his fault. Leon was only here because Marbles refused to drive.

His mind cleared. Right now, they weren't driving. They were running, and it was this that Marbles did best. He vaulted down from the roof, grabbed a chain-link fence halfway, and hung there like a lizard on a wall. He kicked over a dustbin, hoping to trip the woman, who was approaching impossibly fast. She jumped the bin and its contents and plucked Marbles from the fence before he even knew she'd reached him. He rolled to the side and back to his feet, wooden pole in hands. It had been tucked behind the bin, and he hoped its nail-riddled end would prove a sufficient weapon.

The woman turned, calculated the threat, and moved to disarm Marbles. Marbles rolled again and caught the woman in the ankle with the pole, tearing a chunk of flesh from her artificial bones. Surprised, Marbles dropped the pole as thick fluid sprayed from the wound. He inspected the wooden pole and saw a green-blue slime hardening over the end. Clotter-slime.

"No, kid! You gotta run. She's…"

Too late for that. The Neuro had already regained its balance and locked on to Marbles, who was shuffling back into the wall of the alley. It launched a fist at Marbles, grazing his cheek. The Neuro's damaged leg struck Marbles's chest, throwing him back into the bricks and spraying more clotter-slime across his road-sweep jacket.

With barely a second to catch his breath, Marbles sidestepped another blow, pulled his cap down over the Neuro's face, and let the back tighten before hoisting himself up to a windowsill. From there, he jumped across to a gutter, pulled up, and ran. Boss watched the blips spread apart as Marbles fled the scene, and his excitement flooded in as quickly as his anger usually did.

"Damn, kid. You're fast!"

Marbles had no mind to respond. He just focused on the next leap ahead of him. After a minute, Boss spoke again.

"Turn right there. Leon's just ahead."

Marbles did so and crossed another branch of the winding alleys, ending up beside Leon, who was tucked behind a cluster of chimneys. They both slumped there for a while, breathing hard. Leon removed a small water bottle from his supply pack and handed it to Marbles. "Saved my ass back there, man."

Marbles shrugged. "Well that's what you needed me for, right? It's nice to have a purpose."

Leon smiled. He took a swig of water and wished it were something stronger. "How's it looking, Boss?"

"The dot is fading but still on the move. You keep moving and you'll stay ahead of her. Sit there much longer and your body parts are gonna be cloggin' the gutters!"

Marbles looked at Leon and nudged his head back. "Got a way with words, that one."

"Piss off," cracked Boss's voice. Leon snorted a laugh.

"We need to move. Which way, Boss?"

"Follow the alley to the end, then skip left. Ahead's the park you left the car at."

Leon turned to Marbles. "Mind helping me down again?"

Marbles dropped to a balcony below, then to the ground, and dragged a dumpster from the alley and placed it against the balcony. Leon followed, clumsily lowering himself until his feet finally found solid ground.

"Oh no, no, shit, *shit!* I've lost her."

"She's gone?"

"That'd be nice, eh, kid? No, she's just slowed her pace. I can't track her, but I can guess where she'll be heading. You've gotta get to that car first."

Marbles gave Leon a look, and a small sense of pride grew in him. Whereas it now seemed that Leon would like to curl up in a corner, Marbles felt awake, alert, and readier than ever. Leon seemed to sense Marbles's scrutiny and tried to shrug off his fear, making his discomfort even more obvious. Marbles gave him a slap on the shoulder, just as Leon had done to him back at the house. It was enough. Boss's temper boiled once again. "What the hell you guys doin'? Get movin' for Christ's sakes!"

Marbles did his little head tip and eye roll that Leon had seen before and smirked. The two of them began their jog towards the park.

Between breaths, Leon did his best to give Marbles the low-down of the area. "Fences... here... Gotta climb... Car... Over there... No road... Stay low..."

Once Marbles had heard enough, he ran ahead of Leon and ducked into a bed of plastic bushes. Leon followed, flinching as the already spiky branches, made even more offensive by their all-weather coating, ripped at his clothes.

A nearby clinking rattled him alert, and his heart beat loudly. It continued to beat loudly long after he noticed it was just Marbles clipping at the fence with a small pair of wire snips.

Marbles looked back. "You keeping lookout or what?"

Leon shuffled over and peered through the fence, taking deep, slow breaths. He was glancing frantically left and right but saw nothing approaching from the darkness.

A few more clinks beside him.

"How's it lookin', boys?" Boss sounded as nervous as Leon looked. Marbles, however, was on autopilot. No fear, just routine.

"So far so good," he said.

Marbles really *was* in his element here. Boss was right to pick him. With one last snip, the hole in the fence was complete. Marbles folded it towards them and they both climbed through. Between the flowers and hedges ahead, Marbles could just make out the back of the car. He smiled. "Almost there."

"Wait! I've got movement. Damn, it's fast! What is it?" Boss asked.

Marbles shrugged at Leon, who returned the gesture.

"Can't see anything, Boss."

"And hopefully it hasn't seen you. But it's sure as hell lookin'!"

Leon pulled the fence flap closed behind them and kept low, then crawled at a painfully slow speed towards one of the floral displays. Keeping their heads beneath the canopy of petals, they did their best to ignore the pricks of fake thorns on the ever-bloom roses.

Ahead was a very decorative tree, no doubt made of the same material as the rest of the "plants" in this park. Either way, its shape and density made it perfect for climbing, and Marbles's feet began to itch at the sight of it. "Stay low, Leon. I'm gonna get a better view."

Before Leon could protest, Marbles was up and bounding towards the tree. He reached its trunk and scrambled up, hiding amongst the leaves as easily as if he were the breeze itself. Leon's heart thundered once again. He looked down into the painted ground beneath him and closed his eyes, focusing on his breathing.

The earpiece crackled. "Look out, kid!"

Leon snapped his head up and peered through the petals but saw nothing.

"Marbles, it's heading straight for you." Again, neither Leon nor Marbles saw it.

"Boss, you sure someone's here? I've seen nothing at all."

"It says so on my navs. Here it comes again."

This time, Marbles *did* manage to spot something. High up, against the stars, a black smudge was moving across the sky. Surely it wasn't a scanner-craft. He relayed what he thought he'd seen with a questioning tone, unsure as to why the CCD's latest equipment would be searching for a pizza delivery car.

"What? No way! Scanner-crafts, too? You sure?"

Leon poked his head out of the flowers and risked a skyward glance. The silver smudge grew slowly as it lowered itself, closing in on their location. Beams were protruding from its surface and licking the ground beneath in search of whomever it sought.

"Looks like it, Boss. I can see the beams. It's closing in on the park."

"Shit. Didn't leave any DNA in that car, did ya, Leon?"

Leon snorted. "For a scanner-craft of that distance to sniff my DNA inside the car, I would still need to be in there, veins open, squirting blood all over the interior."

Boss pulled a face but said nothing across the comms. Marbles broke the awkward silence.

"Artery."

"What?"

"Arteries are the ones that squirt blood. If you opened a vein, it would just…"

"Shut up, man. You know what I meant."

"Well it's just—"

"Quiet, ladies! This is *not* the time."

Leon let it go. He didn't seem concerned about the scanner-craft. Chances were, it was looking for something else entirely. He spoke again, changing the subject. "Hey, Boss, it possible they're looking for the Neuro?"

"Not likely. Neuros are shiny new, so you know, clean slate and all that. Don't even think they officially exist yet. Plus, if you saw beams, then they're sniffing for DNA, and robots ain't got none, dipshit."

Leon remembered the way Voice had spoken about the Neuro, as if Leon had accidentally woken a mythical being or something. He had a horrible feeling tugging at his shoulders, and he barely managed to spare a second's thought for his partner, who still kept his head low amongst the tree branches. "Marbles, you alright?"

"Just another day at work, dude."

Leon couldn't help but wonder how his partner was staying so calm. At first, he thought that maybe Marbles was used to this sort of situation, but now he wondered if maybe he just wasn't fully aware of what he'd gotten himself into. The scanner continued to fly overhead but was moving only slightly in each direction now. It was homing in. Leon's stomach lurched as it stopped directly above the park, three scanning beams conjoining to create a sort of orange floodlight that seemingly ignited the plastic leaves and branches all around Leon. He heard a clunk from the road behind him, but he dared not turn to look. He dared not even breathe, keeping his head low beneath the flowers and hoping the beam would move on.

"The dot has disappeared from my navs again. The scanner-craft has stopped. What's going on?" Boss's staticky voice was blaring into Leon's earpiece, and Leon forced himself not to yell back at him to shut up.

Marbles replied in place of Leon, who was watching the beam carefully focus on the flowers above his head. "The scanner's stopped right above the park. Beams are on Leon."

"Shit! You need to run. Can't hide from the scanners."

"It's too late, Boss. The ground unit is almost here. If he runs now, they might shoot."

Marbles could almost hear Leon's heart from across the park.

"Ground unit's here. Searching bushes. Found the hole in the fence. Doesn't look like it's coming through. What's it looking at? Something in the bushes? Crap, it's through. Slow movements, Leon. It's about to find you."

Leon, not knowing what else to do, rolled onto his back, hands raised, and caught a glimpse of the metal torso on a uni-wheel. The ground unit rolled towards the movement, gun nozzle tracking Leon's face. A beam jumped from a little light on its shoulder and wiped across Leon, who let out a mouse-like squeak. The beam dimmed, displaying a small holographic message in front of the ground unit: "Mismatch." The unit then turned back to the petals it was previously focusing on. Leon let go of his desperate breath.

A quiet chuckle sounded over the earpiece as Marbles couldn't contain his amusement. "Did you just piss yourself?"

Leon was still too frozen to speak or even move, but his eyes did trace the ground unit and saw what it was scanning: a dark shimmer on some of the plastic petals. Leon felt his leg, where he'd grazed himself on the hard plastic, but he felt no blood. It wasn't his own blood that the ground unit was searching for. That only left one other. He kept his voice low. "Marbles..." Not low enough. The ground unit turned again and raised its gun once more. It didn't scan Leon this time but radioed above for permission to question and pursue. An "affirmative" crackled down from the scanner-craft, and the ground unit's gun flicked alive, lights glowing blue along the side.

"I think we've got a problem, Boss," whispered Marbles from the tree.

"You said it. I've got another mark heading straight for ya!"

Leon put his hands up again, staring straight back into the black screen where eyes would be if the ground units weren't machines. The ground unit said something, gargled and robotic, which translated itself a second later. "You know Marbles." It wasn't a question. "Where is he?"

Leon shrugged, and a lump caught in his throat.

"Refusing to cooperate with police is an offence and you can and *will* be arrested. I ask you again. Where is Marbles?"

Leon's mind was working overtime. Did the ground unit just say "police"? A metallic explosion saved Leon from answering. The gates to the park blew into fragments as the Neuro darted through, Marbles's auto-fastening cap still over her eyes, thwarting her vision. The ground unit readjusted its aim, zapping the Neuro's head and yelling, "Halt, Marbles! You are under arrest!"

The Neuro kept its pace towards the car, and once again, the ground unit beamed a request to the craft above. On receiving an affirmative, a single *whomp* erupted from the ground unit's engaged firearm. A fired orb struck the figure and tackled it to the ground, tentacles unfolding and wrapping tightly around the target, who writhed and managed to clamber back to her feet. Loud cracks echoed throughout the park as the Neuro pulled a few metal tentacles from the orb to free herself. The ground unit fired another orb, then another. The Neuro finally collapsed, almost completely paralysed by the cocoon of tentacles. The ground unit radioed in again and the craft readjusted its beams onto the Neuro. It locked on to her position, acting as a searchlight. The Neuro looked like she was back on autopilot as she fought her constraints. The owner of that piece of equipment wouldn't be happy when he plugged himself into the Neuro and found her stuck in a police holding cell, scratched and crimped all over from the metal tentacles.

"Time to move, I say. What you reckon?" It was Marbles, chirpy as ever, quite enjoying the show from his vantage point. Leon didn't bother responding; he just hopped up from the flowerbed and ran for the car while the scanners and the Neuro were occupied.

18

LAST, LAST TIME

LEON DIVED INTO THE CAR, bouncing in the seat as he frantically fumbled for the ignition. The engine roared alive, the sound forcing even more adrenaline through his body. Out of complete reflex, he swung the car around, drumming on the dash as Marbles hopped from the tree, landed in a roll, and jumped across the back seats. They both whooped and Marbles fist-pumped as Leon accelerated. Seconds later, they were out on the road, laughing like a couple of kids who'd just vandalised a classroom and got away with it. Boss was excitedly bashing the side of his nav-grid screen some more, yelling basically any word that popped into his mind as he watched the speeding dot on his screen.

"Go! That's it! Yeah! Out of there! See ya, scanners. Who's the man?"

The scanner-craft spared one of its beams, which followed the car as it sped away, but there was too much distance for it to get a reading. After a few seconds, the beam faded, and the scanner-craft stayed behind. Leon pulled onto the highway just in time to join the early-morning traffic heading towards the city centre. With their hearts and minds working overtime, the slowness of the stream seemed to get impossibly slower, and Leon was literally twitching as he stared at the red tail lights in front of him. Only after at least an hour of slow driving did either of them manage to speak in a normal manner, the shaking no longer evident in their voices.

"They were looking for you back there. The scanners." Leon had been trying to decide the best way to bring it up.

Marbles responded with a questioning look, though he didn't seem overly surprised. "People are always looking for me, though this is the first time it's been *during* a job, not *after*."

"You usually attract the scanners?"

Marbles thought about this.

"You know why they were after you?" It was Boss this time, who'd been listening in on the conversation. Marbles shook his head, though Boss couldn't see it. Boss didn't seem to care about the non-response, either. He'd become distracted since his delivery boys had escaped the flower gardens. He was having a separate and heated conversation with someone on another line.

Leon looked over at Marbles, eyes darting to the barcode on his neck. Marbles instantly began defending himself. "It was just a misunderstanding. I took my day's pay and a guy thought I was stealing. Chased me down. Someone close by must have seen me running and tagged me. That's it."

Leon considered this. There was nothing there that would warrant sending scanners. Such an expense to the police company for such a small, alleged crime.

Leon racked his brain but also thought this might be a good time to learn more about his partner. "Is there anything else? I mean, if you know but just don't want to tell me, that's okay. But if you honestly don't know, that's a bit of a problem."

"I honestly don't know."

"Hmm. Any previous tags?"

"Yeah, one. When I was a kid, I stole some sweets."

Leon laughed. "That shopkeeper must have one hell of a grudge. Nah, that can't be it. We're missing something. I don't really know what to suggest. You seriously don't have any ideas?"

There were another few minutes of silent thought before Leon offered another suggestion.

"They take tax evasion pretty seriously…"

Marbles gave Leon a look. "Show me someone who doesn't dodge a bit of tax."

"Alright, well maybe not. I'm just trying to think outside the box."

Leon had forgotten Boss was still listening and was surprised when he chirped back into the conversation. "Okay, kids, great job back there. Nothin' seems to be followin' you. Everythin' worked out perfect. Now, I've got some news."

Leon cringed. "I'm afraid to ask what it is."

"I don't like kissin' ass, but the truth is, I need ya, Leon. I'm understaffed, I've got powerful people breathin' down my neck, and now I'm gettin' phone calls and... Ah, damnit!"

Despite the obvious danger, Leon felt exhilarated by the events of the night and was afraid to admit to himself that he enjoyed the whole ordeal with his new sort-of friend. The disguises, the running and hiding, the near misses, and the getaway. Maybe he could help out a little longer. He replied against his better instincts. "Was there something else you needed me to do?"

"It's nothing too major. A business partner of mine is adamant about sending Voice out on a long-distance drop, but he ain't completely fixed up yet. He could do with a hand."

Leon sighed deeply and sat back in his seat, thinking for a moment. "I suspect I'll regret this, but fine. I'll help out Voice."

"Good, 'cos he's already on his way over. Once you're back, let me know, and I'll get his coordinates." With that, a click sounded across the comms. Boss had disconnected.

19

WHO IS THE BOSS?

AN ALARM SHRIEKED above as a red blinker marked its place on the map across the back wall. The onlooker felt his overly large stomach grumble as he saw the whereabouts of the mark. It was getting too frequent. Once every few months now and increasing. The bald man kicked himself backwards from behind his desk and let his chair glide out in front of the map. He made a few lazy hand gestures in front of the screen, zooming the map out and searching the area. His already beady eyes narrowed impossibly more so until they were nothing but black specs squashed into his swollen face. Thankfully, these hideous features of his were almost always covered by round, mirrored disks clipped in place inside his eye sockets. The glass itself had many uses, but the tint was purely to hide his eyes. He didn't like how they betrayed his thoughts.

The man sat quietly in front of the map. His arms grew tired after a few more gestures and he used the last of his energy to kick back again, greased wheels sliding with ease towards his desk. A semi-portable phone lay there, buttons spaced to accommodate the width of his fingers, and he speed-dialled number one.

Before it could finish its first ring, Boss answered. "I'm busy."

The man sighed quietly in irritation. "We've got another."

"What zone this time?"

"C."

"Shit. Well I'm in the middle of something right now. Both my guys are still in the field."

"I'm going to need to use Voice."

"Voice is back? Did you plan on lettin' me know?"

"He's not a hundred per cent, but the general mechanics are ready to go. It's all that I require. We'll finish off the repairs once he's back from the zone. Just give me a couple more days."

"I don't have a couple more days, Dubbs. What I *do* have is a goddamn Neuro up my ass, a missing car, and a shop in lockdown. I'm not making a whole lot of money right now!"

"I will get Voice to you as soon as I can, but let us not forget the priority here."

"You got no one else to send? Or you just like screwing with me..."

"Zone C needs another drop-off, and they are going to get one." Dubbs's tone was as calm as ever, but this last sentence conveyed authority.

A few gargled grunts worked their way across the line, before Boss calmed himself with a few deep breaths. "Don't start trying to call the shots, pal. I'm the one who calls the shots. I'll send my best guy your way once he returns from this little road trip, and he and whatever part of Voice you've fixed up by then can head down to your bloody Zone C."

"That's too kind of you."

"You're goddamn right it is! These repairs are getting far too expensive. And how am I supposed to run a business with you constantly stealin' my staff members?"

"Well, have you tried talking to Voice about it? If he didn't drive so recklessly..." Dubbs's tone was rarely anything but cool and collected, which infuriated Boss more than whatever Dubbs was actually saying.

"How am I supposed to reason with a machine, Dubbs? Why don't you tell him for me in whatever freakin' robot language it is that he actually understands? 'Cos he sure as hell doesn't understand English!"

"I'll see what I can do."

"Yeah, course ya will. Shoot me your address and I'll get my guy there as soon as possible."

"Huh, that'll be the day. I'll have Voice meet your guy at the third place."

With that, the phone disconnected. Dubbs sighed again. He always felt tired after talking to Boss about anything. That man just had to push his luck—every time.

Dubbs glanced around the empty room and shook his head. All the effort would pay off in the end. He wouldn't last forever, but if he could leave behind a functioning team and a decent foundation, then his work could continue without him. That was all that mattered to him now.

20

SOME PLACE

LEON WAITED PATIENTLY, shivering with the cool breeze rustling his clothes. He couldn't pull his jacket any tighter. He pressed himself more tightly against the wall of the building to stay under a window ledge above, the only shield against the drizzle. Boss stood beside him, arms folded, goose flesh from head to toe. He had decided to don his disguise again, which offered hardly any defence against the cold. The wind was picking up now and the odd piece of trash was blowing past, rattling or scuffing the ground as it went.

"So uh… he's on his way, right?" Leon managed through blue lips. Boss snarled and turned, but his words were stopped by a stray lock flicking into his eye. Leon disguised his chuckle, waited for Boss to finish cursing his wig, and spoke again. "Like, he definitely said he was going to be here?"

"Well, I spoke to my partner, Dubbs. He's the one fixing Voice up. He said he would have him here, ready."

"Okay. Maybe you should call this Dubbs guy? Just to double check."

"Nah, he's as paranoid as a fire toad on fool's day. Wouldn't answer a mobile call from his own mother."

Leon squeezed his lips together and eyed the road, hoping to see a pair of headlights. He couldn't wait to have the car's heater blasting him point-blank. If it didn't happen soon, he was afraid his nose would snap off.

Boss was concentrating hard on the ground in front of him, taking deep breaths and tucking the locks of hair under his chin. Leon only realised then just how much willpower it was taking Boss to ignore the cold. "I didn't expect today to be quite this cold, eh? Came from nowhere."

"It's fuckin' freezin'!" Boss shivered. He rubbed his folded arms together as he tried without luck to cause a bit of friction. He cupped his hands over his mouth and blew, ripped off his wig, and wrapped it around his shoulders. "I can't feel my face!"

Leon chortled until the cold air burned his chest. At risk of irritating Boss further, he couldn't help but ask about Voice again. "So this was definitely the place he was heading to, right? Dubbs said 'meet Voice down the random alley behind the closed knitting shop'?"

"Kid, it's not that complicated. We've got pre-planned drop-off points. This is one of 'em. He said meet Voice at the second place, and that's where we are. Dubbs just likes screwin' me around, that's all."

They stood shivering for another few minutes. With each gust of wind, a wave of watery needles was blown into Leon and Boss, who could have passed as statues for any passers-by. But of course, there were no passers-by. Not a soul in sight, and worst of all, no Voice.

"Ah, shit." Boss unfolded his arms and stepped out into the rain. He moved slowly but deliberately, pretending he wasn't frozen from the balls up. Leon watched with confusion. It was only when Boss was almost out of sight behind sheets of rain that he yelled out to him. "Am I supposed to follow?"

"Depends. Wanna freeze to death or you wanna come meet Voice?"

"I thought Voice was meeting us here?"

"Third place. I remember now. Dubbs said he would meet us at the third place."

Thankfully, the third place was only an hour's brisk walk from the second place. Boss had given up on his disguise once his ankles began to rub, and he marched ahead, barefoot. Once they veered off the main roads and down another quiet alley, Boss heard his phone ringing. He shoved his hand down his top and removed the phone.

"What?"

Leon heard a mumbling on the other end of the line, interrupted at intervals by Boss.

"Yeah… We're there… We've been waiting all day. No, I'm right here. I'm at the car park now. Mhm."

They turned the last corner and stopped. Leon looked up at Boss, who stood, just as dumbfounded. Boss's electric eye was visibly adjusting and scanning what was stood before him. There was only one vehicle ahead of them, and it wasn't the one Boss had ordered. The phone was still mumbling away.

"What the hell is that?" screamed Boss down the line. "What did you do to Voice?"

"I told you I needed him. He wouldn't be much use to me in that little sports car, so I've moved the hardware. Don't worry, I will put him back when he's done."

"And how much is that costin' me? Goddammit, Dubbs, stop with the tricks and the doing things and stuff!"

"Don't worry, I'm giving you a good deal." Dubbs made a sound, and Leon thought for a second that he'd actually heard the man laugh. Maybe. Then tapping sounded as

Dubbs typed something across to Voice. A few more taps, and Dubbs returned his attention to the phone.

"Okay, everything is ready. If your man could hop in the wagon, we'll get this moving. Wouldn't want to waste any more time if it can be avoided."

Boss huffed resignedly.

"Voice will get your guy back safely in a couple days' time. For now, why don't you put your feet up? Catch some sleep, drink some wine, whatever. Oh, and Voice wanted me to let you know that he thinks your dress looks lovely." Dubbs choked on another laugh, and then the phone clicked and disconnected.

"It's a skirt, asshole!" But the line was already dead.

Leon burst into laughter but stopped as a stiletto caught him hard in the chest.

"You *seriously* just throw your shoe at me?"

Boss looked to the ground, ashamed. Hydraulics hissed as Voice lowered the shell of the baby monster truck and shortly after sounded a couple of toots from the horn.

Boss hobbled over and leaned in as a window slid open. He exchanged a few words with Voice.

Leon was close behind. "Alright, Boss, I better get moving. I'll call you once we're back."

Boss nodded and walked away. As before, his folded arms were the only rain protection he wore, and it wasn't long before the fog devoured him.

Leon ran to the passenger's side and the door sprung open as he neared. He climbed the step and jumped into the seat, slamming the door shut behind him. Then he noticed he was the only person inside. The whole back segment of the wagon was full of large crates and nothing else. Puzzled, he reached across the seats, preparing to hop over to the driver's side, and the horn sounded. He jumped back, looking dumbfounded at the wheel. Then the engine roared to life and the navs lit up. Leon looked at the screen, and words began to fill the previously empty address bar. "Hey, Leon. Welcome to my ride."

Leon wasn't sure how to respond. He spoke aloud. "Uh… hi? Can you hear me?"

The address bar on the navs cleared and another message replaced it. "Yep. Can't speak, though. Sorry, still need some fixing up, but I'm good to drive. You ready?"

Leon wondered where Voice might be and how he was controlling the vehicle. It took him a little longer than he'd like to admit to realise that Voice *was* the vehicle.

"Oh, so… you're Voice?" He rapped on the steering wheel with his knuckles. "Wow, that explains a lot. I honestly thought you died in that pile-up." He looked around the inside of the vehicle, nodding to himself. "I bet you weren't cheap, huh?"

The address wiped itself again, and more words appeared: "I think I was a five-finger discount type of deal, actually, though that part of my memory is wiped." Then a real address filled the box, and lines began to draw themselves across the map. The car made another few sounds as its chassis rose to maximum clearance. Leon sat back and strapped in. The engine roared and the wagon tore backwards. The steering wheel turned itself, and Leon stared at it uncomfortably, ready to intervene if necessary. He'd seen how precise Voice's driving had been, but he had also seen him skid into oncoming traffic.

"Uh, no stunts while I'm inside, please." Leon's thoughts flashed back to Marbles and how he must have felt when Leon picked him up from Grey Town. Now he understood. The steering wheel wound left, right, then left again as accelerator held itself to the ground. They ripped through the alleys and flew back out into the streets, bouncing back and forth as the shell rocked on its oversized suspension.

21

MISFORTUNE COOKIE

THE DOOR AHEAD SEEMED just like any other door. Dark. Wooden. Weather-worn varnish. Despite its appearance, however, there was something very different about this door. This door resembled a hope for justice, as behind it was a sleeping man who might just have the answers these cops were looking for. Answers to the questions the squadron had been asking themselves ever since the murder of their colleague, leader, and friend. A few rules had certainly been bent—if not completely overlooked—for them to end up here, but as they stood united, so close to the answers, not one of them regretted the risks they had taken.

The squad leader let his battering ram charge. Once its light flicked green, he hit the switch. A pulse exploded from the end of the ram, punching through the bottom hinge and levering the door straight out of the frame. The squad wasted no time, and before the splinters had finished decorating the hallway carpet, they all piled inside, flashlights on and guns glowing ready.

"Clear!" came one voice from the front room as another sounded from the kitchen. The small team tore through the bottom floor in seconds, before regrouping at the foot of the stairway in the hall.

They were saved the hassle of ascending as a light flicked on atop the stairs, revealing a bearded man in pyjamas. "Can I help you?" he managed, sounding genuinely confused.

"Mr. Sven? Hands behind your head, slowly. Turn—back to us—now." The squad leader had leapt up the stairs and cuffed Mr. Sven before he finished turning.

"What's this about?"

"We have reason to believe you have aided in the escape of a criminal…"

"You're mistaken."

"… by the name of Marbles Everlook…"

"I've never heard of that name."

"… and will be taken in for questioning."

"You've got the wrong man. I'm telling you."

"Cut the crap, *Sven*. We know what you've done, and you're gonna tell us what we need to know." The leader made sure the handcuffs were painfully tight and began pulling Sven down the stairs as they cut into his skin.

"I don't know what you're talking about. Do you have a warrant to be here? I demand to speak to my lawyer before—"

The hard butt of a gun caught the bridge of his nose before he could finish his sentence.

"You forfeited your right to a lawyer the day you helped kill our sergeant, motherfucker."

Sven's eyes rolled back into his head. His body became a rag doll. Snorts and mumbled insults surrounded him, but he wasn't sure if he was hearing or imagining them. The only thing he could feel was the cool metal at his wrists, and for a while, which might have only been a split second, he wondered if he were hanging by them. A deep voice, much closer than the others still swirling in his head, punched through.

"Yo, hit him again, man." Another crack with the gun, which Sven heard but didn't feel. He didn't remember what happened next.

Mr. Sven sat, feet bound to a metal chair, which was bolted to the ground. His shivering kept him awake, and he wished he were back in his bed.

"I can see you're cold. Why don't you just answer our questions so we can get you out of here? Help us help you. What is your connection with our suspect?"

"I've been over this. I wasn't there. I don't know a Marbles. It's not me you're looking for."

"Fine. So let's say, for argument's sake, that you weren't there. Could you, at the very least, explain why a fake ID, with your photograph, was found in the coin compartment of the getaway vehicle?"

Sven rolled his eyes in frustration before they settled back onto the cop with a hard stare.

"Oh yeah, you don't know that, either. Is that right? Well maybe you could tell me why you would have such an ID made in the first place. Or how, exactly, you got yourself a false profile in the police files to back it up. This is some sophisticated work, I must say."

The policeman held a driver's license in front of Sven's bearded face. The hologram of a face flashed brightly. Sven recognised the license—it was the one Boss assured him would be destroyed. The name at the top was fake, but the record in the police system should have been enough to satisfy any traffic cop or random breath-tester. Whatever these guys were trying to pin him for was undoubtedly more serious. He thought back to when the squad had entered his house, trying to remember what they said before they knocked him unconscious.

"We had an agent recover this from the wreckage. Seems it's not only the local police department you've pissed off." He looked down at the ID again and let the hologram flash the photo in the air above it. "Did you really think a beard would be enough to throw our face recognisers, Mr. *Cookie*?" He read the name on the ID with a heavy drop of sarcasm.

"That's not mine." Technically, he wasn't lying, as it remained Boss's property until it had somehow ended up in the hands of the cops. "My name is Sven. You said so yourself."

"Yes. That may be your real name, but obviously you operate under a false identification when transporting criminals."

"What? No, that's—"

"That's enough bullshit from you is what that is! Where is Marbles now?"

Sven huffed again, closed his eyes, and sat back. He could tell he was going to be here for a while. Taking a moment to calm himself, he opened his eyes again and continued his stare. "I've told you. I don't know what you're talking about."

The policeman smiled, cool as ever, though Mr. Sven could see the anger boiling up behind his eyes. Sven understood, because he felt it, too. If Boss had bought all new gear like he'd promised, instead of using the old stuff with Sven's

"Cookie" details still programmed in, then he wouldn't be in this mess. What made the situation more frustrating for Sven was that he honestly didn't know what the hell was going on.

The policeman leaned forwards, returning the stare.

"What're you thinking, I wonder? Are you thinking about what lie you could tell that I might believe? Maybe you're working on an excuse? Something you think will exempt you from this little mishap?"

Sven had had enough of this. "I'm thinking you're grasping at straws. I'm thinking you don't have a shred of proof. I'm thinking you've got the wrong guy, and I'm thinking you're wasting your time."

"And you're also thinking you're pretty clever, but we're going to get to the bottom of this." The interrogator nodded at the cameras. "Take him to the downtown lockup."

The door slid open and three men walked in. Trailing behind was an autonomous ground unit. One man unshackled Sven's feet while the others stood closely by, hands on shock-batons, waiting for an excuse to use them. The interrogator left, and the trio handed Sven to the ground unit, who led him out of the steel box and down the hall.

22

DRY RUN

FINALLY, AFTER HOWEVER MANY red lights, Voice pulled the wagon into an open stretch of tarmac. The wagon rocked as gusts of wind slammed the side. Leon looked down at the navs, unsure where their destination was. All he could see was a line across the screen. He was in for a long stretch of silent bobbing through the ocean of sand and dust. It took a while to exit the city completely, but once the buildings ended, there wasn't an awful lot to keep his attention. To make things even worse, Voice couldn't speak. Leon spent a little while trying to get a response, but now that Voice had an address locked in, he couldn't seem to type any custom messages. He gave up in the end and realised he'd be better off sleeping the time away. He certainly felt tired enough.

Just as Leon felt himself drifting off to wonderland, the feeling of falling jolted him alert. The wagon had left the tarmac at high speed and now bounced through the dirt, suspension shrieking. Voice must have seen something up ahead. Leon checked the navs and noticed a marking on the map. Not a moving node like he'd seen before, but a bright red marker that someone had manually programmed in. He asked Voice what it was, forgetting in his half-sleeping state that Voice no longer had a voice.

"I wish I knew where we were going, Voice. I don't know where to look or what to look out for." He kept his eyes peeled on the horizon but saw nothing beyond the dunes. The ground dropped and the road fell out of sight. Not much longer and their dust trail would blend in with all the other walls of dust kicked up by the wind. Voice continued his detour, speed still dropping as he weaved between large rocks and piles of domestic waste.

Another hour passed this way, and the progress was slow and gradual. Another red point appeared on the map. It marked a police checkpoint. Voice responded with a turn of the wheel and bounced right, launching the wagon into a sand dune climb. The engine growled angrily as the wheels sunk into the soft powder, but still they spun, despite the sand's grip. The wagon crawled to the top. Leon made the most of their vantage point by checking all directions for patrols or police—it seemed like that was what they were avoiding—before they dove down the other side of the dune and headed back to the tarmac.

The sand and dust beside the road was a darker colour now. Leon spotted bits of plastic and other scraps all throughout the sand grains. Frowning, he looked around. "Wait a minute. I've seen this on TV. Are we heading for a zone?" Of course, there was no response.

Leon could no longer see the wastes around him. He saw houses instead. His old neighbourhood—trees, dogs and cats, bicycles, footballs, his family's car. Beside him were his parents, smiling and talking to each other. They embraced each other as Leon climbed into a taxi, nervous but excited about starting his new life in the big city. His parents waved him goodbye as he took off towards the highway, warm sun beating from above. He heard a sound in the distance. Rumbling engines. They were definitely petrol and in a hurry. A military vehicle flew past Leon's taxi, heading back towards his parents. Large trucks drummed close behind. Everyone on the street stopped to look as a convoy rolled its way into the town. On the news that night, Leon heard that there had been a parasitic outbreak at the edge of his hometown. To stop its spread, a desiccant foam was sprayed from jet hoses attached to the trucks, sapping moisture from everything it touched and turning all to solid mounds of dust. Like all living things, the parasite couldn't survive without water. Those who ran didn't make it far. Those who barricaded themselves in their houses never left as they became tenants of their own tombs. Screams and cries whirled in Leon's head as he saw images of his hometown's streets becoming mottled and grey. This envisioned nightmare sent him coasting into a shallow, restless sleep.

Leon was shaken awake once more. He wiped the sand from his eyes and scratched his neck. They had arrived at their destination. Around him were dusty, empty streets lined with buildings resembling sun-dried coral. The sun was getting low but wasn't threatening to fall behind the desert plains just yet. With the dark thoughts of earlier locked away in his mind once more, Leon turned to the driver's seat. It was empty, but he felt that this was the right place to direct his speech. "So I guess you aren't going to help me unload?"

The navs lit back up and a response typed itself across the top. "That's why you're here. I drive, you unload :)"

The wagon hissed, masking Leon's mumbling as he hopped from the seat and looked back to the screen for instructions.

"Open the wall panel and switch the dials on. Chuck the crates on the conveyor belt. Done."

Leon did as he was told. Something inside the conveyor belt screeched painfully, but after a few seconds, it gave into the strain and the belt clunked to life. He started unpacking, placing the supply boxes atop the grimy belt that disappeared into the side of a warehouse. It looked abandoned, judging by the chained doors and run-down exterior. Before Leon had time to fall into routine, Voice sounded the wagon's horn. Leon trudged over to the passenger's side and flung the door open. "What's up?"

A fine mist covered the buildings in the distance. Leon had mistaken it for the darkness of the setting sun, but it wasn't that at all. It was rain. Voice's screen said, "Don't get caught in the zone's rain. That's the last thing Dubbs told me."

"Alright, I'll speed up."

Leon ran back and continued offloading the crates, two by two, onto the belt. As he removed the last two, Voice's doors slammed shut and locked. Leon placed the crates down and made for the passenger's side door, but he'd already wasted too much time. Despite Voice's obligation to protect his passengers, Dubbs had added an override code to the program. Under no circumstances could Voice allow himself to get rained on whilst in the zone. The engine came alive, and the next second, the wagon was speeding off the way they'd come. Wide-eyed, Leon gave chase, arms flailing at the speeding vehicle. It didn't stop. Unsure of what was going on, Leon did the only thing he could think of: he ran back to the warehouse, jumped onto the conveyor belt, and curled up to the size of one of the crates.

Flaps of plastic wiped over Leon as he let the conveyor belt slowly pull him into the warehouse. His eyes were clamped shut in anticipation of feeling a speck of rain, but there was none. He heard a clunk up ahead as one of the crates fell from the belt. Then a shuffle as something moved it aside, just in time for the next clunk. He opened his eyes and uncurled. The warehouse was almost completely empty, except for a burned-out shell of a van at the far end, in front of a standalone wardrobe.

He hopped from the still-moving belt and took a better look at his surroundings. The supply crates had started to pile up at the end of the belt. He waited for whatever caused the shuffling sound to clear the way for the rest, but it never came. As if his ears had just switched themselves on, a hard hammering sound pummelled the tin roof above, like an endless roll of thunder.

"Move away from the belt," commanded a muffled voice. Startled, Leon glanced around, wondering where it had come from.

"I said move!"

Leon jumped aside this time, realising that the rain was coming in through the still-moving belt and he was standing right on the drainage slope.

"Help me move these crates back, quickly."

Leon yelped as what he'd mistaken for an old uniform on a hook moved towards the boxes. Seeing the person wrapped in a full-body radiation suit made him feel quite insecure about his T-shirt and cargo shorts. He ran ahead of the rain-soaked panels and helped the suit drag the crates away from the belt as it brought water further into the warehouse. Leon looked over the last crate for splash marks. Leon looked up, ready to share the news of there being no water damage to the crates, but he instead fell backwards, hands waving between his face and the nozzle of the gun. Despite this not being the first time, a gun in his face always threw him off guard. In his defence, though, the situation here was a little different. This gun wasn't a new-age set-to-stun electro-gun, but rather an old-school Smith & Wesson revolver, created with the intention of leaving one hell of a mess.

"Get off the ground!" barked the suit. Leon didn't respond quickly enough and found himself being dragged away from the puddle creeping away from the belt. The suit then grabbed Leon's collar, gave him a hard look in the eyes, and continued carrying the crates, this time placing them in the back of the burned-out van.

Leon stood up, absently swatting dirt from his backside.

"What's going on?"

The suit looked back, and Leon caught a glimpse of red-tinged hair through the visor.

"Reckon you could shift a crate while you talk?"

Leon frowned and made his way to the pile, picked up a crate of his own, and waddled to the van. The suit seemed to make much lighter work of the heavy cargo.

"Why the gun?" he asked.

The suit dropped another crate into the van.

"Had to be sure you weren't carrying."

Leon straightened the pile, trying to make a bit more room for the last few crates. "Carrying what?"

"You know, the Bug or whatever. I don't have the equipment to do official checks right now, but we each have our own methods. It has mutated again recently. We lost two men last week—saw their eyes darken almost immediately. Your eyes ain't dark, but you keep lying around when there's water about and I can't guarantee they'll stay that way."

Leon had thought the suit meant carrying a weapon. The mention of the parasite sent his mind spinning as he saw another flashback of the news clip. Distracted, he loaded the last crate and tried to shut the door, though it jammed a little over halfway. He took a closer look, wondering if maybe it was something he could fix, but the tracks were completely warped by rust.

"Yeah, that's as far as it goes. So did you want to come meet the others? We can have you checked out properly, too. Once the rain starts, it can go on for a day or two. You're gonna get bored waiting up here for it to stop."

The suit creaked the driver's side door ajar and squeezed in through the gap, then leaned across to the passenger's door. Behind was a dirty old sheet that the suit threw over the crates and fastened down inside the van before slumping into the shredded remnants of the driver's seat. Leon hopped in and found that his chair was only slightly better, though both used the crates behind them as backrests.

"This thing even going to start?" asked Leon, looking around the completely wrecked remains of the van. To answer his question, the suit produced a key from the sun visor, which Leon was surprised to see still attached, and found the ignition.

"We keep all the important parts in top nick." With that, the engine turned over and a healthy electric whine came from somewhere beneath them. "The old look is for camouflage. No way you could tell this van apart from the other vehicles out there when the engine's off."

"How many people do you have here?"

"Give me a moment, yeah?" The suit rolled the van forwards and over a solid metal grate that began to descend with the weight. Before long, the van had sunk into almost complete darkness below the ground. They rolled forwards once more and the platform ascended behind them, closing off the tunnel. Leon felt a barrage of questions work their way to his lips. He kept quiet for now, though. A hissing sounded beside him and the suit's headpiece unclipped. On the dash was a comms system that Leon recognised. Most likely courtesy of Boss or Dubbs. The faint glow of its screen was the only light in the tunnel at the moment, and in it, he saw the shine of her hair once again. It was a matted red mess atop a frightened face. The young woman placed the helmet on the crate behind her and sighed deeply, relieved to have the weight removed from her shoulders. "Sorry, it gets really stuffy talking with that thing on."

Leon stared as his eyes adjusted in the darkness, and after a few seconds, he realised that she was looking back at him, eyebrow raised. "Oh, I didn't mean to stare. My eyes were… It's dark. Um…"

She chuckled, and despite the awkwardness, he felt a lot more comfortable at the genuine sound no longer horribly distorted by the visor. "I'm Leon, by the way."

She took his extended hand. "Daiz. Nice to meet you." They held each other's gaze. The moment was cut short by a familiar burst of static. The comms screen brightened and displayed a gentleman with a neatly cropped moustache and proud chin. Despite now living in one of the most hostile environments known to man, he obviously held authority before the outbreak and continued to do his best to maintain his rank.

"Just checking in. Did you get the drop?" Before Daiz could reply, she saw his moustache turn towards Leon. "Who are you?" He wasn't happy.

Daiz spoke quickly. "This is Leon, the supply man. He was stranded in the rain so I've brought him along. His eyes aren't dark."

"And what if he's got an old strain? You could be bringing it back here."

She held up the pack of cookies to the comms. The moustache man huffed. "You had better keep those antibodies strong, young man. We will give you a thorough check when you arrive."

Intimidated by the pixels on the screen, Leon struggled to find words.

"Okay, thanks for checking in. The rain is strong so we will stick to the passage all the way. See you in a few hours," Daiz said on Leon's behalf. She spoke loudly, over the top of the protesting man on the other end. "Talk to you soon." The screen crackled and went back to the ominous glow of standby mode. Daiz sat back and sighed. She looked at Leon. "So you've met Hughey, the overprotective father figure of the group. He's harmless, really, but you shouldn't take his words lightly. Keep eating those cookies, for everyone's sake." She took a deep breath. "You seem like you have questions."

"Uh, definitely."

Daiz flicked on the headlights. The tunnel lit up before them but the van stayed just as dark inside.

"Good. We've got a long drive. Fire away." She flashed him a smile before putting her foot down, van whirring as she tore through the stone archways unfolding in the darkness.

"My parents! They could be here. They were in the first outbreak. Esmeralda and Tock. Do you know them?"

Daiz tried to instil hope in Leon, but the quick reaction of her head told him almost instantly that she didn't know those names. "The first outbreak was hundreds of kilometres from here. That's now Zone A. They have a similar network over there as we do here. Your parents may be among them. There is always a chance."

Leon's eyes shimmered with the onset of tears. "Can't you ask them? Is there any way to send a message?"

"We do have a little contact between zones, but it's costly. You would need it authorised by Hughey. Dubbs can get us food and some water, but the electricity is scarce. I just don't know if—"

"Don't bother." Leon let his tears fall, though he didn't allow his voice to waver. "I know where they are—buried in foam. I was stupid to think…" He trailed off.

Daiz continued driving. Leon sniffed back another wave of tears.

"Am I safe here?" He gestured to her bio-hazard suit.

The young woman took her eyes off the road to flash a cocked eyebrow at Leon. "It's not airborne. It just thrives when it rains. This suit is for precaution's sake, really. In case it mutates again. You will probably be fine."

"Probably? That's the best you can do?"

Daiz hoped to relax her passenger with old-fashioned hospitality. She reached back and punched a hole in the top of one of the crates, then wrestled a box free through the gap. She threw it at Leon, who removed a small blanket and another packet of cookies. "There's medicines processed into all of our foods. Get those down your neck and you will repel the Bug for another few hours, at least. And if it's already in you, it will be incapacitated. There's nothing permanent yet, but Dubbs takes care of us. Your odds are good."

Leon wasted no time in devouring a handful. He was happy to have a distraction and spat his next question at Daiz through a spray of chocolate chip crumbs. "You mentioned camouflage. Are you hiding from the foamers? Who sends them, anyway?" His thoughts were still with his parents as he put them in his situation. Maybe they weren't foamed straight away. Maybe they ran, terrified, surviving an extra day, only to be hunted down by another group. The van's headlights reflected off the shiny surface of the pillars, casting a striped pattern on the windscreen. Leon couldn't help but be captivated by it as it darted up the bonnet. He turned to the red-haired driver and saw the same pattern flicking across her face. He waited for a response. After a short while, she slowed the van a little and faced him, and it seemed she was watching the pattern on his face, too.

"All we know is that if we stay on the surface for too long, we're found and killed. The people we are hiding from... Well, we don't know who they are."

"Have you tried leaving?"

"We can't. They find us. It's like they can trace us somehow."

"But if Dubbs can get a driver in and out with these supply drops, surely he can—"

"It doesn't work. They find us. Every time. Us zoners cannot leave." With this, she changed gears and sped the van along even faster. She was driving as if her life depended on it, and Leon grew more concerned, wondering if maybe it did.

23

INCUBATION CUPBOARD

Daiz pulled into a side tunnel. It was similar to the first one, but this was an old train tunnel, and Daiz was bouncing the van along the tracks, trying, without much success, to line the wheels up with the rails to smooth out the ride. Leon rubbed at his numb backside, complaints drowned out by Daiz's laughter. At least one of them was enjoying the ride.

Dots of glowing paint that reflected the headlights indicated the way. Daiz tore the van left, bumping up an access ramp and driving through the low-ceilinged walkways of the subway station. Finally, she pulled into a parking spot that made the van look as if it had crashed into the wall back when the foaming began.

"Well, this is it," Daiz said. She kicked the rusted van door open and climbed through, then walked to the back of the van. Leon joined her and made to pick up one of the boxes, but Daiz stopped him.

"Maybe let them check you first."

Daiz picked up the crate instead and shuffled over to the barricade of rubble. She moved about in the dark, doing something Leon couldn't quite make out, then waited. She held up an all but invisible hand to Leon, then walked further behind the bricks and twisted scraps.

"Hello?" No answer.

Daiz moved her hands around again, trying once more to activate what Leon assumed to be a doorbell. This time, he did see some movement, but it looked more like the shadow of a figure than an actual person. The only light now came from the small gaps in the blocked stairway behind him. He turned to see what had caused the shadow and found himself face-down on the cold tiles of the subway floor, arms twisted behind him. He called out to Daiz, who had turned, but her protests went unnoticed. Leon was being painfully dragged back into the darkness, echoing sounds adding to his disorientation.

Leon wasn't sure how much time had passed when he finally became aware of himself once more, tied to a chair and stuck in what looked like a broom cupboard. His head was hazy and he wasn't certain it hadn't been split in two. A light bulb hung from a cord above him and swayed slightly, making shadows duck for cover behind every surface, then peak back out and check if the coast was clear. Over and over. He wanted to throw up. The shadows played with his vision even after his eyes were closed, but he held them shut nonetheless, concentrating on his breathing. Only when the nausea subsided did he test his voice. No one responded. He yelled again, louder this time, though more questioningly than angrily.

"Hello?" Nothing. "Anyone there? I'm Leon, with the supplies. I'm with Daiz."

A bolt screeched beside him and he turned his head. The door seemed strange, like it was vibrating. The nausea tugged again at his mind and stomach. "Hello?" he whispered, eyes blurring. The door swung open and the darkness entered the room, enveloping Leon and dousing the hanging bulb above him. The only light now came from a device that seemed to float towards him. A beam of blue light sliced at him. Leon began to struggle against his binds but he could only move his head. Before long, an invisible force held his head, and his cries were muffled and painful. Something was blocking his airways. The blue beam made its way to Leon's face and shot into his eyes, one at a time. Then, as quickly as it had come, the thing left, the door closed, and the shadows once again hid from the swinging bulb. He could breathe again now. The dizziness returned and he slumped forwards as much as he was able, colours cutting their way across his eyes. His vision seemed to tunnel. All he could see was a bright pattern of the thin square box open at his feet. A circular grease stain had bled into the bottom, and the inside of the box's lid showed an overly friendly-looking man with a robotic eye. His bright red mohawk reached the edge of the box. He wore a cheesy grin and held both thumbs up. Underneath were the words "Pizza Boss, open 24/7" written in mock Italian font. Leon's throat burned. He decorated the box with the semi-digested pizza and fell unconscious.

Leon awoke, shivering. His feet were bare and his hair dripped water into a pool on the floor around him. His arms had been freed—the extra rope now tied around his shoulders, holding him upright. The door beside him was open. Someone peered in from the darkness and swiftly came to his side.

"You're awake." The voice was familiar. Leon could make out the faint shimmer of red hair. It was Daiz. She threw the blanket from the van over him and untied his shoulders.

"You were thrashing about a bit."

Leon dried his hair and wrapped the damp blanket around himself. "It's cold."

"Yep. You get used to it."

"Where are we?"

Daiz paused for a moment, thinking. "I'm in a service tunnel near the escalators. You… Well, you are in a cleaner's cupboard." She chuckled.

"What did they do to us?"

"To me? Nothing. You're down here for the incubation period. We hold for twenty-four hours, just to be safe, although the new strain has been knocking people out in a minute flat. I wouldn't be worried anyway; I fed you a cheesy pizza, just to be sure. Some of the folks down here might not be happy if they knew that, but we've got enough problems without adding "recreationals" into the mix. Know what I mean?"

"Not really."

"That pizza, man. Best medicine we've got, but too many of our guys were getting hooked on the stuff. Most of us don't want too much of it floating around down here, so… you're welcome."

"You drugged me?"

Daiz made a strange noise with her lips and her eyes drifted to the recent past as she remembered something funny. "Oh, and sorry about the water. You chucked up all over the place and all I had was the pressure hose."

Leon could sense her concentration and wished he could ignore how hard Daiz was trying not to laugh in his face.

He hadn't found it funny in the slightest. All he could remember were horrible noises, sharp colours, and dizziness.

A clunk sounded behind Daiz. Footsteps rang from the walls as a suit emerged from the shadow, blue flashlight flicking on in hand. The suit leaned into the cupboard. Through the reflections on the visor, Leon could just make out a cropped moustache. The old man shone the light into each of Leon's eyes in turn and saw nothing out of the ordinary. With that, he stepped back, removed the headpiece, and smiled warmly at Leon, his hand held out in front of him. "Leon, wasn't it? Sorry about dragging you in here like that. Got to protect our own, you understand. Anyway, you're clear, so… welcome to Zone C."

24

DOWN TOWN

T HE SMALL AMOUNT OF SUN that remained for the
day cast a large circular shadow over the police
station. The officer at the front desk was still getting used
to the occasional visit from a scanner-craft, and when he
noticed the shadow, he poked his head out of the window
to get a better look. As expensive as they were to hire, he
couldn't help but be impressed by the new technology.
There were plenty of good changes on the horizon. The
lieutenant didn't quite share the same view, always
cursing the "good for nothing" scanners and ground units
for their slow, overly cautious approach, but the theory
was that he just didn't like the fact that they weren't
capable of filing paperwork. That meant that the human
police officers wouldn't be completely out of a job — for the
time being, at least.

The scanner-craft had stopped moving now. It hovered, high above the station, spitting out orders to all ground units below. The door to the station buzzed itself open and a ground unit rolled in. A muddy track was left on the entrance rug behind it. The officer added "wiping feet" to the list of things that humans could still do better than robots. The unit was gripping at a long metal bind, which was wrapped tightly around Cookie Sven, who trailed behind. The ground unit turned to face the police officer and clicked and beeped, then waited for the scanner-craft to beam down a translation. "I need an empty holding cell for one dangerous suspect."

The police officer raised an eyebrow at this, curious as to where the "dangerous" description was coming from. The man seemed completely compliant. Nothing further was said, though, so he tapped at a keyboard and had a gate fling open down the hall. He then pointed the ground unit in the gate's direction. "Number twelve."

The ground unit dropped a computer stick on the counter, tugged at the tenta-binds, and deposited his detainee in the cell down the hall.

The officer began typing out the file for the detainee, filling in blank fields with the information from the unit's report. Around halfway through he was interrupted and sat back, thankful, as the door swung open once more. Another two ground units entered the station, also holding tenta-bind cords. Thrashing around closely behind was a Neuro-surrogate still sporting Marbles's garbage-man hat. The officer considered the Neuro's face. There was something strange about it. Something he recognised. He had seen this suspect before, but last time she was in here, she wasn't wrapped in metal tenta-binds.

"Wait a second. Wait." The officer climbed out from behind his desk and stumbled around in front of the ground units. "Who is this woman?"

The ground units stopped but ignored his question. The Neuro continued to writhe.

"You need to wait a couple of minutes. I've got to call the lieutenant. Something's not quite right. Please, take a seat over there." He instantly felt stupid for offering seats to the chrome unicycles and scurried over to his phone on the desk.

"Yeah, I'm at the front. Some ground units just brought in a suspect, but I'm sure she was with that fed the other day. I've seen her before. No, she's not talking. They've still got her in binds. Yeah. Okay, make it quick."

The officer looked over the counter at the units, waiting patiently. "Excuse me. What has this woman been arrested for?"

There were a few more beeps before the little speaker by one of the unit's shoulder joints burst to life. "This machine has been arrested for attempted job thievery. We are preventing robotic homelessness and stopping newer models leading to our redundancy. This machine had also interfered with a police crime scene, destroying evidence and potentially even the suspects themselves."

The officer's face screwed up as he processed this information. "Job thievery? Did you get sent out into the field for that? What do you mean *machine*?"

Beep beep click pop. "We were pursuing a suspect in the police sergeant murder case when this machine, also pursuing our suspect, crashed into the scene."

The door behind the officer hissed open and the lieutenant stepped through. "What've the bloody ground units done this time?"

The officer repeated the brief conversation that he just had with the ground unit, and the lieutenant's face burned red. "Useless pieces of trash! You're tellin' me you let our murderer go so you could arrest a federal agent instead?"

Beep beep buzz. "We ran a risk assessment, and this Neuro-surrogate was deemed to be of higher risk to our immediate well-being. Yours, too. We defended ourselves on behalf of all ground scanner units and employees—the police company and its shareholders."

"Neuro *what*?" The lieutenant had clearly never even heard of such a thing. He grabbed the phone off the officer's desk and called the fed who'd been at the station earlier that week. After a quick few words, he replaced the phone and spoke to the officer. "Okay, he's on his way. Hopefully he can sort this out. For now" —he turned to the ground units—"I'm going to need the two of you to head through to cell sixteen. And let this woman out of those binds, for Christ's sake. She's a federal agent!"

The units began to protest in angry beeps and clicks until the scanner-craft, still monitoring the situation from above, beamed invisible new instructions down to its ground units. The beeps stopped abruptly, and the units wheeled themselves out of the lobby and down the hall. The Neuro also stopped struggling as the binds fell. She twitched a bit, stretched her arms, then walked obediently behind the units. The lieutenant apologised to the Neuro, reassuring her that a representative from the federal agency was on his way. The Neuro nodded and continued her march towards the empty cell. The officer tapped at his keyboard and the door swung closed. Only after the situation had been somewhat handled did he let out a large breath and sit back in his chair, shaking his head. He looked at the lieutenant, who was also in disbelief.

"I'm telling ya, some things machines can do perfectly well, but other things are better left to us."

The lieutenant had a quick peek over at the officer's computer screen. "Who have we got in number twelve?"

The officer brought up the logs he was midway through typing.

"I recognise that face. Is he the guy from the driver's license that got turned in? Cookie or something?"

The officer beamed. "Ah, that's where I've seen that woman. She's the agent who handed in the driver's license. Number twelve might be our getaway driver."

The lieutenant gave a short "good" in response and stepped out of the room, door hissing closed behind him. The officer sat back in his chair, still thinking about that woman and clearly remembering her now. She hadn't said a word last time, either, which the officer remembered thinking was unusual. She relied on the other fed there to speak on her behalf. The officer shrugged and returned to his paperwork.

The federal agent stepped into the police station and glanced at his watch. The officer behind the desk recognized him immediately.

"They are in cell sixteen, sir." The officer pointed down the hall. "Two ground units and the other agent. Your partner?"

The officer buzzed the fed through and contacted the lieutenant. Once the lieutenant re-emerged, he and the fed stepped into cell sixteen. The fed dialled a number and left the phone call connected as they entered the cell. First, the fed addressed one of the ground units. "Why did you arrest my Neuro?"

"This machine was arrested for attempted job thievery. We were trying to prevent homelessness and redundancy."

The fed looked at the Neuro, who was shaking her head. The fed thought for a moment, then spoke into his phone. "Why was permission for that act granted?"

The commander of the scanner-craft above made a panicked noise. He clicked through his logs before reading back the conversation that had taken place between the ground units and the scanner-craft itself. "Says here that they were apprehending the suspect. They asked a *Marbles* to halt and then requested permission to fire the binds. Nothing about a Neuro in my logs here, sir." The fed could almost hear the "phew" follow the commander's statement. The mystery was partially solved by what the ground unit beeped next.

The scanner-craft commander translated over the phone line. "GU013 says, 'We didn't mention when the suspect turned out to be a Neuro, as it would have cost us the permission to pursue.'"

The fed's mood soured. "It seems that they've been making decisions without you. Take units GU013 and 014 back and demand a refund. I recommend you pull any active units off the streets for now until you can be assured that this is an isolated case."

"Yes, sir," said the lieutenant.

The fed looked up at the Neuro. "Looks like it's just you guys for now."

The Neuro nodded.

"And what were *you* doing at the park?"

A different voice sounded across the phone line now. It was the Neuro's operator. "After dropping that ID card back here, I programmed the Neuro to head back to the wreckage and see if anyone else turned up. Seems that while I was away from the console, my Neuro pursued a suspect and got itself caught by those ground units in the process."

"Did you manage to identify who the Neuro was chasing while you were neglecting your station, leaving a multibillion-dollar piece of equipment to operate by itself?"

The Neuro operator cringed and his reaction mirrored onto the face of the Neuro-surrogate. "I've got two results here. One guy remains unknown. The Neuro never got close enough to get a proper reading, though a blurred image is stored in the visor's internal snaps. Maybe those ground units could fill in some blanks there. But the other is in our database. Goes by the previously mentioned name *Marbles*. I've seen the extracted video from his barcode. Been circlin' the office for the last few days. He's our killer."

The fed looked thoughtful once again, which the Neuro operator witnessed through the Neuro's eyes. The operator spoke. "I know. That's the part that has us stumped, too. No one knows who extracted the barcode. We found it in an unnamed folder on a scrambled server.

Someone had the piece of shit close enough to scan his barcode, then just let him slip away afterwards."

The fed tapped his lips with a finger and hummed as before. "You think he's still got his barcode?"

"Shouldn't think so. We tend to remove it straight after the information is extracted. This one obviously wasn't done exactly by the book, though."

The fed nodded. He was satisfied for now, and he readied to leave.

The lieutenant extended a hand to the fed, who looked at it but made no move to meet it.

"I appreciate the agents taking such interest in the murder case of one of our own," the lieutenant said. "I promised the boys here that I would do what I could. I rented these ground units and I even called in a scanner-craft for Christ's sakes, but as they've demonstrated, they are less than capable. I hope you get to the bottom of this."

The fed took the hand. He couldn't have cared less about the dead sergeant, but he hoped that the death might just lead him to the actual man the fed sought, and so he shook on hopefully discovering his ex-partner Dubbs's whereabouts. Then he turned towards the exit, still speaking to the Neuro's operator through the phone line. "Leave this 'unknown' to me," he said. "I need you to go and find me Marbles."

"Yes, sir." The Neuro gave a lazy salute to the fed's back and headed towards the exit.

"Just a second. This unknown guy you mentioned. I'm pretty sure we've got him. It's the man behind that fake ID you found."

The Neuro stopped and shrugged, no longer able to communicate with the lieutenant since the fed with the phone had left. The lieutenant continued anyway. "We had a volunteer squad track him down, and he was brought over only this afternoon."

The Neuro nodded and gestured for the lieutenant to lead the way. They marched down the hall and stopped outside of the holding cell of Mr. Sven, aka Cookie. The Neuro placed her visual sensors against the small hole in the door and shook her head almost instantly.

"You sure that's not him?"

The Neuro stopped moving for a moment, and the lieutenant assumed its operator was doing something behind the scenes. As if hoping it would encourage him, the lieutenant spoke again. "If you can't tell me that this is our second guy from the car, then I'm afraid I'm going to have to let him free."

The Neuro looked back through the eye hole, and as before, she shook her head. The latex face morphed into a mockery sadness, and the lieutenant couldn't believe that he hadn't realised before that this wasn't a real human.

Now that he knew, it seemed so obvious, even ignoring its inability to talk.

"Well, you can't change facts. Thanks for your help."

The Neuro saluted as before and took off down the hallway, exiting to the streets. She had a cop-killer to find.

25

PARASITE

MOONLIGHT ENVELOPED THE MAN as he ascended the steps to the entrance. The bag over his head had long ago grown itchy. He wondered why it seemed necessary to drag him so far out of the city each time they wanted to meet with him. Only once the sliding doors were pressure-locked behind him did his cuffs loosen. A heavily edited voice granted him permission to remove the hood.

The man found himself in a familiar room, one which contained nothing but a steel chair facing a large mirrored wall—that and a small glass of potent liquid, the fumes of which he could smell from the moment he passed through the doors. He took a seat. Despite the dryness of his throat, he didn't dare take a sip.

The scrambled voice spoke. "Our last meeting was less than satisfactory. I hope for your sake that you have a better report prepared this time."

The man shivered. "Well, I've had a Neuro on me ever since that dead sergeant…"

"No more excuses. Dubbs has been on the run for far too long already."

The man spoke quickly to defend himself. "I've gotten close this time. I thought I would fall a bit behind schedule, as we have only just got the petrol car back in action, but everything has caught up and is moving along as planned."

"Good. And what of the blood sample?"

"It's being collected as we speak."

"Very good. Will you be delivering it yourself?"

"I thought it would be less suspicious if I didn't, you know?"

"I agree. No time for mistakes anymore. We must find Dubbs's whereabouts. You know what happens to you if you don't deliver?"

The man bowed his head. "I know."

26

DOWN THE RABBIT HOLE

DUCKING, LEON FOLLOWED Daiz through yet another archway, which led to a wide opening in the underground. They had been visiting various places and chatting about life in the tunnels, though despite the grand tour, Leon still didn't feel confident that he could navigate the tunnels by himself. They shuffled over to the collection of blazing drums in the centre—the biggest fire they'd come across so far. A few small groups dotted the current room, gossiping about whatever, and a lonesome guy propped up near the central fire was listening quietly to a radio show. It didn't take long before one of the groups noticed Leon as a new face and moved their group to him. He was quickly swept up in people asking for the outsider's opinion on things, followed by questions on how the world was getting on without them. He didn't have the heart to tell them that the world didn't seem to care, so he only mentioned that there'd been the odd news reports about certain preventions and breakthroughs. They seemed happy that something was being done. A voice behind interrupted the discussion.

Once a small amount of warmth was circling inside Daiz's suit, she dropped to a nearby mattress and stared blankly at the dark ceiling, waiting for sleep to come. Her place in the circle was quickly filled by another, who greeted Leon with handshakes and smiles. The people's friendliness fought off the otherwise bleak atmosphere, and Leon quickly forgot that he and the others were holed up in what used to be an underground train station.

"Sorry about the unending list of questions. Don't very often have newcomers down here. Oh, no sir!" At some point, Hughey had glided up behind the group and was listening in. Despite his face struggling to hold a tough-guy look, Leon could see that he was just as happy to have someone new to talk to as the others. Leon stepped aside, widening the circle. They all talked for a long while, with another occasional survivor joining the conversation. There was no way for Leon to know the time down there, and it was only when a few of the group began to retire for what must have been the night that Leon was shown to a small side room. It looked like it might have been a ticket office at some point before being converted into sleeping quarters. It still had the security window looking into the hall, which was perfect for letting in just enough light so Leon didn't trip over the other occupants.

"Hope you don't mind sharing, but this is actually our most comfortable room. It holds the heat better than most."

Leon thanked Hughey and threw himself down onto the vacant cushion pile in the corner. As he made himself comfortable, one of the younger guys he'd been talking to out by the fire stumbled in, a grin spreading across his face and colourful box in hand. He dropped down onto his little patch of soft ground near Leon and opened the box. It showed another ridiculous picture of Boss, this time in a grass skirt and doing the hula. He still had the same misleading smile and a thumbs-up as if he were the kindliest, most chilled out guy in the world.

"Pizza? It's a Hawaiian."

Leon scrunched his nose and glanced between the box and the guy in front of him. He almost reacted with a polite "no thank you" and a well-practised wave of the hand. As if reading his thoughts, the guy with the grin nudged the box a nanometre closer and nodded at him. "Help yourself."

A gust crept under the door and blew past Leon, sending a small shiver down his shoulders. He looked about himself, taking in what he could see of the damp walls and their dark corners. He heard but didn't quite see whatever was scurrying across the floor behind him. He looked back at the smile on the guy's face.

"When in Rome."

With the first bite, the colours of the pizza and the box itself jumped alive and smothered the shadows. The pineapples multiplied and stretched across the ground. The ham flipped up, mixed with a dash of pink and orange from the box, and filled in any gaps it could find. With the next mouthful, something wispy appeared on the back wall, painting clouds across the sunset which had formed from the ham and cardboard. The pineapple ground was gritty now, and Leon could feel the sand beneath his body. When he tried to look back down at the pizza, it no longer existed. In its place was a rug stretching far across the beach, filled with all sorts of edible treats. Someone grabbed a piece of cake, and Leon looked up to see a grinning surf master sitting opposite him. Tattoos of waves and shark teeth covered his arms, similar to the ones that were springing up over Leon, too. They compared them casually, as if only just discovering their tattoos was the most normal thing in the world.

Leon sat with his back to the straw hut. He had been there for what felt like forever, speaking quietly to the surf master, who was whispering back; neither wanted to wake the sleeping occupants of the surrounding dream-pod hammock-cocoons. Leon glanced back at the surf master's grin, wondering how his jaw wasn't aching. Then he began wondering for the second time if he was grinning also. The first time this came to mind, he tried to check his reflection down at the ocean, though it was a much further walk than it looked and he just couldn't quite make it to the water.

Leon opened his mouth again and words escaped. He spoke with the surf master of all things. Things too important not to talk about. Things that would make gods and politicians cry if only they knew such things even existed. They figured out how to cure all diseases, defeat world hunger, and end the war in the central east. But all conversations were forgotten now. Leon lifted another plate of food from the rug and laughed at the picture of Boss's face. The surf master began to tell Leon all about that strange fellow on the box. Leon cut him off.

"Don't worry, I know who he is. That's what makes it even funnier. Don't think I've ever seen the grumpy bastard smile like that." He pointed down to the box.

The surf master's eyes widened and his mouth changed shape for the first time.

"You know the Pizza Boss?"

"Well yeah, he's my employer."

"I thought you were Dubbs's guy."

"I guess they work together, though I hadn't heard of Dubbs till just before coming here."

The surf master nodded to himself. "Have you ever seen the Pizza Boss kill anyone? I've heard he's badass!"

Leon laughed. "No, I haven't, but it sounds like the kind of thing he would do, with that temper of his."

"I certainly feel sorry for whoever was on shift the day he busted out of jail."

"Jail, huh?"

"Yeah, about a year ago. Plenty of rumours about how that went down, but I heard that his escape was pretty rad. Practically punched through the gate, jumped over the walls, snapped some necks, and stole an auto-driver."

Leon's thoughts drifted to Voice. "He stole a car?"

"Apparently he had to wrestle with it the whole way because it kept trying to turn itself around." The grin was back.

"I suppose that explains the disguise whenever he leaves the shop."

"Oh yeah. We've heard about that, too." The surf master's teeth glinted in the sun. He was full of new questions, but it was Leon who seemed to be out of the loop. All that

Leon knew was that he worked for a very suspicious pizza delivery business. The bombardment of new information confused Leon and made him drowsy. He thanked the surf master for the banquet, bid him goodnight, and curled up into his own dream pod. It was a lot comfier than the ripped foam sheets and concrete floor that he could barely remember.

27

FAST BUS

COOKIE HIT THE PAVEMENT, clutching at his ribs. Despite the pain through most of his body, he felt as if he'd just dodged a bullet. He needed to contact Boss as soon as possible—partially to warn him and partially to find out what the hell was going on. His brisk walk became a jog as he made his way home. He knew the police would have bugged it by now, so he emptied his squirrelled-away emergency kit into a backpack, grabbed a few circuit boards, and left the building. He screwed an aerial to the top of the pile of seemingly useless electrical chips, then tapped two contacts together in a coded sequence. If he made the device correctly, the sequence would have fired off to the nearest submersallite, where it would be redirected through DJ T's radio show and find its way to Boss.

Cookie set his watch to 00:00 and continued towards the main street. Boss would have an hour to contact him now that the code was sent, which meant that Cookie had just under an hour to get an untraceable phone. Shouldn't be too hard, though it would mean a trip to China-Ville, his least favourite place on earth—of all of the two places he'd ever been.

Cookie made to hail the passing cab but thought better of it as he observed the tinted eyes of the driver. If the police were watching him right now, it wouldn't have been a stretch for them to organise undercover cab drivers to circle the area. He lowered his arm and the cab continued by, unhindered. He wanted to move in a way that the cops wouldn't keep up with, so instead, he broke into a run. He darted around arm-locked children, wheelchairs, and slow walkers. The occasional glance down at his watch showed that he still had plenty of time remaining. Rubber burned ahead as an infuriated businessman pulled out of the traffic jam and risked a long-distance over-take in the fast-bus lane, giving Cookie an idea. He headed for the fast-bus post and readied a jump as a monstrous vehicle dropped a little speed and swung in close to the post. He launched himself at the fast-bus and grabbed the edge of the back platform. A barrier folded from beneath, holding him aboard while it accelerated once more.

"One for China-Ville, please."

A robotic face on the side of the fast-bus ticket machine asked for payment. Its mouth lit up, suggesting that

Cookie should insert a note. After he did, the machine regurgitated a ticket and bid Cookie a nice day. Cookie stood there, waiting for the barrier to let him into the seating area, but it didn't lift.

"You gonna let me in?"

The screech of unoiled metal came from beneath the robotic face, and a small compartment door slid open. The ticket machine's face lowered its speaker volume as it spoke to Cookie.

"Psst. Need any supplies for China-Ville? Three per cent discount for fast-bus customers."

The open metal chest contained various items, all very suspicious, most very illegal. Unbranded holographic stickers hung at the top, ready for any face photo to be inserted. They were convincing enough to fit most ID cards almost perfectly. There were also various electrical chips that, when in the right hands, could surely wield a destructive power. A couple of them Cookie recognised, though he was only a dabbler in electronics himself. On the bottom hooks were seductive business cards and various packets of jellified goods. Cookie glanced around him, but the fast-bus had reached top speeds now, and the people they passed were nothing more than blurs. He quickly snatched a silver ring from one of the hooks and fastened it onto his finger. With a twist, it glowed blue, showing that it had a charge. He poked a note into the ticket machine's mouth.

"Thank you!"

Cookie stood there, waiting for it to regurgitate change in the same way it had done with the ticket. Nothing happened. He prompted the machine. "No way is this thing five hundred bucks."

"If you were expecting a receipt, you've shopped at the wrong place."

Cookie felt his face boil and he raised the fist that bore the ring, aiming it at the ticket machine. In response, the machine lifted the barrier and Cookie was flung inside as the fast-bus collided with a car in front. The angled scoop at the front of the fast-bus tossed the car aside whilst still accelerating. Cookie fell into a passenger as another car was shunted out of the way, but the passenger's insults were lost on him as he focused on climbing into a vacant seat. He managed to clip himself in, just in time to be squashed hard against the harness as the bus threw a hard right turn. It took a while before he felt his stomach contents settle, and only then did he look up from the ground. The woman opposite him was still staring at him with deathly intent while mumbling something to her seemingly hearing-impaired husband.

Cookie flashed a smile. "It's called the fast-bus, lady. You pay for speed, not comfort."

The woman scrunched her mouth into her nose, looking at Cookie with pure hatred. She made to deliver another belt of insults but was cut short by another collision. All she managed was "oof!" as her false teeth flung from her mouth, a last strand of drool hanging on for dear life. In complete surprise, Cookie exploded with laughter. The toothless woman spat something or other in his direction, but he couldn't hear a word of it over his own cough-laugh and the rattling of her teeth bouncing their way along the fast-bus floor.

Another hard lurch and the fast-bus had arrived. It slowed a little but never fully stopped. The ticket machine yelled from the back, swivelling its face towards Cookie. "China-Ville, get off the bus!" Cookie unstrapped and headed for the exit.

"Too slow, let's go!" the rusty voice rattled.

Cookie leapt from the back of the bus. He landed awkwardly, but it was still one of his more graceful exits. He turned and saw that no one else had left the bus at this stop, which he hoped meant no police tail. *Perfect.*

He twisted the ring slightly on his finger, deactivating it. The glow faded quickly and returned to looking just like any other ring. He wouldn't need it for now, at least. He had a while before anyone could regain the ground that he had just covered, and he should be long integrated with the chaos and crowds of China-Ville by then.

28

CHINA-VILLE

AFTER FIGHTING HIS WAY across a main road, Cookie emerged on the same side as China-Ville. The place wasn't hard to miss, standing many stories high, with thick cables strewn from the corners and outer solid concrete walls. The concrete wasn't visible until a few levels up, though, as the bottom floors were completely wrapped in colourful flags, pictures, lights, garments, billboards—basically everything. Despite all of those things, though, it was something else that made China-Ville so hard to miss. The mega-complex seemed to have a life of its own. It was like a parasitic organism that relied on other, weaker, and often unknowing creatures to keep itself alive. It seemed to be of infinite size and complexity. This structure called out to people from all walks of life, drawing them in from the world over. At its outer perimeter, there were mostly tourists or those who exploited tourists. Cookie took a quick glance from one end to the other, far in the distance, and tried to estimate how many Hawaiian shirts he had just mentally ingested. The fads changed from year to year, and the market changed its stock to suit, though there was one constant that he couldn't deny, and it was what Cookie despised the most. While still about a block away, Cookie could smell China-Ville, strong as ever. It smelled of nothing in particular—not just weird foods or unwashed inhabitants—but more of the combined smell of everything that happened there. It consumed the entire area, and he wondered how the people living nearby ever could get used to it.

As he pushed past the first row of shops, he couldn't help but marvel at how clever the residents here really were. It was absolutely a matter of hiding in plain sight. So much was going on at once that so much could pass by right under one's nose. It was a criminal haven in disguise, with walls not only of concrete but of civilians buying pirated goods. First things first, Cookie purchased a scarf from one of the street-level stores, which was now wrapped around his shoulders and nose. It would help with the smell, keep his identity covered, and keep the grime off his back, all in one. A trick learned years before that he still swore by.

Cookie squeezed through one of the entrance gaps, almost becoming wedged between a store and a support pillar. Even the walkways were a defensive mechanism. They acted as funnels, growing narrower the further he advanced. Defending this structure wouldn't take Spartan inhabitants, just patience and large ammo magazines.

The market stalls had begun to thin out, and straggling tourists were diverted by strategically placed whorehouses or other slightly more illegal goods and services. After what felt like another layer, though Cookie couldn't be entirely sure, he became aware of the burning eyes all around him. Shopkeepers had dropped their friendly acts. The fake watch vendors had long since disappeared. Tourists generally didn't travel this far. This was where he needed to be to see if he could find what he was searching for and make it out again. Above him, window slats were slammed closed. Clicks of what sounded like firearms being loaded echoed down the halls. A man was sitting nearby, acting casually like he was drinking a glass of wine and reading a good book on a balcony. Though there was no balcony here, just an uneven ground of concrete slabs and bamboo weave, the smell of various dead things, and grimy, stale air that begged for a breeze. The liquid in the man's cup wasn't wine, either. It was black, thick, and shiny—a cup of pure grunge.

"I'm looking for a phone."

"You look around. Phone shop everywhere." The man's voice was raspy. Just listening to it made Cookie's throat hurt.

"No, I need one of these phones." Cookie made to remove the transmitter device from his pocket. The man stopped him with a strange sound and a raise of his eyebrows. He seemed surprised that anyone would be stupid enough to reach for their pockets here.

"You move, you dead."

Cookie raised one hand in surrender but knew that if he didn't explain himself fast, they would most likely kill him anyway. His free hand moved slowly to the pocket, and he removed the three-beep transmitter he'd used earlier to contact Boss. The man snatched it and scanned it closely. Once he found whatever he was looking for, he tossed it hard to the ground. An armed ex-military type stepped from the shadows and kicked it through a broken drain cover. The grunge drinker barked an order at the soldier and had him lead Cookie away.

Cookie recognised none of the area and hoped that he wasn't walking straight into a trap. The walkways widened, and he wondered if the soldier was leading him to an exit, back towards the streets outside. The soldier pushed him into the shop front of a reverse-engineered movie boutique. He then spoke in hushed tones to the engineer at the counter, who nodded. There was another person in the store who Cookie hoped was an oblivious browser, though he kept his ears trained on the area behind him, just to be safe. The engineer tapped at a glass cabinet in front of him, and Cookie leaned in for a closer look. He heard the engineer whisper something but looked up to find that his mouth wasn't moving. He looked down at the cabinet and once again the voice sounded. It was coming from inside his head. Cookie's R-chip was being overpowered by a transmitter hidden amongst the gadgets in the cabinet. To indicate that he'd heard, Cookie glanced up at the engineer and gave a short nod.

"Three or five beep?"

Cookie placed three fingers on the glass in front of him. The engineer removed the front row of computer chips and held them out to Cookie. Cookie frowned, unsure as to what he was being shown, but he realised as the engineer pointed to the contacts that the different chips were indicating varying levels of encryption. Cookie selected the largest chip and the voice entered his head again.

"Meet me around the side in twenty minutes."

The engineer exchanged the chip for a small empty box and placed it in a bag, then passed it over the counter to Cookie. Aloud, he said, "Thank you, sir. Tell your friends."

Cookie left. A few others had joined the other shopper, but all were too busy checking out new release movies to spare him any attention. Cookie set a GPS mark on his watch so he could find his way back here, then stepped out into the quiet walkway, following the sound of bustling hustlers. It didn't take long before he was back at the outer layer and all sorts of useless things were being shoved in his face for a "good price, good price!"

The smell of dead things was temporarily overthrown by the smell of living things defecating. The whiff of questionable foodstuffs blew past occasionally, offering some respite. The only pleasant smell that Cookie came across was from a perfume cloud of an exotic-looking woman. She walked far faster through the crowd than Cookie could manage, and he wished that he had the time to chase her down for his nose's sake. His watch vibrated and the screen lit up, indicating that he ought to head back to the engineer. In the rushed evacuation from his house, he forgot his lenses, so he couldn't see the directional arrows projecting from his watch. He had to stop pushing through the crowds at each fork in the path to check the tiny screen on his wrist. It took a little longer than he hoped, but he made it back to the store without the engineer having waited too long. Cookie slipped down the side of the store, scarf scraping grime from the wall as he pressed against the narrowing passage. The door was already open a crack, and the engineer must have seen Cookie approaching because he opened it the rest of the way immediately, thrusting a small, crudely taped-together device into his chest. The door then slammed closed.

Cookie continued shuffling along to the back of the shop and, ignoring the family perched around a small bowl of chow, began to transmit some more beeps to Boss. After he'd transmitted only a few beeps, the engineer's voice crackled in his head, just as before.

"If I'm picking up that signal, then you're too close to my shop. Piss off. I won't warn you again."

Cookie checked his watch. Fifty-five minutes had passed since he first beeped the Pizza Boss. He didn't have time to push his way out of the layers and find somewhere safe to transmit from. He set to work ripping his new phone open, memorising where the parts belonged so he could reassemble it later. The engineer must have put a bug in the phone itself because there was no way that the same one from inside the glass cabinet could overrule his R-chip from this distance. He thought back to the small gadgets he'd seen in the window and tried to find anything in the phone that looked similar. He couldn't risk the engineer recording the supposedly encrypted call to Boss and selling it to the highest bidder.

Fifty-seven minutes had passed now. If he didn't send his digital key to Boss immediately, he would need to find a new way of contact.

Fifty-eight minutes.

Cookie gave up and reassembled the phone. He tapped at the keypad and watched the time as the message flew from his screen, down to the submersallites, and across to Boss's receiver. The phone rang a second later.

It was Boss. "Jesus, kid. You're cutting it fine."

"Listen, I'm tapped. We need to meet."

The voice of the engineer spoke over Boss's response. "Get away from my shop, man! I don't need your pirate signals drawing attention this way!" the engineer yelled directly into Cookie's head.

"Just shut up a sec. I'm going to be quick."

Boss was fuming. "Don't tell me to shut up, you—"

"Not you, Boss. It's the engineer giving me lip over my R-chip."

The engineer was furious this time and continued yelling through Cookie's R-chip, drowning out Boss's voice yet again.

"Boss, repeat that?"

The engineer was still yelling and behind Cookie the side door was kicked open. It took the engineer a few seconds to squeeze into the side alley, but the open door was now blocking Cookie from view.

"Where are you, ass wipe? I know you're close." The engineer was shuffling his way down the alley towards the front of the shop, looking around for Cookie. His string of insults didn't stop, and Cookie couldn't press the phone any further into his ear as he struggled to hear Boss over the engineer.

"Meet… at… place… First… place…"

"Got it, Boss. Give me twenty."

With that, Cookie ripped the back off the phone and crushed a couple of random chips. He discarded the rest in the gutter and started running, the engineer's voice fading quickly as his signal emitter fell behind. Once Cookie was beyond range of the engineer's signal, static erupted in his R-chip, and Cookie couldn't help but yell in agony, clutching his hands to his ears. That did nothing, of course, as the chip was in his head, and it took him all his willpower to think through the noise and ask the chip to switch itself off. He clambered to his feet, only now aware that he'd even fallen to the ground, and continued running. Risking a glance behind him, he saw a crowd of people disperse as the bulk of the engineer charged through. He must have heard Cookie cry out. Ahead was another cluster of stalls, and it wasn't long before Cookie was also ramming his way through a crowd, leaving a clear path for the engineer to follow. It took a few last-minute turns to dodge and duck the main influx of people, and once again he was somewhere in the second layer of China-Ville. After a long few minutes of regaining his breath behind a thick binding of cables, Cookie stood, flicked off some of the grime, and checked his watch. Because he had previously set a waypoint at the engineer's shop, he could use that as a landmark for navigating his way out of this endless twist of alleys. He selected the shop from the recent locations menu and waited for something to happen, but nothing did. The screen flashed a few times, then went blank. After a second, the power light turned itself off. The watch was dead.

Cookie punched a tin wall, harder than he meant to, and cringed as he heard it echo in all directions. He paused, listening for footsteps, but heard nothing. He sat back down behind the cables, deciding to take cover before he tried fiddling with his watch. Chances were, it would take a while to reset.

"Jammers, I'm afraid."

Cookie jumped, not realising there had been somebody nearby. He looked towards the voice but saw nothing except grimy pipes and piles of trash. He shuffled a little closer, focusing between two support beams, and to his surprise, he saw that one of the rubbish piles was sporting a pair of goggled eyes. Cookie looked at the pile, dumbfounded. He began to wonder how many other homeless people he'd passed today without even noticing.

"Jammers, you say?"

"Yep, best jammers there are."

"Well they've buggered up my watch. I'm trying to find my way out of here. Do you know where we are?"

"Sure do."

"Where?"

The small person in the rubbish pile smiled. "I'm awfully hungry." A leaf of paper lifted and a cupped hand poked its way through.

Cookie patted down his pockets and found a ten-dollar note, then placed it between the trash-dweller's fingers. The hand retracted quickly with the money. Then the trash offered an answer.

"China-Ville."

Cookie waited for the person to continue, but it seemed like that was the end of it. He stood, preparing his angry voice.

"That's it? No shit we're in China-Ville. How do I get out of here? C'mon, I've got somewhere to be."

The paper lifted again and out popped the cupped hand.

"You're kidding, right?"

The goggles held the stare. Cookie removed a twenty and made it quite clear that was all he had left. Before handing it over, he activated his shock ring in front of the trash and let it glow blue. He couldn't tell if the person was intimidated or not, but he hoped they knew it wasn't an empty threat. He didn't have time for games, especially in his least favourite place on earth. He handed over the note, and the trash nodded a sort of thank-you, though no words were spoken.

"Well? How do I get out of here?"

The trash replied in his same steady tone. "You will find your way."

Cookie had had enough. He lunged forwards, rearing his arm, ready for a hit. As he slammed his shock ring into the pile, it leapt alive. Energy exploded from the ring and tore the trash into millions of new pieces, which caught on a breeze caused by the sudden energy pulse and scattered all along the alley. Cookie watched the pieces drift as gravity barely bothered to pull them back towards the ground. All kinds of things floated there—discarded paper items, bits of cardboard boxes, torn metal from cans, shattered lids of bottles—but nothing that made up a human.

Cookie looked down, directly at where the pile had been sat. He wiped the ground clear with a foot, revealing a solid metal drain cover sealed tightly from below.

With a beep, the screen of his watch blinked back to life.

29

NO EXIT

LEON FELT AS IF THE FLOOR had risen and hit his face. It was cold and hard and his cheek was squashed into his eye. He took a breath and felt the dust from beneath him fly into his lungs, causing a weak cough. He tried to sit up but failed. Slowly, his brain prodded further downwards and discovered that his arms were still attached. So were his legs. He lay there for a while, just being aware of himself and trying to draw a mental image of his current pose. A drip of water nearby told him that his ears were in fact working. He felt the electrical signals push their way through his swampy brain, getting lost in the fog on the way. Water dripped nearby. He sat bolt upright, ignoring the nausea that followed. He fell backwards as he looked around, his balance not correcting itself quickly enough. As he lay there, the ceiling began to spin, and another sound came through the bleakness. It was a voice. The nausea returned. He couldn't focus on the face that now leaned over him. It distorted as it swirled, and he was suddenly aware of his need to throw up. All he could focus on was where should he do so and if he would make it there in time.

"What?" It was Daiz's voice that Leon heard, and he wondered if it came from the face he could see but couldn't focus on. She laughed, looked up at someone, and shrugged. Leon had been mumbling his thoughts aloud. Another face formed beside Daiz's. *Surf master?* But there was no grin or golden hair or shark tooth necklace, man.

"Okay, I think he's gonna hurl. Help me out here." Daiz pulled him upright and wrapped his arm around her shoulders. "I'm blaming you for this, Lung, and don't think I'll forget."

"Empty threats, as always." Lung smirked at Daiz as he grabbed Leon's other arm. They tried to drag him to the drainage gully a few doors down, but Leon didn't hold his late-night snack for that long. He shortly afterwards fell unconscious.

A commotion had started further down the hall, and most residents of the underground living quarters began making their way into a central control room to catch a whiff of the latest news. It was the only room that received twenty-four-hour power, as there were a few vital instruments inside that kept the water purifiers and air filtration systems running. To keep power consumption to a minimum, however, all visual displays had been traded out for Morse code switch displays that showed nothing but bright or dim lights for dots and dashes accordingly. On one particular display, hooked up to a large dish, the switches flashed away as they received a message from the outside world. It came from a trusted source via China-Ville's submersallite. A message from the chief of communications over at Zone A.

"Zoner inbound. Possibly foamers following. High alert. Sealed medical room."

The translator stood in the control room, confused. Hughey tapped his notepad irritably, scribbling down the words being read to him. "Read it again," he commanded, sure that the translator had gotten something wrong.

"Sealed medical room. Zoner inbound. Possible foamers..."

"That can't be right. Move aside." Hughey pushed the translator away and stared at the switch display, struggling to catch the words that flashed before him. He did manage with a few keywords, however, which confirmed what he'd been told.

"A zoner heading here? Is he insane? He's going to drag an entire fleet of foamers with him! What's he thinking?" He ran to the power bank, ready to plug in the transmitter and satellite dish, but the translator stopped him.

"Look at the time here. The commander delayed the message. It was sent over twelve hours ago."

Hughey twitched his moustache, forehead creasing as his eyebrows became one. "Why in God's name would he have done that?" He looked back at the switch display, which still flickered away as the message repeated itself. "Turn that off, for now. If the message is true, we might just need all the power we can get."

The engineer set to work on the power bank, being careful to only disconnect the cables for the receiving panel and let them hang beside the cables for the transmitter instruments. The rest of the room's occupants, some panicked, some excited, and some plain confused, were chattering energetically.

"Okay, listen up!" Hughey roared over the racket. The room quieted to a busy hum. "It's important that no one panics. Continue as we have, and all shall be fine. If a zoner really is heading here, it's his own loss. He won't find us, but the foamers will find *him*. No more supply runs to the surface for now. Let's get a full inventory count."

A woman at the back raised her hand. "I will get counting right away."

"Thank you, Doris. We should also get to work moving everyone into the three main chambers. We can cut cost on heating and filtration for the next few days."

"What about the medical room?" someone cried out. "We could use the old offices."

Hughey felt the eyes of the group resting on him. "Okay. Prepare an old office as best we can. We're also going to need a scout topside to guide the zoner to our entrance, but only once it's confirmed that he is completely alone." He clapped his hands once. "Let's get moving."

Leon awoke in a cold puddle, shivering. It felt all too familiar.

"We got some dry clothes for you this time, at least."

Bare-chested, Leon was sat against a concrete wall. He lolled his head to the side and saw Daiz standing in the doorway.

"Try these." Daiz threw some crudely sewn garments at him and stepped outside the door. Leon wrestled with damp trousers and the oversized sacks that were his new clothes. They were heavy and rough, making them uncomfortable but strangely quite suitable for the lifestyle down in the tunnels. Leon called down the passage to Daiz.

"So what's the plan for today?"

Daiz laughed. "Oh, now you want to know? I've been trying to tell you all morning."

Leon yawned and felt the cobwebs in his mind loosen. He slapped a wet hand in his face and rubbed his eyes. "Yeah, sorry."

"That's alright. Lung told me about the pizza. If he had seen you last time, he may have thought twice."

Leon stumbled out of the room.

"Then again, you didn't have to say yes." She turned and gave him a look up and down. She pouted subconsciously as she judged his new outfit. This ended with a nod. "Suits you." Then she continued her walk. Leon jogged after her.

"So what *is* the deal today? Safe to go up top?"

"Only if we leave now. Like, right now. We got a message this morning from Zone A. Some nutter's cut his losses and is making his way over here. We need to bail before he drags a fleet of foamers right into our path."

Leon's heart imploded at the mention of Zone A. "I thought no one could leave the zones?"

"I didn't say that no one tries to from time to time." She handed him a bottle of purified water and he drained it dry, not a single drop escaping his lips. He passed it back to Daiz.

"Thank you," he said.

"Yeah, no problem. That was only my *entire* morning's ration."

"Oh." He looked at the ground. "So um, this guy, did he say why he's heading down?"

"Nope, just to be prepared in case someone's chasing him and to get a medical room ready. He must be joking if he thinks he's got a shot at coming this far. Anyways, your driver's back. I've packaged the blood sample for Dubbs, so… just waiting on you."

"Blood sample?"

"Yeah, Dubbs is still working on a permanent cure, so we give him samples of this and that for his research, whenever he needs them."

They headed down the passage, past many bustling bodies going about their duties. Hughey was eagerly waiting by the van, moustache shining and parcel in hands. "A very unusual method indeed. We were lucky to find some of the materials, but rest assured, we followed the instructions to a T."

Leon shrugged. "They never mentioned a pickup to me. Just the drop-off."

Hughey's eyebrows tightened as he considered this, but a moment later his concern fell away. It wasn't an unheard-of request. He gave a sharp nod and patted Leon once on the shoulder. "Safe travels, sir. Stay out of the rain."

Leon returned the gesture and bid those around him farewell with a quick, all-inclusive wave of the arm.

Daiz was getting impatient. "We've wasted enough time as it is."

She pulled the protesting van door open and squeezed into the driver's seat. Leon used his belt to fasten his wet clothes to the roof rack, hoping they might dry in the breeze of Daiz's relentless driving. Then, with barely enough time to shut the passenger's side door behind him, the van tore backwards, lights flicked to full as they disappeared through the turns of the tunnel.

The journey seemed much quicker on the way back, but Leon was sure that Daiz couldn't possibly be driving any faster than before. She definitely seemed more determined, though, and Leon was afraid to speak for fear of interrupting her intense concentration. He recognised the odd landmark here and there as they flew by and remembered to brace himself at a few of the more obvious turns. All in all, though, he had been slammed against the side of the van more times than he could count. His brain was still struggling to process the quick reactions needed for this kind of drive and was relieved when Daiz slowed and the metal grate rose beneath them. They were back in the warehouse.

"That seemed a bit better than last time."

"Yeah, somehow it always does." Daiz hopped from the van and unbuckled the shirt and shorts from the roof. Leon stepped down to the warehouse floor, carrying with him the delicate package for Dubbs. He shoved it into the only pocket sewn into his baggy pants.

"They are still a bit wet." Daiz handed the other clothes over to Leon. "You can keep those others on, if you need."

Leon smiled but said nothing. They both stood, facing each other.

Daiz broke the silence. "Well… um, thank you for making the drop. Have a good drive back to the city."

"No problem, and uh… thank you, too. It's been fun." He instantly regretted his poor choice of words.

They stood there facing each other for an awkward moment before Leon extended a hand. Daiz blushed and jumped at him, swinging her arms tight around his neck. "Take care now, and stay out of the rain."

With that, she climbed back into the van and it whirred awake. She rolled it forwards over the metal grate, and Leon watched her descend into darkness. Despite only meeting one day prior, the idea of leaving Daiz to the zone sat poorly in his stomach. With all that he saw and learned, he felt as if he'd known her for a lifetime. He spared a moment to consider just how different his life could have turned out, if only he hadn't been lucky enough to leave his parents' suburb when he did.

Leon headed back to the conveyor belt, ready to make his exit. Climbing atop the belt, he briefly remembered that he left it running. Maybe the morning scout had switched it off when he passed earlier. Poking his head out through the plastic flaps, he was surprised to see Voice, despite being told that his driver was waiting. It felt strange for Leon to see him there, as if Voice were the only thing except for the damp clothes in his hand that grounded him to the world from which he'd come. The place he had just been seemed more like an alternate planet than just a couple of days' drive from the city.

Jumping into the wagon and taking great pleasure in the softness of the seats, he hadn't noticed that Voice had a typed message for Leon. It wasn't until Voice beeped that Leon turned to the navs screen.

"Good to see you."

"Good to see you too, man. I thought you took off back to the city without me. Where'd you get to?"

The words on the screen backspaced and new ones appeared. "Somewhere with a roof."

Leon looked around the car, nodding. It didn't look like it had any water marks on the windows. Then he frowned.

"Why'd you leave me? You can't get infected, but I can, and you left me!"

Voice apologised, explaining as best as he could in the small text box about his priority settings that couldn't be overwritten. Voice could only speculate that it was to prevent carrying the virus back to the city with him.

"Well, we're bringing the Bug back anyway." Leon removed the small parcel and placed it in the glove box. "One infected blood sample. Hopefully it will be what Dubbs needs. He really gives hope to these people, you know."

Voice's navs lit up. "Dubbs doesn't often work with blood samples. Too dangerous. And he never mentioned it to me."

Leon shrugged. "He left a note in one of the crates. Made it quite clear what he needed. Very specific on everything, from the blood extraction method to the delivery." He tapped at the parcel. "Some state-of-the-art heat-wrap parcel it's in, too. It's what we use for the pizzas, I think."

The navs remained blank for a while and Leon assumed that Voice was rummaging through data files or something.

"I can't reach Dubbs from here. I will call him when in signal range to clarify."

"Fine by me. Lead the way, Voice."

With that, a landmark in the centre of the city appeared in the address bar and the navs' screen filled with lines and directions. The engine roared and they bounced their way past the destroyed buildings and abandoned cars. Leon found himself being rocked into a trance-like sleep by the swaying of the wagon. He wasn't sure if he'd been properly sleeping or not when a rude turn threw him against the door, crushing him in his seat belt. He opened his eyes and stared ahead, trying to see whatever had caused Voice to swerve. The wagon slid to a halt, body arching forwards on the suspension. A wave of dust smothered the windows as it caught up from behind. It took half a minute for the cloud to thin enough for Leon to see ahead, and he didn't like what he saw. A roadblock had been set up across the only road in and out of the zone. Barricades had also been thrown together in a large semicircle around the roadway to prevent an off-road escape. Such a blockade would have taken a while to prepare. Someone knew they were on their way out of the zone today.

Every few barricades were manned by an armed patrol officer. All were looking at Voice. A megaphone beamed its painful and unclear sound as someone belted into its mouthpiece.

"Step out with your hands up. We have you surrounded."

Leon looked down at the console for guidance, but all he saw were the directions to the city.

"We are authorised to shoot if you do not comply. Step out of the vehicle with your hands above your head."

Leon was still waiting for Voice to type something. He was unable to. Leon made the only decision he saw available to him. He opened the door.

"Slowly."

Leon stepped out of the wagon and onto the sandy road, hands above his head. Voice's radio clicked and static screeched from inside. The volume adjusted and so did the channel until Voice found whatever station he was looking for. The radio was silent now. The megaphone blared again. "That's good. Now the driver."

Leon looked back at the wagon. In hindsight, he thought he probably should have climbed over and exited through the driver's side door. He didn't like how this looked and wondered if it were even worth trying to convince the officers that he was the only person in the wagon.

"Don't test our patience. Driver, exit the vehicle."

What choice did Leon have? "There's no one else."

"I'm warning you…"

"It's automated. It's only me."

The officer spoke into his radio, and his words resonated through Voice's speakers now that Voice had tuned into the patrol unit's frequency.

"Looks like they aren't taking the bait. We can't risk them getting out. Get ready. We're gonna have to shoot them from here. You can draw straws about who fetches the bodies after."

Leon felt the blood drain from his face. These guys weren't messing around.

The megaphone clicked on again, the captain not realising that Leon had heard his transmission through the speakers. "You've got five seconds."

"There's no one else!" Leon yelled desperately. He knew that, even if they searched the wagon itself, they wouldn't believe it and would think the driver had just slipped away.

"Four…"

With that, Voice launched the wagon at the row of officers. They opened fire, and from the sound and the chunks of metal flying from the wagon, Leon guessed that the weapons weren't set to stun. He dived to the ground and covered his head, not really sure what else to do. He could hear Voice roaring in the distance and the occasional clang or scream in between bursts of gunfire. A stray bullet skimmed across the soft ground and sprayed sand at Leon, who had begun crawling towards a small cluster of rocks. It was the only cover around and he hoped it was all he needed.

Time seemed to stop, and he wondered how long he'd had his head pinned against the sand and stone. When the sounds finally stopped, Leon felt a jolt of fear through his heart. An engine was idling in the distance and he pictured Voice, torn to shreds, petrol leaking, computer chips fried. He lay in the sand, eyes clenched, waiting for the dreaded sound of footsteps to approach him and finish him off with a bullet in the head. Instead, he heard a familiar beep.

Voice dragged his ragged tyres awkwardly through the sand and pulled up next to Leon. The passenger's side door creaked open, dropping onto one hinge as it did so. Bullet holes littered the exterior. No windows remained intact, and only one tyre was fully inflated.

"Oh man, Boss is gonna be pissed!"

Leon lay there for a moment, just admiring the sight despite the destruction. He had never felt so close to certain death, yet here he was, with his enemies down and his chariot awaiting. Legs shaking, Leon managed to climb to his feet and hop back into the passenger's seat. He glanced at the navs screen, but it still just showed an address and directions. The wagon strained as the wheels dragged its weight through the soft sand and back onto the road, and Leon couldn't help but wonder if they would make it back at all. The road was slightly denser than the sand on its sides, but having only one tyre would prove a challenge, even on a paved road.

"Maybe stick to the centre, where you can."

Leon sat back, vibrating violently as the wheels jutted along. With any luck, that was the last of the patrol officers and they could have a slow but safe journey back to the city.

Leon peered over the dashboard, looking through the roadblock debris and at the officers on the ground, who rolled, whimpered, and clutched at broken bones. Voice had left them alive from what Leon could see.

"Why shoot at us?" Leon blurted and wondered if any of the officers could hear him over the menacing sound of the damaged wagon. Mumbling to himself, he shook his head in disbelief.

An officer growled in response. It was all he could manage through the agony of whatever part of him Voice had run over. Leon couldn't believe that he had come so close to being murdered by patrol officers. Voice slowly accelerated until he was comfortable. Leon's eyes kept darting down at the navs screen in the hopes that Voice would make any comment about what had just happened, but it only showed its coordinates and landmark address.

Leon closed his eyes, hoping to shut out the world around him, but it only made it more vivid. With no visual distractions, the recent events mapped themselves out inside of his eyelids. He saw some connections between pieces of information but couldn't understand the overall narrative. He shifted his thoughts and focused on a new piece of information. This piece involved the barricades. If they were put in place solely for Voice and Leon, then someone had been aware of their presence. How long until that person sent backup to investigate the patrol group's silence? Leon opened his eyes.

"Toot once for *yes* or twice for *no*. Are we in range of Dubbs yet?"

Voice sounded the horn in two quick bursts.

"I'm thinking that if we are out of range, then so are these guys. That means they can't make calls for backup, but I'd say it's only a matter of time before someone else is sent this way."

Voice beeped his agreement.

"Got any spare tyres back here?" Leon was looking around the empty compartment behind him. Voice beeped twice.

"Okay, so no off-road. Shit. It's going to take us a while to get clear of this open strip. If anything comes at us, we're going to meet it head-on."

Voice dropped to neutral and revved the engine in a "bring it on" sort of way.

Leon hummed to himself. "Yeah, but I can't just go and get myself fixed up, same as you can. I would rather steer clear if possible."

He closed his eyes again and dared another look at the puzzle inside his eyelids. "I see why the zoners can't leave now. These guys knew we were coming. That's for sure. They were waiting for us." Again, Leon tried to connect the recent events in a way that made sense. "No one saw you through the rain, did they? While you were looking for a roof?"

Two beeps.

"You sure?"

Beep.

Leon took a deep breath. Not being able to get a response was frustrating him. He started to wonder if Voice found it frustrating, too. Leon's head began to ache behind the eyes, and he did his best to force the questions out of his mind for now. He just wanted to focus on getting back to the city or at least to within communication range so he could possibly get some answers from Dubbs.

Around half an hour passed in this silent contemplation, and Leon was glad of the quiet, as eerie as it made the trip feel. The horizon distorted as the heat rose from the ground, and Leon stared, mesmerised by its movements. The road waved upwards and disappeared into the sky. It looked like the road was being lifted from in front of them as they approached. Because of this, it took him a little while to notice the structure at the side of the road. He could feel himself tensing up as he stared at this metal box through the frame of the windscreen. Breeze drying his eyeballs, he strained to keep them focused.

"That the checkpoint?"

Beep.

Leon found himself praying—something he hadn't done since moving to the city. He prayed that the checkpoint was empty. Let the officers be away on lunch break or distracted by television—anything. He thought back to the roadblock of earlier, mentally counting the number of people he'd seen. It was quite possible that the guys from this checkpoint had been at the previous blockade, leaving this one unattended. Leon hoped.

The box was in plain view now. Leon could see its window and door and blue and white checker paint around the top. Voice kept his speed steady. There was only one way past, and it was straight through the gate. No one was in sight. So far so good. And then he saw it: a dust trail, not far beyond the checkpoint. Something was moving fast towards their location.

An officer, who had been tucked away with a magazine, burst from the door as Voice smashed his way through the gate. Leon thought the engine was making strange noises before, but now it sounded purely animal. Injured animal. Bits of the gate flew towards the windscreen frame and Leon ducked as metal shards sliced through the top of his seat. The officer was too slow to drop the net on the wagon, but he didn't seem to mind, as he had also seen the dust trail in the distance. He laughed, dropped his magazine, and hopped up on the gate's control box, watching with anticipation.

A person was causing the distant dust trail. They were running. Fast. Leon knew what it was immediately. He yelled, "Neuro's coming!" and pointed, though it wasn't necessary. Voice had seen it long before and was preparing his next manoeuvre. He slid the wagon sideways and collided with the Neuro. The wagon, pushed to its limits, threatened to roll over. Voice kept his foot down and focused on getting back to the centre of the road as the wagon swayed and skidded to the other side, digging trenches with its bare wheels. Just as Leon thought the wheels were about to bog down, another slam came from behind. The wagon bounced into the air, as if it had just hit a curb full speed, and Leon jumped across the two front seats so as to not crack his head on the roof.

Leon let out a yell as another slam came from behind. He craned his neck to check the one remaining wing mirror, seeing nothing but dust. Once the wagon managed to pull back into a straight line, Leon sat up and braced himself, one hand on the ceiling and one on the door. He risked a peek behind and wished he hadn't. Seeing the figure hurtling behind terrified him. He looked ahead and swallowed a hard lump in his throat. "It's real close, Voice."

With the next glance, the Neuro had vanished. "I don't know where he went!"

As if to answer Leon's query, a loud clang came from the back of the wagon. The dented doors were dented some more as something bashed at them from outside. Voice began swerving while the clanging continued. Leon looked around the cab for anything useful, but it was bare. The wagon had been completely emptied at Zone C.

A chunk of metal caught Leon in the side of the head as the figure smashed a hand through the door. The hole was small, but there was enough of a gap to see an upside-down face. The view was interrupted by the occasional fist as it continued to pummel the weakened spot, bashing the hole wider.

"It's on the roof!"

Voice swerved again and applied the brakes, hoping to fling it forwards, but the Neuro had found a good grip on a few of the bullet holes. With one last thump, the door caved in and bent at the hinges. It screamed as the metal tore and flapped about in the breeze blowing in from the front.

"It's going to get in!"

Voice dropped gears and opened up, digging new trenches as before, one good wheel struggling to keep the wagon on course. It locked up and spun out, fish-tailing the wagon as it bumped out of the trenches and dug fresh ones all over again. Leon heard clanging above and pictured the Neuro riding the wagon like it was a bucking bull. It was only a matter of time. Eventually, everyone fell.

The door completely snapped free, leaving the back of the wagon exposed. Leon watched as the Neuro, still hanging upside down from the roof, flung this way and that with the erratic movements of the wagon. Slime poured down through the bullet holes where the metal was cutting the Neuro's desperately grasping fingers.

"Keep it up, Voice! We're losing it!"

Leon watched its face as it slid left and right. There was no doubt that this thing was a Neuro, but only now did he realise that this wasn't the same one as before. Its features were different, though just as generic. It was made to look male. *What does this one want? Who's sending them?*

A final lurch sideways and another belt of clotter-slime sprayed into the van. The Neuro remained upside down as it flew backwards and landed far behind the wagon, disappearing into the dust as it rolled. His severed fingers rattled loose and followed shortly after. Leon didn't bother concealing his amusement. "He's gone, Voice. You cut his bloody fingers off. Haha!"

Leon wiped a few specks of the slime off his new shirt before it dried. He kept an eye on the dust behind him, but nothing re-emerged.

"You know what he wanted with us?"

Voice beeped a *no*.

"Something weird is going on here. Surely that thing's not after me. Maybe he thought that Boss was in the car. We should warn him as soon as we get back. He might be able to shed some light on this blood sample, as well."

Voice got back up to speed and continued towards the city. Much to Leon's surprise and pleasure, the next twenty-four hours were devoid of patrols and Neuro attacks.

30

FREEDOM

DAIZ PARKED THE VAN in the usual spot against the wall and leapt from the driver's seat. She ran to the doorbell and rang it furiously, wanting to get back to the relative safety of the underground before anyone else showed up. The door swung wide, and a frightened Hughey stood before her, pistol raised. A few more armed civilians stood closely behind.

"Oh, you're back! Excellent. My gosh, that was quick." Hughey pulled her inside. "If you're helping, now is the time to suit up. Everyone else, stay back," he barked.

Daiz ripped open a cupboard and pulled free her usual bio-hazard suit, then began the tedious process of fastening herself into it. Not long after, a red light flickered on a small display unit beside the door. Someone else was approaching. The people of Zone C began converging on the entrance, walking softly and listening for whatever might have been on the other side of the door.

The doorbell angrily rattled again, and Hughey slid to the door, pistol at the ready. Counting down from three in his head, he swung the door wide, raised the gun, and had it ripped from his hands. A young man tumbled inside and fell into Hughey under the weight of a large sack of something wrapped top to bottom in a thick black material. Hughey cried out and crawled back from underneath the crushing heap. Daiz slammed and bolted the door. The scout climbed to his feet, apologies flying from his lips as he tried to help Hughey off the ground.

"I'm alright. I'm fine. Leave me!" Hughey huffed as he picked himself up. "What in the hell?"

The scout stepped back, revealing the package to the crowd. It was twitching, shivering, and wheezing for breath. "The zoner. Looks like he made it."

Hughey's eyes widened, matching his mouth. He ran to the display unit and saw that the light had stopped flickering. No one else approaching. Perhaps the zoner hadn't been followed, after all.

"How…?" He stopped himself. He could ask questions later. He looked down at the zoner. Although he was almost completely wrapped in the material, Hughey could see by his exposed lips and nostrils that he was disfigured.

They were bloated and ulcerated. The mouth held no teeth.

"What's this crap he's wrapped in?" Lung asked.

"He's badly burned. Get him to the medical room at once, and bring fresh water!"

Daiz and Lung carried the zoner into a side room. With the zoner securely on the table, Hughey began unwrapping the writhing body. Its convulsions seemed to be getting less severe but showed no signs of stopping altogether.

"Can you hear me? This is Hughey, Zone C commander. You're safe now. Relax. How did you get here?" Hughey removed another layer and the body's shape became visible through the thick cloth. "How did you leave? You must tell us. How did no one find you?" One more layer, and the thin waist and wide hips were apparent. This was a woman. She croaked, and the room hushed, waiting for her to speak. A few moments went by.

"Get out," she managed through a splutter of blood.

"Pass me the water," Hughey demanded. He held it to her lips and she drank greedily.

"You need to get out!" she said again through a ruined throat.

Hughey lifted the wrap from the top half of her face and a large clump of hair fell from her head. The burns looked recent. She managed to lift her eyelids, revealing pink, bloodshot domes.

He looked away involuntarily. "Okay, everyone, let's do as she says." The group backed out of the room. Once it was clear, Hughey flicked a control switch and allowed the glass shutters to hiss themselves closed.

"Do you think this is the Bug's newest strain?" Daiz whispered to him.

Hughey shook his head slowly. He thought about the message they had received. At first, he thought the medical room should be sealed in case of a new strain of Bug, but now he saw that it was for something else. He looked through the glass door at the woman, who still twitched but had regained some motor control. She fought off the rest of the wrap from her torso and revealed blood stains all over her shirt. "She's irradiated."

The onlookers stood by as she took another swig of water and coughed up more blood. She turned her blind eyes towards the door.

"What happened to you?" Hughey raised his voice so she could clearly hear him through the thick glass.

She took another drink. "This cloth. It's more radioactive than I hoped."

"What is it?"

"It's what Dubbs wraps the blood samples in. I requested a roll from him last supply run. Don't you recognise it?"

Hughey did recognise it. He thought back to when Dubbs had blood samples collected in the past. The couriers had always been wearing protective suits, but again, he'd assumed this was to stop the Bug, not radiation. "Why are you wearing it?"

The woman's eyes shadowed over. "We are all already infected with the Bug. There are just many different strains. The Bug emits a signal… It keeps us traceable. This stuff scrambles that signal." Her voice wavered, and tears would have welled in her eyes if her ducts hadn't been melted shut. The onlookers gasped and a few stepped back, not believing what they'd heard.

"You're lying," Hughey said, trying to sound strong and sure. The woman shook her head, and a silence fell over the group. He was running it through his mind and saw that what she said made sense. It explained how foamers caught them whenever they tried to leave the zone. Once they set foot above ground, a marker appeared on a digital map somewhere and someone could track them down.

"I wish I were," she managed.

"How do you know this?"

"My husband was commander at Zone A. He asked a lot of questions. Eventually, Dubbs confessed. He told us things…" Her voice softened, and the group had to strain their ears to hear. "He told us what he had done. He told us about the wrap."

Hughey gave her a minute to catch her breath before urging her to continue.

"My husband experimented with ways to use the wrap. Many risked their lives to test out his work. All were found and killed. He too died from overexposure. I realised then that there could be no workaround. The only way to fully distort the signal is to wrap yourself up completely." She took another sip. "Dubbs mentioned that a supply run was coming to Zone C, and just by chance he mentioned the driver's name. With nothing more at Zone A to lose, I wrapped myself up, grabbed a car, and headed straight over."

Hughey found himself holding his breath as the woman whispered her story. "Why did you come here?"

A smile cracked her lips, and the fissures grew as her smile widened. "Is my son still here?"

Daiz gasped. "Leon." Her hands covered her mouth as her jaw fell. Her stomach churned, causing her to bend at the middle. "Esmeralda?" she cried. The woman nodded. Daiz felt ill. It was her fault that Leon had left the zone so quickly. She had been thinking of herself, wanting to get back before the foamers arrived. She assured Leon the zoner wouldn't make it this far and sent him away. Her eyes blurred and she wept. Lung threw an arm around her and pulled her close.

"It's not your fault. You could never have known." He spoke softly as she continued to soak the front of his shirt. Hughey was watching, concern and sympathy working clearly through his moustache. He looked at the ground. "Take her somewhere quiet. Make some tea."

Lung nodded and escorted Daiz to an adjoining room. Esmeralda's smile had shrunk back, lips tight, eyelids sagging. "He's not here?"

Hughey shook his head, unsure if Esmeralda could see, but she knew the answer by the silence.

"I'm so sorry," he managed. He meant it sincerely.

The woman lay back and closed her eyes. "I couldn't die without trying. If you see him again, tell him that not a day passed that we weren't thinking of him."

"I'm sorry," Hughey tried again, but it caught in his throat as he turned away. "Doris, fetch me my radiation suit. I will stay with her until it's over." Doris shivered and darted away.

Lung walked back into the room, looking awkward. "Sir." He swallowed hard. "I'm sorry. But, sir, she said something about wrapping the blood samples."

Hughey looked at him hard in the eyes. It wasn't an angry look. More a look of disapproval. "Her name is Esmeralda."

Lung looked back to the floor. "Sorry. Esmeralda said something about wrapping the samples. But the one that Leon took… Well, the method didn't mention a scrambling wrap. It said plenty of other stuff, but nothing about dampening a signal."

Hughey nodded, understanding. "He could've been followed out of here." He raised his voice so the rest of the room could hear him. "Okay, we are going to initiate phase one. Seal off any unused space. We're going to divert some power. Lung, fire up the transmission's panel. We should let Dubbs know what's heading his way."

31

SLOW COOKER

B OSS TRIED COOKIE'S NUMBER again, his fury reaching new heights as his phone beeped and redialled. He stood there, chest puffed, neck veins throbbing, and ready to release his rage. If Cookie didn't answer soon, he might just have to start cursing and lashing out at the drain pipes or the recycling bins.

The auto re-router was kicking in now, connecting to different submersallites around the globe and testing different signal strengths. If anyone could find a way to call Cookie's phone, it was Boss—and he couldn't.

A steam vent opened somewhere in his mind, and he prevented an all-out explosion by throwing a few air punches and making strange gargling noises. "Goddamn… twenty minutes… my ass!"

The sun, which had still been fairly high in the sky when Boss arrived at First Place, had now completely set, and the blond wig was struggling to hold in any heat. He reached up under it and smoothed his mohawk flat to one side. That would help warm half of his head, at least. He tried Cookie again, and as the no connection tone sounded, his muscles tensed and his anger grew anew.

"Where the hell is that son of a bitch?"

32

BLOOD SAMPLE

"**C**RAP, IT'S STILL ENGAGED. Who could he be talking to?"

Leon tossed the dialler back into the glove box beside the parcel. If Boss wasn't going to answer his phone, then Leon would go to the shop in person.

"Let's go find him."

Voice continued his speedy manoeuvres around the streets, which seemed to grow denser by the rev. He aimed to get so surrounded by traffic that even if a policeman were to see the state of the wagon or recognise its description from the checkpoint, they wouldn't be able to reach him if they tried. Leon heard a noise rattling at the front of the car. He listened carefully and realised it was his phone. Voice must have connected it through to Dubbs, who was now screaming down the line and trying to be heard from the glove box. Leon spoke hesitantly. "Uh, hello?"

"I've just received word of a blood sample. Explain," Dubbs bellowed.

"The one you asked for? There was a note in the crate saying you wanted a blood sample. Very specific, apparently. You make cures, eh?"

"Young man, what I do is of no concern to you. You barbaric types are always undermining my work. Just like your boss. The egomaniac likes to think he's in charge. Does things without running it by me first. This must be one of those things. The blood sample needs to be destroyed immediately before you cause another outbreak."

"And how am I supposed to do that?"

Dubbs thought about the best way to explain the steps to Leon. "Firstly, where is the sample now?"

Leon explained that he had it secured in a vial prepared by the zoners, which was now sat in the glove box. He described the vial, strange as it looked, and described the custom-made container that held it, too. Dubbs seemed to consider this and ran a quick calculation on his end.

"Fine. That should be safe enough, for now. I will send coordinates to Voice of where to take the vial to be disposed of correctly. Wouldn't want you accidentally unleashing the Bug upon the city. I will contact Boss. If he pulls any more stunts like this, then he, and ultimately you, will be out of a job. Remember that next time he tells you to do something so foolish."

"Well good luck getting a hold of him," Leon remarked.

Dubbs ignored this and disconnected the line. He had tests to prepare. The message from Hughey said that the blood might be transmitting a signal, so Dubbs sent coordinates for a decoy laboratory to Voice, where it would be securely scrambler-wrapped before being delivered to Dubbs's main hideout. Since the sample was already collected, he thought he might as well put it to good use before disposing of it. Plus, as unconventional as the vial and container sounded, it was definitely an angle that Dubbs hadn't tried before. Maybe it could give him new information and aid in the development of a permanent cure. He spared a moment to chuckle to himself at this thought as he imagined a Neanderthal like Boss cracking such an intricate problem.

Once he finished mocking Boss, Dubbs became consumed by preparation. His mind was working at a million miles per minute as he clanged tubes and needles and vials and everything else onto the desks in his office. Once his area was prepared, he began the next part of his ritual—taking a minute of silence to honour all the victims of the Bug that he and the fed had created.

33

WHERES THE BOSS

"**H**E DIDN'T SOUND HAPPY." Leon shook his head and glanced down at the navs, still hopeful for a response from Voice. He saw the directions refreshing and redrawing themselves a few times, and Leon assumed that Voice and Dubbs were having a quiet conversation about where Voice should head. Leon also noticed that Voice kept the stop-off at the pizza shop in all of the possible navigation decisions, and he respected him for that—if it were possible to respect a machine. He remained true to his binary word, at least.

He left Voice to the navigation and tipped his head back in what was left of the cushion of the seat behind him. The road ahead was gridlocked and progress through the city was slow. Much the same as when Leon first headed into the zone, it was a shaking that pulled him awake before he even knew he was sleeping. The wagon ground its way into the car park of the shop, the now completely rubber-less wheels making a teeth-rattling sound along the gravel. Leon jolted upright with the feeling of falling and yelled. He couldn't help but feel stupid for doing so, and he imagined Voice chuckling away in some dark, microchipped corner of his robot brain, quickly overwriting the evidence as he did so.

Leon slapped his face a few times. His eyes adjusted, and he unclipped his belt and hopped out of the wagon. He only noticed then that the light nearby was coming from Voice's high beams, not the shop. Shutters covered the doors and windows. Lockdown. Exactly what Boss had ordered the last time a Neuro was on the scene. Maybe Boss had been tipped off. Leon breathed a sigh of relief.

Just to be sure, he gave a few solid thumps to the shutter and let it rattle through the entire building while calling out to Boss. There was no response.

"Well, he should be safe in there for now, at least."

Before Leon could climb back into the wagon, Voice had slammed his door closed and flicked the locks. Through the window, Leon spotted that the GPS showed a destination not too far ahead.

"That where Dubbs is?" He tapped the window. No response. "I'm not supposed to know that, eh?" Leon tried the door again.

Voice pulled away at speed, dragging Leon a few steps down the road before ripping the handle from his grip. Leon stumbled and swung his arms up in disbelief. He followed the smoke trail halfway down the road, but it was clear that Voice wasn't returning any time soon. Not knowing what else to do, he started walking in any direction in search of a good cup of coffee.

34

STREET RATS

BOSS LINED HIS BLEEDING HEAD up with the dent in the cable cover. It was an old metal casing, and Boss liked metal things because he could leave more of a mark on metal than on brick. He lunged his head forwards again and heard a crack as the pipe broke right through to the cables. He reached his sausage fingers into the gap and pulled out a few random wires, growling as he did so. The steam vent in his mind had found new ways to relieve some anger.

"Yeah, that will show 'em," came a mocking voice from the end of the alley. Boss turned to see Cookie stood there, a sly grin on his face. Boss marched forwards, breathing deep and heavy.

"Think you're real smart, do ya?" He was shoving his finger towards Cookie. "Oh, look at me. I'm gonna tell Boss twenty minutes, then take more like twenty hours!" His imitation of Cookie's voice would normally have been more than enough to ignite laughter in Cookie, but he knew when to keep it subdued.

"Sorry, Boss. I ran into some trouble. You wouldn't believe—"

"You're not the only one, kid. These last few days have been lethal for the business, and now you have me wasting an entire afternoon hanging out back here, waiting for you. You know how many perverts and weirdos I've had coming up to me?"

Cookie gave Boss a quick look over. The fishnets, the short shorts, the belly button, the muscles, and the stubble. "None?"

"That's beside the point." He waved a dismissive hand and began pacing, working on keeping his temper at a manageable level. "What's so damn important, anyway?"

"I got arrested the other day. Said I helped a fugitive by the name of Marbles escape in a petrol car last week. Something about a dead cop. What've you done this time?"

"I didn't know Marbles was involved. He's new to the team. It was my driver Leon who found the dead cop."

"So a guy kills a cop. The crime scene is found by one of your guys. Then, and unbeknownst to you, the newest guy you hire is the cop killer? Sounds like one strange coincidence to me."

"No shit. You think Marbles was a plant?"

"I don't know what I think. But I definitely think something. It gets weirder. While I was locked up, some chick came around. Carried herself weird. Looked too symmetrical. I only caught a glimpse. She was the one who identified me as the wrong person. Let me go. Know what that's about?"

Boss stopped pacing and racked his brain cells. The steam vent opened again, easing his anger. "May have been a Neuro. I've had one interfering recently."

"What, as in a surrogate machine?"

"Yeah."

"Damn, Boss, they must really want this Marbles guy. That's some new-age shit."

"Uh-huh, except they were snooping around *before* Marbles was on the scene. They were the reason I hired him in the first place. He's a duck and diver. Best chance of not getting caught while out on a delivery."

"And where is he now?"

"Delivering. He's been running them all day. I'm trying to make up for a bit of lost profits, you know?"

"You've left your shop unattended?"

Boss had done quite well at releasing his anger through concentration and thought, but now it flared up again, a growl readying itself in his throat. "It wouldn't be unattended if you hadn't left me out here for the last—"

"Okay, okay, got it. You're pissed. This was important. Listen, I can't think of a next logical step for them other than releasing more ground units or maybe renting another Neuro, so you need to be on high alert. If they don't get Marbles soon, they will try other, less direct methods. That could be bad news for the shop."

"I'd crush your windpipe right now if I didn't know you were right." Reluctantly, Boss extended his hand. Cookie could see that it pained him to pull such a humanising gesture. Cookie said a quick prayer for the bones in his hand and took Boss's.

"It's good to have you back, kid. What's the plan?"

A vehicle rushed past the alley entrance that led to First Place, followed by another. They both turned to watch the road as another vehicle flew past. They were police cars, though their sirens were silenced and their lights were dim. Cookie looked at Boss.

"Let's start by heading in the opposite direction, eh?"

Boss nodded in agreement and began jogging away from the police officers. Cookie kept pace. As they neared the back exit of the alley, another vehicle whooshed past, and Boss dove aside, flattening his back to the wall.

"What are you doing? It looks a lot more suspicious if you're jumping behind bins every time someone passes," Cookie hissed.

"I'm on probation here, kid. I could be arrested just for looking at you."

"Probation?"

"Good behaviour. I don't think walking in dark alleys with past criminal associates counts as such."

Cookie made to speak, but Boss shushed him with a gesture. They listened carefully to their surroundings. The approaching car veered off early. The next few were slow pedestrian vehicles. The coast seemed clear of police cars, for now. They sprinted across the road, jumping between swerving and tooting cars before hiding down the next alleyway along.

"We can't sprint the whole way out of here, Boss."

"I just want to put a bit more distance between us and the cops."

"*Really* don't want them to see you, huh?"

"I really don't want them to see *you*. Solitary confinement wasn't built for guys like me."

Cookie pulled a face. "Uh, yeah, I think it was built exactly for guys like you."

"You know what I mean. Let's go."

"Are you going to explain this probation deal of yours?"

"Now isn't the best time, Chef."

Boss hadn't called Cookie "Chef" since the early days. It was Voice who had come up with "Cookie," and since then it just seemed to stick. Boss calling him Chef struck a chord with Cookie, and old memories came flooding back. He stopped moving then, only for a second, as his mind took in his surroundings again—really took them in. Alley-running, bad disguises, police cars. It was so different to when they were younger. Boss sensed it, too, and this was the first time in years that Cookie had seen him show an emotion other than anger, even though it was only the slightest hint in the corner of his human eye.

"We've gotta make do with what we've got, kid. Same as always," Boss said. Cookie understood. There was a task at hand, and it required full attention. One thing at a time, and right now, that thing was putting as much distance behind them as possible.

"Where do you think they're heading, Boss?"

Boss let out an awkward, on-the-run shrug. "Whatever they're doing, it's a large-scale search. We ought to get off the streets."

"Can I help?" echoed a voice through the alleyway.

Boss and Cookie skidded to a halt and turned, readying themselves for a final showdown before being dragged to jail, but the alley seemed completely empty. They looked around, trying to pinpoint where the mysterious voice had come from, but neither could make out much in the darkness. After a few clumsy seconds, something dropped from above, landing a few steps away from the pair. It unfolded as it rose to its feet, and only when Boss's robotic eye switched to warm tissue mode did he see the familiar face of Marbles. He gave a nervous grin to Boss and hesitated when his gaze fell on Cookie.

Cookie didn't wait to learn who this shadow alley man was and lunged at him. Marbles sidestepped easily, and Cookie flew past, landing face-first on the ground.

"Wait, wait!" Boss barked. He ran over and helped Cookie to his feet. "Cookie, this is Marbles. Marbles, Cookie." Marbles kept his eyes to the ground but managed to squeak out a greeting.

Cookie made a strange face at Boss, unsure of how to take this information. As if in response, Boss pulled a cigarette from his purse and lit up. Cookie recognised the gesture. *Keep a close eye on him.*

With that, Cookie turned to Marbles and nodded. "You've been causing me a bit of trouble, Marbles."

Marbles's cheeks glowed red. He pressed his lips hard together. "Sorry."

There was a long pause as Cookie examined Marbles. When he decided that "sorry" was all he was going to get, he continued. "Okay, so you've probably noticed the cops everywhere. No doubt looking for you." Cookie said that with a little point of his finger, a habit he long ago picked up from Boss. "That could mean they are indirectly looking for Boss, too."

Marbles turned to Boss with surprise. "Do they know I work for you?"

"They don't seem to know much about you at this point," Cookie replied.

"Well, those cops are heading straight to the shop. I saw them setting up a perimeter."

Boss's jaw dropped and he pounded the wall in front of him with his clenched fist.

"You sure?" Cookie asked.

"Positive. I've left the shop locked down and thought to find Boss myself. It's lucky the cops can't hunt like I can."

This word "hunt" made Cookie feel uneasy, though he did his best to hide his feelings. "So they just let you wander out of a sectioned-off area?"

"No way would they have let me, but I left before they put everything in place."

Boss was still preoccupied with ramming his bloody knuckles into the wall. Cookie slid over to stop him and whispered quickly in his ear. "I don't trust him."

Boss stopped his fist short of another collision, but a few flakes of brick fell away anyway, as if they knew their fate. He looked up at Marbles's absent face, then across to Cookie's.

"I know he's strange, but I just don't see him as a killer. He doesn't seem to know anything about what's going on, and I think I believe him."

Cookie shook his head. "I trust you, Boss, but I think this is a mistake. Something is definitely up. Don't let him blind you."

Boss winked, and that was the end of it. He raised his voice to re-include Marbles. "After you."

Marbles smiled. It was time for him to do his thing. He ran ahead, looking for ledges and hoists as he went, keeping Boss's lack of athletic abilities in mind. Sure, the guy had muscles, but imagining Boss climbing a drain pipe to a windowsill made Marbles almost laugh aloud.

35

SHOWDOWN

THE LAST HALF HOUR passed slowly, and despite feeling that they'd been moving nonstop, the trio hadn't travelled overly far. They were off of the ground now, though, and the chance of being found atop this roof by anyone other than a resident was slim. Boss collapsed back against an air vent, gasping for breath. Cookie fell beside him and lay flat on his back, panting like a dog. Marbles just huffed and took a seat on a chair that someone had left out.

Getting bored waiting for the other two to catch their breath enough to talk, Marbles turned his chair towards the edge of the rooftop and looked out over the city. They weren't too high up, but high enough for Marbles to appreciate the size of the city. Even Marbles was rarely on a building of this height, as he preferred the smaller ones he could scale and launch himself from more easily.

Cookie finally felt he had enough strength to lift his head. It was still a bit hazy, but his eyes gradually adjusted, and he looked over at Boss. Boss was breathing hard, as if he had just run a marathon.

"Since when did we get so unfit, Boss?" Cookie laughed tiredly, unable to believe that only half an hour of exercise had drained him so much.

"Since cars got me places faster," Boss managed to mumble between breaths.

Marbles sat by the ledge, hunched over something indiscernible in the moon's glow. A burning sensation grew across his neck, and he turned to meet Cookie's eyes, who stared intently into his own. With fumbling fingers, Marbles tried to hide what he was holding. Cookie was on his feet and ran over in two large bounds, then slammed Marbles down against the ledge. His eyes beamed, soaking up the intimidation and fear coming from Marbles. The updraft caught Marbles's hair, making him look even more fragile in the twilit glow. Cookie played on this weakness and tightened his grip on Marbles's jacket, forcing him further over the edge.

"What have you got?" he screamed at Marbles, face twisting into hatred. "I saw you. What did you do?"

Marbles was in shock, his mouth barely moving, and he couldn't form words.

"Either you show me or I remove it myself. If I do that, I will need to let go of you first."

Marbles let out a sound then, which might have been a *no*. Cookie wasn't sure. He let go with one hand and Marbles slipped further. With that hand he felt around in Marbles's jacket pockets. Marbles squirmed, gripping at the ledge and trying to pull himself back to safety. He managed to wriggle free of Cookie's grip as Cookie pulled a bag from his pocket. It flew from Cookie's fingers and he watched helplessly as it plummeted to the street below.

Cookie stared over the edge for a long moment, though whatever was in the bag had collided with the pavement, its splattered contents too far away to see. The remainder of what he held was a small slice of pizza he recognised as one of Boss's. He looked down at Marbles shaking on the ground.

"What was it?"

Marbles hesitated. "I'm sorry… I know… I shouldn't…"

"What did you do? What was it?"

"Margarita with extra mushrooms."

Cookie looked at the crust in his hand, wondering if Marbles had in fact only ever had a pizza. He threw it over to Boss, who picked it up feebly and inspected the contents.

Cookie continued his bluff. "I know you're hiding something! What else was in the bag?" He took a large step towards Marbles, towering over him with his chest puffed. If Marbles wouldn't tell the truth, then he would beat it out of him. Marbles had never felt so trapped. He tried to get up and run, but his legs were disobeying his orders. Cookie readied to deliver a pummelling with the works. Marbles closed his eyes. He was a runner and couldn't deal with being confined. He pissed himself.

As Cookie wound back his fist, a wide beam of light washed over the rooftop. Cookie stopped and looked upwards. Boss tuned back into the present, and he too tilted his eyes to the sky, jaw going slack. Above them hovered a scanner-craft which had made its way down from the edge of space. Boss's eyes began to water. He had never seen one so close. He doubted many people had. It stayed at altitude as taller buildings stopped it from descending further, but from one end to the other, the craft took up the entire width of his vision. It was the aircraft carrier of scanner-crafts. The mothership.

Two large glass domes protruded from its bottom. From both of those, three DNA beams glared downwards, licking the rooftops. The six beams quickly conjoined on the roof where the trio resided. Boss looked over to Cookie, who looked back, seemingly just as blown away by the sight. He would have loved to just sit there and admire the spaceship-esque creation hanging above, if only it weren't trying to find them.

Cookie ran to Boss's side and helped him to his feet.

"We've got less than a minute before it locks on to us. Another couple of minutes before anyone gets up here. Maybe longer if they send ground scanners—can those things even climb? Anyway, we need to ghost before then."

Boss nodded and looked over Cookie's shoulder to see Marbles dancing about, trying to lose the beam that was locked solidly on to his sodden shorts. He felt their eyes on him and yelled, "Can we go yet?"

Boss nodded and started running on tortured legs. Cookie pulled at his shoulder and spun Boss around.

"Look, they're locked on. They are clearly after *him*. Let's leave him here."

Another beam locked on to Marbles—his face this time. Boss flinched. He didn't like leaving team members behind. He hesitated, not knowing what to do. Then instinct made his mind up for him. He ran back to Marbles and grabbed his wrist. He gave a daring look back to Cookie, who didn't protest, but Boss explained himself anyway.

"If one is caught, we may as well all be caught. Everybody talks, eventually, and Marbles already knows more than I want to hand over."

Boss wasn't sure if Cookie understood or if he just didn't want to waste more time on chatter, but he began fleeing alongside Boss and Marbles anyway. Pushing off Boss, Marbles launched himself ahead, scouting the surroundings and looking for the easiest way down. They climbed across to an adjacent building, only a couple of stories lower, and continued their sprint. They passed a few doors that Boss rugby-tackled, but when they hardly budged, he decided it would take too long to cave one in. He kept running.

Another beam washed itself over the building and followed closely behind Boss. Sweat poured from his head, and the low altitude of the scanner-craft meant the beams could pick up an otherwise diluted DNA trail.

"Shit." Boss slowed to a jog.

"Don't stop. They haven't caught us yet," Marbles screamed.

"No. But they will."

Boss felt a stitch burning up in his side as exhaustion fought its way back. A string of crashing and shattering echoed from between the buildings ahead of them. Marbles reached the edge of the roof and peered over. What he saw threw him backwards, and he landed with a heavy thud, winding himself. A Neuro, climbing the side of the building, threw herself into the air and landed where Marbles crouched only a second before. The firearm at her side activated, no time wasted in beaming the scanner-craft for permission. A police-approved operator must have been in control this time. No autopilot. She snapped the orb-launcher in line with Boss's head and took a stance.

Cookie was stunned by the machine, recognising it as the federal agent who had identified him while in jail. Despite Boss telling him that it was probably a Neuro, it was only now, when he saw it in action, that he completely appreciated what that entailed. In the split second that Cookie stood dumbfounded, gazing at the Neuro, she had readjusted the gun nozzle and fired two orbs into Cookie, tackling him to the ground as metal tentacles wrapped themselves around him. Boss dove aside, keeping his head down behind a satellite dish. Scrapes, bangs, and clunks compelled Boss to peek at what was going on behind him, and he saw that the Neuro was now fully concerned with Marbles.

Deciding it was now or never, Boss shuffled his way over to Cookie and began ripping the tenta-binds from the orb at Cookie's chest. He had never before mustered so much strength, and by the time the last bind came free, his arms felt like trees rooted to the ground. Marbles was still hopping around the rooftop, a tentacle wrapped around one of his legs. Boss made to move in, but Cookie grabbed Boss's shoulder and pulled him backwards. They both tumbled down an access stairway, rolling and clanging floor after floor. Boss growled and tried to stand up, ready to climb the stairs and help Marbles, but he couldn't move.

Cookie crawled to the edge, where a ladder led almost to the ground. "You tried, Boss, but there's nothing you can do for him now. You can't fight a Neuro. Not in this state."

Boss pulled himself towards the ladder, aching all over. "We don't leave men behind, Cookie. It's never how we've done business."

Cookie's face turned solemn. "I'm sorry, Boss, but I can't let you go back. You've never trusted me enough, but I'm telling you now that our best chance is to split up, and that's what we're gonna do." With that, he kicked Boss over the edge. He watched the giant fall. The drop was significant, and Boss sunk deep into the heaping pile of trash bags below. Cookie waited, peering into the dark and straining his ears to detect any sound of movement as time slowed around him. A rustle washed up from the laneway floor, followed by a few clinks. One of the bags fell from the pile as Boss swam to the top. He was alive.

With no more time to waste, Cookie clambered down the ladder, sped off down the lane, and disappeared into the night.

36

SLEEPING SPIDER

THE CIRCLE OF PATROL UNITS closed in, slowly narrowing in on the area marked on their handheld screens. The area was a circle, somewhere within which a signal had initially appeared on the grid—the same signal that ploughed its way through the roadblocks, outran the Neuro, and was now trying to lose its tail through the city.

"Just another building, same as the others." One of the officers approached the chain-link across the door and gave it a hard tug. It was rusty but held its strength. "Not been open in years."

"There's gotta be something around here. Keep your eyes open."

The officers continued their search, not really knowing what they were looking for. The misty visors pressing against their faces made this even harder. One of them noticed the conveyor belt poking out of the side of a warehouse and climbed across it. He pushed his head through the plastic flaps awkwardly. His oxygen tank lay beneath him, jabbing him in the back. He readjusted himself to get a better look.

"Anything in there?"

"Whole place's empty." He climbed all the way in and walked around the inside of the warehouse, looking for *anything* that might tell him *something*. None of them seemed happy with the task at hand. Patrolling the road was one thing, but gearing up and slinking around abandoned zone buildings was another. He helped his partner through the conveyor belt opening, and the two of them kicked dust around the floor, bitching about their vague orders.

"I don't get it. If the buggers already left, what we doing here?"

"The others have been talkin' about a whole group of them livin' round here."

"Get off it! This place was wiped clean. Truth is, I saw a car enter here a few days ago. I bet it was that same car leaving today."

"You let a car through?"

"Didn't let it, did I? He sped on through, across the dunes. Naught I could do. Nothing for him to find here, anyway.

Chains and dust. And the bloody virus, of course. Don't he know we're here for his own well-being? They want to get through, let them through, I say. Don't come crying to me if they get infected or shot on the way out, though."

The other officer wore a concerned face. "But we don't know if he *did* get infected, since we didn't get chance to scan him. And he *didn't* get shot, did he? Because you aim like a computer nerd playing tennis. So he's tearing through the city as we speak. What if that car starts this whole epidemic all over again? Seniors won't be happy knowing that you let him through—twice."

"They don't have to know, do they? Anyway, naught I could do. We're wasting our time in here. Nothing but chains and dust."

He turned back to the ground and kicked another flurry into the air, watching it erupt and slowly settle as it succumbed to gravity. The other officer shook his head and turned back to the conveyor belt, ready to leave. Then he noticed something. He squinted at the ground, and it took him a moment to realise what he saw—or, rather, what he didn't see. The entire conveyor belt had a cleanly washed floor beneath it. No dust. Even if it had rained, the water wouldn't have travelled so far into the warehouse.

"What you looking at, Kev?"

"No dust. Look."

"Well there's more than a shitload over here, if you want it." He kicked another firework of dust into the air. "I hope this doesn't clog my filters."

"No, look. The conveyor belt has been washed clean. Right to the end. Someone's used it recently."

The dust-kicker leaned in closer and realised what Kev was saying. The conveyor belt must have been running the last time it rained. He looked up and gave a nod. "I think you've found something to report, Officer."

Kev nodded in return and shuffled through the flaps, then called for his supervisor. It didn't take long before an entire search team was poking around inside the warehouse.

37

FEDERAL CUSTODY

BOSS STEADIED HIMSELF against a dustbin. His breath left him long ago and he was now running on pure stubbornness. Even *that* had started failing him once he realised the only way out of his current, cornered position was up and over. He could barely lift his feet, let alone his entire body, over yet another fence.

"Halt!" It was a trio of police officers.

Boss growled. "Way to interrupt my evening's jog."

"Don't move. Hands above your head."

Boss raised one hand but kept another on the bin. Now that his legs were turning to jelly beneath him, it was all the support he had. The police shot the lock off the gate and moved in, regardless. They were quick and rough, despite Boss's obvious exhaustion. They didn't want to take any chances with someone his size. A police officer ripped off the golden wig to reveal a flattened mohawk. It took only a second to identify him as the Pizza Boss.

"We hunt for an escaping zoner and find the Pizza Boss. What are the odds?"

"That's a pretty big search team for one person. It almost smells like something else is going on here."

"Well we're going to find out. Bring him in, fellas."

Boss spat a large jellyfish globule at the cop's feet, then followed him back to a van with the aid of the detaining officers. His neck bent forwards as they threw him into the back of the van and shut the door so fast behind him that Boss was surprised his ankles weren't caught in the slam. After a moment of using the last of his energy to throw himself at the door, he realised he wasn't alone in the mobile cage.

"Even if you *could* knock that door open, what exactly would you do next?" the voice said from the shadows.

Boss huffed angrily. He could do anything that he wanted; how dare they try to confine him. He thought back to the last time he'd been this powerless—it was the last time he'd been arrested. He found a way out last time, and he would do the same this time. All he needed to do was focus and control the anger. Boss turned to the federal agent across from him.

"Sometimes, *Pizza Boss*"—the fed soaked the name in sarcasm—"I wonder what goes through your mind. You understand what probation *means*, right? Benefit of the doubt and all that?"

Boss glared hard at the fed, trying to read him, but adrenaline continued to cloud his mind. The fed laughed complacently. Boss resented the idea of cooperating with the man he hated more than anything on earth, but in the back of this van and with a city full of cops on high alert, he knew he'd lost this battle. He gave a short nod.

The fed continued. "Your problem, Mr. Boss, is that you're assuming I care about you. I don't. Your release had conditions which, need I even remind you, are unfulfilled. And those conditions weren't to be carried out *at any cost*. We've just received reports of a large-built hooker on a rooftop with a suspected murderer. Are you even going to bother trying to convince me that wasn't you? There was another member of the little trio, too. Ex-criminal associate. One Cookie Sven. You've directly violated our agreement. Not to mention the smuggling from a zone…"

"Woah, hold up now. Zone smuggling? I don't know what you're talking about, and neither do you."

The fed smiled. "Well, we need something to tell the press. How else can we explain the signal that we traced leaving Zone C? Was that Voice, by the way? I recognised the driving. I hope you're taking good care of him…"

"What Dubbs does with Voice is none of my business. All I know is that I've had nothing to do with zoners, man, and I don't know anything about a signal."

The mention of Dubbs sent a pang through the fed's chest. He leaned forwards, his stare matching the intensity of Boss's.

"You don't seem to understand how thin the ice is. In fact, I would be surprised if there was any ice left. You're balanced on surface tension, *man*. Do you really want to make waves?"

"Are you coming on to me?"

The fed caught Boss along the side of the head with an open hand, dislodging his robotic eye. It flung from its socket and rolled to the fed's foot. He stomped down hard. Boss was stunned. A second later, his brain caught up with the present. "Fuck!"

He poked a finger at his now empty eye socket, not able to believe what had just happened. "You seriously just took my eye?" The empty socket sparked as the chips and boards tried to rewire themselves before deeming it useless and going dead. He looked up at the fed with his remaining eye and saw him sitting there, so still, cool as ever.

Boss waited for the familiar rage to boil up inside him and lend him the strength he needed to cave open the van's door with the fed's head. But nothing happened. He was completely burnt out. Instead, what he felt was a strange, unwelcome feeling joined by the stiffening of his muscles. His chest burned with each breath and his feet joined his now useless metal eye socket in becoming nothing but dead weight. The unwelcome feeling was fear.

He looked down at the ground with his good eye, and the fed smirked just enough to taunt Boss. He knew he had him now.

"Now that you've given it some thought, I believe it is safe to say you will be a little more cooperative?" He waited for Boss to respond before continuing. He wanted Boss to know who controlled this situation.

"Your little hiccup can be forgotten…" He paused here and waited for Boss's head to twitch or his ears to prick. Boss was desperately trying to keep himself composed, but all he wanted to do was ask him what he could do— anything—to stay out of jail. Right on cue, Boss's head jerked upwards a little before he stopped himself, but it was too late. The fed was reading him like a book.

"We need you to get to Dubbs…"

"What's new?" Boss mumbled.

"We have new intel. He should contact you soon. When he does, you need to convince him to meet. You will only get one chance at this." He removed a phone from his pocket and placed it down on the bench next to Boss. Clipped to the side of it were a small dish and a signal booster. The fed played around with some settings on its small display and tuned into the frequency the robotic eyeball was spitting out in desperation. This allowed the phone to pick up on any incoming calls that the eyeball would have usually directed to Boss's R-chip. "Ready yourself. It won't be long now."

38

DELUXE EXPRESS DELIVERY

DUBBS BALANCED THE RECEIVER between two of his chins as he assaulted the dial box with a wide finger. He was mumbling something under his breath, and although he wanted to announce his complaints louder for all the office block to hear, he was worried that the excess jaw movement might crush the device at his neck. Once again, the phone rang out, and Dubbs felt a slight shift somewhere in his mind. He hoped it wasn't his sanity. He didn't very often lose his composure, but Boss had a way of pushing his buttons. He hit redial and took the receiver out of its sandwiched position so he could safely munch on a Choco-Corn Crunch. As the line disconnected again, the office door opened, and Dubbs instantly felt his rage directed at the old man who now stood in the doorway. It took a few moments of concentration to disassociate the old man from the engaged phone, and when he finally spoke, the man could tell that the calm in Dubbs's voice was forced.

"Yes?"

"Sir, we've got that parcel you asked for."

Dubbs looked behind the man and froze solid in his chair. The man had wheeled in a trolley, which held the small parcel that Voice delivered, and there was something unwelcome about it that had drawn Dubbs's attention. The shades over his eyes were filtering certain light patterns, revealing a faint infrared glow. The parcel was emitting light in all directions, and it was fading out quickly, but in the centre, a solid beam shot upwards and penetrated the ceiling.

Dubbs squashed back further into his chair, the plastic joints groaning with the added pressure. "That's not just glowing. It's got a direct signal…"

"Sorry, sir?"

"It's emitting. It needs to be dampened, immediately!"

The old man looked confused while what Dubbs had said sank in. After a few seconds, his eyes widened. The old man couldn't see the beam with his un-lensed eyes, but he knew by Dubbs's panic that it must have been different to the samples he'd dealt with in the past. The man hurriedly began throwing protective gear over himself in preparation for handling the dampening wrap.

"No time for that, you fool! Dampen the signal *now,* or every officer in the state is going to know exactly where we are!"

Tossing the protective gear aside, the old man pulled the scrambler wrap from its thwart box and wrapped the vial. He placed the thwart box clumsily back over the top and hit the one button on the front. The red glow dimmed, though not enough. Dubbs could still see it. He shook his head and realised he was holding his breath. He gasped, still staring and completely stunned at the red air above the parcel.

The old man tried to regain control of the situation and prove his worth to his employer. "I'll have it destroyed right away, sir."

"No!" Dubbs was surprised to hear the words escaping his own mouth. "For a signal that pure… maybe it's… I need to test it… Wrap it thrice more and leave it in the vault below. That should buy us some time. Maybe I can retrieve it later. Come straight back. I've got something I need you to do."

"Sir?"

"Go!" Dubbs kicked himself backwards, rolling towards the big screen on the wall. He activated it with some hand movements and watched the surrounding streets through the numerous cameras around the block, plus whatever other cameras he'd acquired access to by permissible means or otherwise. So far, things looked in order. He glanced at the clock and decided that if someone had picked up the signal already, he would only have seven minutes at most before the authorities rolled up. He had a decision to make, and oh did he hate making this decision. The previous times his hideout had been possibly exposed, he had taken the cautious route, had all files and records destroyed, fled into hiding, and started somewhere new from scratch.

Dubbs tried to calculate his odds in each situation by quickly adding an estimated weight of influence to every factor that came to mind and comparing the results with each other. He was surprised to find that his subconscious mind had added a large numeric value to Boss as a positive influence factor. He glanced back at the phone and wondered why he held so much faith in the aggressive, unreliable asshole.

A bead of sweat formed on his brow and made its way along the creases of his nose.

Six minutes.

He looked up at the screen. Still no cops. No scanners, no beams... No anything. Dubbs frowned and switched cameras. An empty road. He viewed another cam and saw nothing but parked cars and plastic trees. It appeared that the surrounding twelve blocks, at least, had been sectioned off. He didn't even have five minutes—he was already surrounded.

Kicking his way back across the room, Dubbs tried Boss once more. This time he heard a successful click.

Boss answered. "Yeah?"

"I wish you would have told me about the sample," Dubbs blurted. "I haven't got anything in place."

"Oh yeah. Sorry…" Boss looked at the fed opposite him and shrugged. The agent just stared back.

"Listen, Boss, they're closing in. The blood has led them to my area. It's only a matter of time."

"Oh yeah?" Boss was genuinely confused. He'd slipped the note between the zoners' crates under the fed's instruction, but he had no clue what it actually said.

"You made a grand job of the method. Strongest signal I've ever seen from a blood sample. I need to know how you did it…"

Boss went quiet as he looked for guidance from the fed, who sat silently, staring into Boss.

"Boss?"

Boss had to improvise, so he stuck to what he knew — aggression. "Always making me bend over backwards for your damn science. I can't send you anything now. I'm not at the shop…"

"Listen, Boss, I need to nuke this office, and when I say nuke, I mean everything destroyed, including my phones.

I can't take this blood sample with me. The signal is too strong and they will just follow it. I will need a new sample like this for the next time I set up shop. We won't be able to contact each other, so I need to know how you collected it. I need your method. Now."

Boss froze as an unfriendly hand gripped his wrist a little too tightly. He winced, holding in his yelp, and looked up at the fed, who gave Boss one distinguished nod. Boss understood. Dubbs fidgeted in silence. Something strange was going on. He could feel it.

Boss managed to speak. "Then I will jot you down a copy of the recipe while I head over. Where can we meet?"

"You know I don't do face to face, Boss."

The hand on Boss's wrist tightened even more.

"It doesn't sound like you've got many options, Dubbs. How long will it take for you to wrap things up? Maybe I can get a driver to—"

"I can be out of here in three." Dubbs tapped furiously at his keyboard. "I have transport waiting. It will take me a while to get through the checkpoints. You will find me in sixteen hours."

"Where will you—" The line went dead.

The hand on Boss's wrist let go, and the federal agent nodded again, slightly impressed. The van slowed, and the inside of the mobile cage was assaulted with flashing blue and red. They had arrived at one of the checkpoints. Boss peeked through the tinted view slot and saw the huge backlog of drivers, all waving frantic arms or tooting or cursing. The agent smiled. "Somehow, I don't imagine Dubbs *will* be working his way through any of these checkpoints. Would put you in an awkward situation if we brought him in without you, eh? Don't worry, though. I've heard they've been renovating. New padding, thicker chains. Everything you will need for the remaining hundred and fifty years of your sentence."

Boss felt the thing in his stomach again and began to wonder what his chances of avoiding jail were, even if he brought Dubbs to the fed single-handedly.

Desperately, he stared out of the slot in the side of the mobile cage, hoping to spot someone who looked like an illegal scientist. He squinted, his missing robotic eye no longer able to zoom in for him, and spotted a fire truck causing another roadblock across the way. Ordinary Joes were queuing up or pushing through or yelling abuse. Dubbs could be any one of them—or not. Boss had no idea, and all he could hope was that the authorities didn't, either. He had to find Dubbs first.

Boss could make out beams of scanner-crafts penetrating the grey sky. He couldn't believe it. Feds, fire trucks, local PD, scanners. They really wanted Dubbs's head on a pike.

"Well this is where we part, *Pizza Boss*. I'm done with you, for now. We will be in touch." The fed rapped at the side of the cage that backed up to the driver's seat, and the van's door clicked open. "Just remember, I've got eyes on you. More than you know."

With that rattling around in his mind, Boss clambered out and onto the road. An ambulance flew past, its siren muffled by the rest of the chaos, and almost knocked Boss flat to the ground. He recovered and looked back at the van to see the rear door had already clamped itself shut. An armed passenger hopped out of the side door and ran towards the commotion. A moment later, the van bumped up the curb, weaved through the still partially present gap carved by the ambulance, and disappeared behind a wash of people.

Someone approached Boss, a question obviously balanced on the tip of his tongue, but stumbled back as he received a one-eyed stare and a bit of a sneer. This returned an ounce of ego to Boss, who strutted in his fishnets away from the crowds and back towards his shop.

39

NANNY STATE

THE MUG SLUMPED between his fingers. He swirled it, watching the black liquid completely devour the grains of sugar as he poured them from a sachet. Leon had recognised this café from a visit a long time ago, and with most other places closed or barricaded off, he decided to stay put and enjoy the chaos—for the time being.

If not for the scanner-craft above acting as a street-wide umbrella, the rain would have soaked Leon. He snapped up his collar and nestled in. Nothing felt better than a warm coffee on a cool night and out on the pavement of a usually busy street during its quiet hours. The road wasn't completely empty, of course. There were the odd couple here and there, stumbling back from a night on the booze and clutching at each other's arms, oblivious to the situation on their doorsteps. There was also the occasional vehicle of a local who had managed to argue their way through the blockades and, after God knows how much questioning, been granted access to their own driveways.

Leon sat and watched, amused by all the small details that made life what it was. He thought of Marbles and wondered if he would still be running deliveries for Boss. A parkour deliveryman would be more useful now than ever. Leon missed talking to Marbles, as wacky as he was. It was refreshing not to feel like the only outcast among this infinite herd of city sheep.

The deep rumble of a petrol engine brought Leon back from his daydream, and he was quite surprised to see a large wagon rocking against the breeze and tearing up the tarmac. He finished his coffee and sat back, hands resting on his head. Voice pulled up beside Leon and the door sprung open. He expected the one they called Dubbs to emerge, but nothing happened. Voice beeped.

"Oh, you want me back in now?" He stood and walked over to the door, then peered inside. It was empty.

"Where's Dubbs?"

The screen on the dashboard flashed.

"You and Boss first."

Leon smiled to himself as he got into the wagon. "Whatever, I'm giving up on trying to work this out. Let's go."

The caffeine buzz suddenly struck Leon and he began twitching. He drummed on the dash as he looked around, taking in the increasing chaos as they drove closer to a diversion point. A policeman stood with a glow stick and waved cars to the right.

"Damn, looks like we're taking the long way around."

Voice didn't respond. Leon thought that maybe he was concentrating. He then realised once again that Voice wasn't a person, and he hated how his mind treated him as a human or, worse, as a friend. He tried to keep quiet, but his heart was pumping louder. That was some strong coffee. The twitch in his fingers reached his lips. "Had you been looking for me for long?"

No response.

Leon looked down at the screen and realised that Voice couldn't respond because the GPS was active. A dot, not far up the road, was flashing. Leon watched as it moved slowly but at a steady pace. After a second, something in Leon's mind clicked. He was about to ask Voice how he was tracking Boss by GPS, but a pang of something in his gut kept him from disclosing his recent discovery. Probably best he pretended not to notice, but he'd make sure to mention it to Boss later. He then wondered if Voice could track him, too.

They neared the policeman slowly as the queue shortened—one car at a time. Leon checked the screen. Boss was up ahead and to the left. This cop was diverting right. One more car forwards and the queue stopped completely. Leon poked his head out of the window to see that the cop was staring straight at the bullet-riddled wagon.

"Act casual, Voice. I think he's spotted us."

Voice must have been processing the same information. Using the quickly closing gap ahead, he accelerated and swung the wagon to the side, up the curb, and around the roadblock. The policeman was yelling somewhere behind, but the sound of the exhaust quickly drowned him out as Voice slid around the next bend and took off down the road.

"Not quite what I meant!" Leon yelled as he grasped at the doorframe, trying to keep himself upright as he was forced aside. The small amount of traffic on this side of the blockades meant fewer obstacles, and Voice roared along and skidded one last turn, then stopped dead ahead of Boss.

Leon popped the passenger's door open and, sticking a thumb up, leaned over it.

"Oh, Leon! Good to see ya, kid. I need a ride."

Boss ran to the wagon, where another door popped open for him, and climbed in. "Can you take us somewhere away from all this bullshit, Voice? Need to rest up. Meeting Dubbs tomorrow. Did he tell ya?"

Voice beeped, and Leon explained their beep-response system.

Boss nodded. "Good, good. I was hoping he sent you some coordinates. I don't have a bloody clue where to find him." He looked over at Leon.

Leon shrugged. "I've just been getting dragged all over the place by Voice. I stopped asking questions a while ago." He gave Boss a quick look and hoped Boss realised what it meant. It was true that he didn't know what was going on, but he certainly hadn't stopped wondering. In fact, a few new questions were brewing in his mind after he saw Boss's coordinates on Voice's navs screen. He decided that his silence probably wasn't the best thing for the situation, in case Voice was studying their behaviour, so he went straight into some general chatter with Boss.

"What happened to your face?"

"What?"

"Where's your eye? That's gross, man."

Boss had forgotten about the empty socket where his robotic eye had been. "This goddamn federal knocked it right out of my head!"

"A fed?" Leon's face twisted at the mention. "What happened?"

Boss felt his stomach knot. He wasn't too sure if Leon would care about the truth behind Boss's plans, but he wasn't about to start explaining anything in front of Voice, since anything Voice knew, Dubbs seemed to know a half-second later. Boss grew angry in an instant, which showed in the sudden reddening of his face. He made up a quick tale and changed the subject, aiming it back at Leon. "You wanna speak about gross? What the hell are you wearing?"

"This is because of your damn pizza. Threw up all over my other clothes."

This eased Boss's nerves as he felt a laugh growing inside. "It was at least a Mexican, I hope?" he asked mockingly.

"Hawaiian."

The laughter escaped.

The mood was contagious, and Leon began chuckling as well, though after taking about a year's supply of ridicule, he turned back to the missing windscreen in front of him. The smirk took another few minutes to leave his face as he reflected on his visit to the zone, which naturally led to thoughts of Daiz. The rest of the ride passed in silence.

40

GOT A PLAN?

THE SUN SHONE THROUGH empty window frames, warming Leon and Boss, who were sprawled across the seats, as they continued to snore. Voice was contemplating moving them to a shadier spot, but his battery cells benefitted greatly from the sunlight and his priority program was kicking in. Leon awoke first, due to the light directly in his eyes. He yawned and stretched, a sharp pain in his back limiting his movement. He managed to wriggle into a slightly less awkward position and glance back at Boss, who clearly didn't have sleeping troubles in the light or the heat. A sliver of drool shimmered in the glare of the sun. Leon couldn't dare to look any longer. He turned back to the windscreen.

"You awake Voice?"

"Yeah, I don't sleep…"

"Oh yeah. But I didn't know if you had a standby mode or something."

"I do. And you just pulled me out of it."

"Oh… Sorry. So what's the deal today?"

"Dubbs gave me a location. We're going to meet him later."

"What until then?"

"Well you need a change of clothes. Also, Boss needs to work on a new transmitter for Dubbs. I have the specs."

Leon smiled at this and looked back at the snoozer.

"You want to wake him up, then?"

"HELL NO."

Leon leaned across the car and beeped the horn, then withdrew his hand quickly when he saw Boss stir, acting as if he too were just rudely awoken.

"Argh, what the fuck, Voice?" Boss stretched, much more violently than Leon had, and rubbed at his face with his knuckles. Leon stepped out of the car, breathing in the strange city smells and taking a seat on the curb. The car park they had overnight-camped in was almost completely secluded, and Leon was surprised at how alone this made him feel on the edge of such a busy city.

Boss exited the car and took in the surroundings in one quick sweep. "No cops here? Good. Apparently, they sectioned off my shop at some point last night. Marbles said he had barely made it past."

"Where is he now?"

Boss's face drained of colour. He had completely forgotten about the Neuro last night. "Last I saw him, he was with me and Cookie on a roof, tackling a Neuro." He watched Leon's face drop. "He beat one before. He can do it again. I'm sure he's fine."

Leon didn't believe Boss's words, and Boss didn't either. Truth was, he had hoped to have heard from him by now. Silence was rarely a good thing.

"What was Cookie doing there?"

"Trying to help me out. He had a warning for me, though I think it came a little too late. He's the only man I trust with my life. You know that?"

"Why'd he leave the business before?"

"He left with everyone else when the business was shut down. I got arrested, and the gig was over. I don't blame him for running, though. I would have done the same thing. I don't doubt for a second that he would have helped me bust out of there if I hadn't got out myself anyway, and that's what counts."

"Aren't you worried they will arrest you again?"

Boss pushed the thought aside a little too casually, and Leon realized that had been haunting Boss ever since he left jail the first time. He slapped Leon on the shoulder, giving him a wide smile and lighting a cigar. "I'm invincible, kid. You not figured that out yet? Plus, I've got a kick-ass team." He nodded sincerely at Leon before turning back to the car park.

"Who is this big softy beside me, and what did the federal agent do to the real Boss?"

Boss snorted. "Don't push your luck, kid. I just got a good feeling about today, is all."

No elaboration followed, and Leon didn't ask for any. The scanner-crafts above were still low over the rooftops, but their frequent movements allowed rays of sun to wash down over most of the city. Boss and Leon sat there quietly, soaking up the sun on this unusually warm day.

Not wanting to break the silence but knowing it needed to be done, Leon spoke in a whisper. "Hey, Boss, I can't be certain, but I'm pretty sure Voice had you tracked. You know about that?"

Surprised but not concerned, Boss turned slowly to Leon. His head shook a little and his lips tightened. After a moment's thought, he said, "Oh yeah?"

"Yeah, there was a moving marker on his GPS just before, and it led us right to you."

"Strange. With my eye gone, I shouldn't be giving off any waves." He felt around in his pockets and found the temporary beeper phone that he'd used to contact Cookie. Removing it, he snapped it in half and tossed it aside. "Not impossible to trace a beeper phone, I suppose. Not that Voice has access to a submersallite that he can just hijack and reprogram whenever he wants."

"Maybe Dubbs has one?"

"No way. Too paranoid about someone reversing the signal and finding him or something."

Leon shrugged. "Well, it seemed like Voice was tracking you somehow, so just… be careful."

Boss leaned in close. "You're a natural, kid. Keep those eyes and ears open. They've served you well so far." He took a moment to breathe and almost looked hesitant to continue. "Something else is going on here, and I'm sorry that I've dragged you into it, but as big as this mess seems, it will be over soon."

Leon looked asquint at Boss and soaked up the cryptic compliment, wondering what the underlying message was that he was meant to decipher. He chose to take it as it was, for now, and see if it fit into his mental puzzle later.

"I better head off, then. Are you meeting Dubbs on your own or do you want me to swing back later?"

"You're definitely forbidden from not coming back."

"So… see you later then?"

"Yeah. Just use that grandma car of yours for now. People will be looking for petrols, and, uh"—he looked across to Voice—"big-ass wagons with bullet holes an' shit."

"Good thinking! I can see why you're the boss. Catch ya'." Leon took off before Boss could retaliate to the sarcasm.

41

ANY TINTED GLASSES

LEON DROVE AHEAD IN HIS LITTLE box on wheels, keeping an eye out for police. He didn't know where exactly they were heading, as Voice was keeping that information strictly to himself, but the now closed-circuit navs that Boss had spent the day modifying were letting Voice ping forwards an occasional direction to Leon's screen. They were taking the most intricate route that Voice's mind could compute, and after a while, even Boss was worried that they'd gotten themselves lost. He half expected to see foreign faces in an uncharted land. A sharp screech and a loud smash quickly brought him back to reality, though, as he realised they must be near central city. The drivers there never ceased to amaze Boss as they tempted the fast-busses in their little eco-friendly cars. *No chance…*

Another ping on Leon's navs showed what looked like the main road into China-Ville. As expected, it was swarming with tourists, providing good cover from any potential pursuers. Leon pushed his way through. Progress was slow from there on, but he felt safe behind the thick wall of consumers.

Once Voice stopped updating the navs, Leon assumed that they had arrived and pulled into a side lane that even his tiny car struggled to fit into. He hopped out of the driver's seat and looked around, amazed at the colours and smells and accents echoing all over. Voice pulled up behind, all but blocking the walkway, and Boss fell out of the door, eye rolling. "Jesus, if I had known we were going for a city-wide tour, I would have thrown us a few comms together. I was bored half to death."

He slammed the door behind him. Voice backed up and disappeared down one of the many turns ahead. Leon watched, long after the dust settled. "Think he's coming back? Or we got to find this Dubbs dude ourselves?"

Boss shrugged. "Either way, I'm going for a stroll. Can't sit still any longer."

"I hear that."

They walked slowly, glancing down each turn as they searched for clues about where to go. "While we're here, you should get yourself a pirate eyeball or something. Anything. Just cover up that hole in your face."

"An eyeball from China-Ville? You kiddin'? Who knows who else could be watching through it. That's like paying for someone to spy on you."

"That's what the brand names want you to think so you buy theirs for an extremely inflated price. It's all the same gear."

"Eh, either way, I don't want just any old eyeball. Last one was custom design from Dubbs. If I get a new one, it will be from him."

"Can you at least get some sunglasses or something? It's gross, man."

"Sunglasses? What you think this is, the seventies?"

Leon pulled a face. Someone had once told him never to argue with stupid people, and he was beginning to see why.

"You realise that eye tints are only a year or so old, right? Sunglasses are still the most common—"

"Alright, kid, cool it. I'll get some damn sunnies."

"Thanks."

"But they're coming out of your pay."

Leon shook his head. The duo walked a little further down the lane, eyeball arguments left behind. After another turn, they heard a rumbling sound coming from an unknown source, and they stopped and looked around. It sounded like a distant earthquake. After a few disconcerting seconds, a hissing came from beneath Leon as a manhole cover lifted itself. Boss pulled Leon aside and stared at the cover, peering through the gap as it continued to open. The tunnel was completely dark, and neither Leon nor Boss saw anything except for a dirty little face peering back. This person was small but not young. The goggles perched on the end of a button nose were covered in grime. Two round eyes stared over the top. A piece of rag fastened over the head concealed long, matted hair, and it took Boss a moment to realise that this face belonged to a woman. He didn't know what to say, being so taken aback by this half mole who had just popped up from the floor. The mole broke the silence.

"You Boss?"

Boss nodded dumbly.

"Come down, quick-like."

Leon rolled back his sleeves, readying himself for the descent.

Boss looked at him sideways. "You don't seem as weirded out as I feel."

Leon shrugged. "Working for you, I've become immune. Just add this to the list of weird stuff I've seen these last few days."

Boss couldn't argue, so he followed Leon underground.

They walked quietly for a while, following the glow strips and the sound of mole-lady's footsteps through the shadows.

"Reminds me of being back at the zone," Leon said, though it was more of a thought out loud. He realised then just how much he missed it.

Boss scratched his head. "Oh yeah? The TV showed a bunch of tents and aid work shelters. I didn't picture it like this at all."

"I was surprised, too. The survivors are hiding in places like this. They said they are hunted. I wasn't convinced until the checkpoint guards pulled their guns on me and Voice."

"Strange."

The mole-lady quieted her footsteps to catch the end of the conversation.

Boss continued. "As much as I hate to suggest it, I wonder if the police could help them."

The mole-lady stopped altogether now. "The police are the ones doing the hunting. Or some other government section is, at least. I guarantee it."

"Why's that?" Leon asked.

"They are always covering something up or working on some new secret. When was the last time you saw them doing any good?"

Leon shrugged.

Something loud happened in front of the group, and after a few last moments of darkness, a beam of light flooded the hall, burning Leon's unadjusted eyes. Only after a half-minute of agony did Leon realise that the mole had placed the goggles over her eyes before the door opened. *Thanks for the warning,* he couldn't be bothered to say.

From the newfound light, a silhouette approached. It looked familiar. Much like Hughey from Zone C, his posture said more than enough about the position he held in this underground facility.

"Welcome. Good to see you again, Pizza Boss. Just a shame it's under these circumstances, know what I'm sayin'?" The man extended his hand to Boss, who took it firmly and grunted.

Leon rubbed at his eyes, hoping to speed up the adjustment process. "Tyrone?"

The man grinned and extended his hand once more. "Leon. Good to see you again, too, my man." He looked across to Boss, then back to Leon, acknowledging something that neither of the others saw. "You've come a long way since we last met."

"I've been busy right around the clock after taking this new job," Leon said.

Tyrone's grin widened. "I knew that Moppers Anonymous was the place for you. Didn't I tell ya, man? When was the last time you had a drink?"

Leon was taken aback. He eyed Tyrone suspiciously.

"Now let's bring this baby back to the ground with the soothing sound of a warm breeze on a cool night. That's right."

A thousand words crashed into Leon at once, and he spat out a gargled mix of nonsense as they all combined in his mouth. He took a breath and tried again, barely able to contain his excitement. "DJ T? Really?"

Tyrone stepped forwards, his arms wide. "Yeah, it's me, brother. I'm glad you found your way." He stepped forwards and gave Leon a strong hug. "Now let me show you how our radio station works down here." He turned back to the woman who had led them through the underground passage. "Could you grab that gate for us, Molly?"

Boss snorted at goggle-girl's name. He couldn't have thought of a more fitting one.

The walkway quickly widened, and Boss and Leon marvelled at the sight. The next room looked like how Boss imagined the inside of an alien spaceship might look, and for a moment he wondered if he were indeed inside one. The room was huge, at least five stories high, and resembled an auditorium. They were halfway up, on the same floor as the balcony walkway that circled the entire space. In the completely hollow centre was something resembling a satellite dish. Lights flickered all over it, different colours at different intervals, conveying messages to those who could understand them.

Tyrone watched their gleaming eyes. This was the part he loved the most. "So what do you think?"

"What is this?" Leon asked.

Boss backhanded Leon's chest. "Do you need to make us look so damn stupid?"

"Well, do you know what it is?"

"No," mumbled Boss.

Tyrone explained. "She's a beauty, huh? It's China-Ville's submersallite. Any information we don't want filtering through the big corporations' satellites gets pumped through here instead. Okay, I can give you the rundown later, but the man Dubbs is waitin' and I've got a show to put on, so let's keep scurryin' along."

42

DUBBS

A DOOR HISSED QUIETLY behind Leon and Boss as they stepped into the last room in the hall. It housed large terminals and pillars of cables with idle screens attached. A cough signalled Dubbs's presence. Boss stepped a bit further into the dimly lit room, Leon close behind. In the centre was a large object darkened against the stark brightness of the screen behind it. Another belt of coughing shook the object alive, and only now did Boss see that what he had mistaken for a computer terminal was in fact Dubbs.

"Jesus Christ, man." Boss gasped as he looked the figure over. It moved again, and Boss had to squint through the wash of screen glare to see that this figure was indeed human. It vigorously rubbed its eye lenses on an excess fold of shirt. Boss continued to stare, wondering if maybe his human eye was struggling to interpret what was actually in front of him. Surely this mass of skin and sweat wasn't the genius he had been working with all this time?

"Sorry, I can't…" Boss leaned his head forwards even more, making it obvious that he was struggling to see in the dark. "Is that you, Dubbs? I'm missing an eye."

"Ah, that explains why you didn't see my directions while you were wandering around up top."

The voice was familiar. This was Dubbs. Leon had kept quiet, and he couldn't honestly say if it were out of respect or fear. With introductions complete, Leon stepped out from behind boss and looked directly at Dubbs. He wasn't anything like Leon had imagined. What he had imagined was someone not too dissimilar to Hughey. The figure that towered over him was absolutely hideous, with a body more suited to a bug than a human. Leon couldn't help but stare into those deep, narrow pits above his cheeks—not even a faint glimmer of life in them. Dubbs spoke again, though Leon didn't hear him. He was too distracted by Dubbs's chins dancing beneath his face.

Thankfully, Boss was paying attention and gave an appropriate response on Leon's behalf. Leon wondered if Boss was struggling as much as him. For now, he found himself forced to look away to avoid staring. Some more words were exchanged, and Boss held up a fresh transmitter with a new encryption key. Dubbs stopped scrubbing his eye lenses for now and let them rest on his stomach. Boss threw him the transmitter. "That's as secure as you can get. Once my shop is no longer surrounded by cops, I will get the method and radio it across."

"That wasn't the deal," Dubbs snapped.

"It's a complicated method and I don't have it on me. I would have brought it, but the shop is still locked down. Give me a few days." With that, he turned to the door they'd entered through. "Let's go, kid." Then he lowered his voice. "Before this guy mistakes us for an entree."

Leon instantly broke out in sweat, afraid of what Dubbs might do if he heard that remark. He usually felt safe around Boss, but Dubbs seemed to reduce the badass Boss to nothing more than a mohawked mouse. When the door to Dubbs's office hissed closed behind them, Boss let out a chest full of air and relaxed. He patted Leon's back as he shook his head. "Can you believe that?" He turned to Leon, who was still completely dumbfounded. Boss laughed. "You look more terrified than me, and you weren't even the one talking to him!"

"But I had to watch him respond."

Boss burst into laughter. "I feel bad for you, kid. One eye was enough for me, let me tell ya."

Leon continued to follow Boss as he led them to the safe-room Dubbs had specified. Ahead was a smaller door, and an assistant was waiting nearby to open it as they approached.

"I tried not to laugh when I asked Dubbs how he got out of that search area. He starts going on about ambulances and emergency rooms, and I'm just thinking, 'No, how did you get down the bloody stairs!'" Boss roared with laughter, clapping his hands and walking in zigzags, a lone tear venturing down his cheek. Leon laughed as well, then suggested that Dubbs might well have used an elevator. Boss lost his laughter then and stared at Leon.

"Moment's gone, kid. You ruined it. Congratulations." Boss had nothing more to add as they quietly entered the room.

43

THE THROAT

T HE SCREEN PULSED, and a siren blared to life overhead.

"Already?" he huffed to his assistant, who stood a safe distance from Dubbs.

"I think it's those other two, sir. They seemed... off."

"I had Voice bring them here. No one could have followed."

"Maybe they tipped someone off on the way somehow?"

Dubbs thought about this for a half second and wasn't convinced. "That doesn't add up. Voice would have noticed something and led them astray, if so." His face seemed to change completely as he focused on the facts around him. If he didn't have such a distinguishable look, his assistant might have thought that for a moment he was looking at a different person. "We are missing something."

"Either way, sir, the people are preparing to resist. It won't be long now, and I would like for you to be out of here before it starts."

"I don't like the idea of moving again so soon. Plus, we chose this place for its defensive capabilities, did we not?"

"That's true, sir, but these are larger numbers than China-Ville has ever faced before. Better safe than sorry."

Dubbs fastened his eye lenses back over the black pits in his face and surprise struck him instantly. The lenses reactivated and revealed a beam directed straight upwards and coming from the assistant's room.

"Wait!" he roared. The assistant stopped dead, too frightened to even turn around. Dubbs's face burned red. "Did you bring the blood vial? Imbecile! You may have just infected us all, not to mention allowed our position to be broadcasted!"

The assistant did spin around, now, and spoke quickly, fumbling through the words and barely making sense. "No! The box, uh, blood... I wrapped and left... in the vault. I didn't..."

"The signal is too strong to be handled so carelessly. It's emitting again. You've led them straight to us!"

The assistant's legs shook so much that he fell backwards, his words a complete jumble now. Dubbs kicked off of the desk beside him, propelling himself towards the terrified man. The wheels of his chair caught on the tassels of a rug, jolting the chair back as Dubbs continued forwards. A horrific scream echoed through the room and beyond as Dubbs landed on the assistant, who popped under the pressure, spraying blood up the wall.

Dubbs looked up to see the red beam now on the move, and he shouted at the traitors beyond the walls of his office. He grew dizzy and strained, but still he belted his insults towards the beam-carrier over the still screaming sirens. In his fury, he hadn't realised that the beam was heading for the door to his office. The door hissed open and Boss came running in, worry on his face. Dubbs was lying on the ground, opposite the door, a layer of clothes and bloody pulp beneath him and splayed in all directions.

"What the hell happened?" Boss dropped to his side to try and help him up, but Dubbs yelled and thrust him away.

"Get away from me!"

Boss couldn't help but look away, confused and a little disgusted. He glanced around the office but nothing explained what was going on.

"What happened?" he asked again, taking a step back.

"You're infected?" Dubbs gasped. "Do you realise what you've done? You've led them right to my doorstep!"

"Infected? What the hell are you talking about? Let me help you up."

The sirens were now blasting through the entire underground's PA system, indicating that the threat had moved from potential to imminent. Leon shot into the room and, shocked by the sight of it, skidded to a halt through the streak of blood. He opened his mouth but didn't know what to say. He watched Boss struggle with one of Dubbs's arms while they mumbled something to each other, which Leon couldn't hear over the sirens. Boss's face went through a strange string of changes. Whatever they were discussing, Boss found it hard to deal with. There was another moment when they were both in thought, and then they were firing short sentences back and forth. They were devising something, and Boss didn't seem overly happy about whatever it was. Leon heard Boss mention Marbles, and a stray thought flashed to the last time Leon had seen his delivery partner. *Where had he gotten to?*

Feeling like he'd finally regained motor control, Leon was torn between helping Boss lift Dubbs or just fleeing China-Ville altogether. He leaned towards the second choice but hesitated. It just felt wrong to leave a morbidly obese man in a pool of blood while he ran for his life. Thankfully, he didn't have to decide as a small squadron put in charge of protecting Dubbs entered the room.

"We need to leave, now!" the front man screamed over the siren as all but one member of the team began pulling Dubbs back into his chair. They all seemed oblivious to the chunky mess beneath him. The remaining man pulled Boss away and pushed him and Leon towards the door. "We've got Dubbs. You get yourselves out of here."

Boss nodded and ran, trying to catch up to Leon, who was already powering ahead. Various soldiers were beckoning and directing them through the underground walkways—some of whom Leon was sure he'd seen before.

Leon rounded a sharp bend and saw a small huddle of people watching one of the monitors on the wall. It was a live news broadcast. A woman was explaining how a "most wanted" terrorist had been spotted. A crude montage of China-Ville splayed across the screen, interjected with snippets of footage of people running and screaming. An army of police surrounded the disguised fortress. The queues to leave China-Ville had grown by the thousands in a matter of minutes as every resident, tourist, unfortunate passer-by, or disguised criminal tried to flee the area. All sorts of underground kingpins were cutting their losses and sneaking out among the chaos, none of them knowing if this "most wanted" person was in fact them.

Each faction in China-Ville had decided to temporarily blow the dust off of their truce and combined their militias to lock the Ville down. All arms aimed outwards at the invading police force.

Even as Leon watched the screen, the people around him were suiting up and gathering their gadgets. Molly the Mole was tapping away at a custom-built machine, activating a Ville-wide scrambler on as many electrical devices as she could. The Ville's inhabitants were used to living in the dark, but the authorities relied heavily on their technological advantages, so the more she could shut down, the better.

The television crackled and skipped, and Boss caught up with Leon just in time to catch a glimpse of the outside world before the screen went blank. They both just stood there and stared at the black, empty rectangle on the wall. The lights flickered and went out, replaced by glow strips and the very infrequent glow orbs, a few hours of dim light stored in their warmed shells.

Boss huffed. "This shit just got real, kid."

Leon struggled with his increasing heart rate. He stared across Boss stood in the dark and saw a flash of a grin as the light reflected from his teeth.

"Just like the good ol' days." He reminisced and jogged to the exit, where someone passed him some information. He gestured to Leon, and they climbed out of the darkness and up to street level.

"Stay close and keep your head down. Talk to no one. Let's go." As Boss spoke, another team of armed locals jogged past and took up position at the start of a few of the busier alleyways.

"Should we have a weapon or something?"

Boss shook his head. "We've got more chance without one, unless you're prepared to go to war with the entire goddamned city. It won't be long before the army shows up. You feel like taking them on?"

Leon shook his head, the answer obvious, and continued down the lane. "It's important to make sure we keep heading in the same direction. This place is designed to disorientate. Don't let it get you, and if you think I'm going the wrong way, then tell me."

Leon had hoped he wouldn't need to worry about navigating while with Boss. He hadn't considered that Boss knew just as little about the layout. "My internal compass isn't so good, Boss."

Boss frowned and shook his head. "A delivery driver with a bad sense of direction? Once this is over, remind me to reconsider your place in the business."

They passed another team, who took a quick glance at Boss before pointing to another alley and continuing on. Boss nodded and altered course slightly, checking that Leon was still with him.

"Shouldn't be too bad if people are giving us directions."

"Not everyone cares if we make it out of here or not, kid."

They kept their pace and took a few more turns. Leon had a question burning in his mouth, and despite being almost out of breath, he had to ask. "What is this really about?"

Boss's face tightened and he kept running.

Leon pushed the subject. "Who's going to all of this effort for a drug-dealing ring?"

Boss skidded to a halt and faced Leon square-on. "It's not about the high, kid. That's just to get people coming back." He looked around the empty laneway, dragged Leon to the side, and lowered his voice. "I told you before that you were part of something bigger now. Dubbs is just using my channels. He needs something distributed, and I'm a distributor of sorts. He must have guys like me all over the country."

"He distributes medicines for that zone parasite, though, right? So why hunt him?"

"I'm sketchy with the details, kid. He paid well and so I didn't ask questions. Apparently he's ex-CCD, and I get the impression that he knows a lot more about this Bug than he should. I don't understand the link there, but I think that all of this is to stop him from mass-producing a vaccine."

"CCD? As in the Crowd Control Division? That what he was telling you just before?"

Boss's eye twitched as he recalled his rushed conversation with Dubbs. He was still struggling to come to terms with whatever had been said. "Yeah, that was part of it."

Footsteps echoed down the lane. Boss didn't like the sound of it, though he was glad to have something end the conversation. Some more militia jogged nearby. "They didn't sound like our guys. Keep your ears open, kid. Let's move."

They progressed further still, keeping their eyes peeled for anything that might let them know where they might be. The next few minutes dragged on as they continued unhindered through another lane. They heard noises above as a few windows were slammed shut and people rummaged around indoors, boarding up possible entrances and the like. Generally, peeping eyes and the whiffs of passers-by made China-Ville feel alive. Now, though, despite the grimy and obviously worn clothes suspended all across the slit of sky above, Leon was hard-pressed to imagine this place as anything but long abandoned. Even the rats, usually in abundance, could sense a change in atmosphere and were refusing to leave the warmth of their nests.

More footfalls trudged towards Boss and Leon, but due to the reverberations off of the angled walls, they couldn't pinpoint the direction.

"Shit. Here we go."

The approaching rumble led Boss to estimate around ten people in the group and was quite surprised to see only three men turn the corner beside him. The guy in the middle stopped dead, where the other two completed a triangle, surrounding Boss and Leon. In unison, all three raised their firearms. "Name and business."

Boss took half a step forwards. "We are with Dubbs; we're trying to leave the Ville."

"No one is leaving. We're locked in."

Boss glanced at the badge on the man's arm. These guys weren't playing. Ex-military. Only one man could afford such a team, and he and Dubbs didn't have the best working relationship.

"We know of an alternate exit, and I believe you do, too."

The man said nothing.

"In fact, you've got your guy heading there now."

"That's enough." The man raised his weapon to his eye, setting his crosshairs on Boss's face.

"That'd really piss Dubbs off, you know."

"If you're with Dubbs, then where is he?"

"You know I can't tell you."

"Then we've found ourselves in a bit of a situation."

It took a little over an hour for the third man of the patrol to run back to his hideout and ask to be advised on the Boss-and-Leon situation. Boss was doing his best not to complain. The reason that the third man ran back to the hideout instead of just making a quick call was that Boss's "team" had scrambled the electrical devices earlier, but being patient wasn't exactly one of his preferred pastimes. Forgetting that he was being detained by men under siege, whose trigger fingers grew itchy around sudden movements, Boss, unable to contain his relief, jumped to his feet at the sight of the returning soldier. He was lucky to have only caught a rifle butt to the back of his neck for the effort. He tumbled to the floor.

The returning soldier spoke. "I have requested a member of a neutral party come to identify you."

Behind him came another man, machine gun in hand, though no uniform like the others. This man looked at the crumpled body and nodded. "It seems to check out, gentlemen. Dubbs is actually with your guy as we speak, and he's looking to leave ASAP. I can confirm that this angry bastard is the one they call Boss."

He slid over and helped Leon pull Boss to his feet, who swayed as he rose.

"Well, look who we have here." The machine gun man flashed his golden tooth at Leon and waited to be recognised.

Leon remembered the smirk, and it inspired as much hatred this time as it did the first time he saw it. "King Neptune?"

"That's right, baby. The one and only."

Leon looked down at his gun. "You've upgraded your equipment."

"Don't get me wrong, I love my mop, but I gotta make a mess first, right?" The gold tooth again. "Though I don't think I'm gonna be able to clean up the mess today will bring." He looked away and seemed genuinely upset that the bloodshed of today might go beyond his cleaning capabilities.

King Neptune turned back to the trio of soldiers. "Better not keep the VIPs waiting. Need anything else, sir?"

The leader of the soldiers shook his head and saluted. King Neptune saluted in return and jogged off the way he'd come.

Boss still leaned on the wall of the alley, unable to fully support his own weight. His eye rolled aimlessly, but he managed to hold on to his consciousness. Leon felt bad for him. If the stubborn asshole had just passed out, they would have carried him through, but like this, he was going to have to stumble the whole way.

Leon grabbed one of Boss's arms and slung it over his shoulder, his back straining against the weight of the giant. The third guy of the soldier trio very unhelpfully prodded

Boss at intervals, making him squirm almost right out of Leon's grip each time.

After a few more laneways, the leader stopped at a gate, and Leon noticed the shotgun barrel poking through, wide enough to take out the five of them in one pull of the trigger. The leader displayed a small note and flashed his shoulder patch through the peephole. After a moment's consideration, the barrel disappeared and the bolts of the gate unlatched. Before stepping through, though, the leader retrieved a large folded flag from his khaki trouser pocket and tore it into strips. He handed one to the prodder with a stern look on his face. The soldier retrieved it with a nod. The other soldier looked as nervous as a poppy on Remembrance Day, and the leader gave his shoulder a quick squeeze before handing him a strip of flag.

"Remember what we spoke about."

The soldier nodded unconvincingly. The leader gave the spare two strips to Leon.

"They're a nervous bunch in here. Best you keep your eyes down… if not completely covered. Keep one arm out in front of you and stay close. You get lost in here, you're on your own."

Leon felt a panic rising inside of him as the three soldiers began tightening their strips of the cloth across their eyes. He fumbled with his pieces, trying to tie one around Boss's head as it lolled left and right. Boss groaned in pain and fidgeted as Leon covered his eyes. In the jostle, Leon felt something squash in Boss's side pocket. He rummaged through to find a doggy bag with one rather deformed slice of pizza. It looked like it had been there a while. Hoping it might help Boss with the pain in his head, he fed him a few small bites. Hoping it might help with his own nerves, Leon took a bite for himself.

44

THE HEART

LEON WALKED ON IN THE DARKNESS, staring at the feet of the soldier in front of him, all sense of time lost. Through his blindfold, he glimpsed nothing but blotches and imagined his surroundings based on the sounds he heard. The further they walked, the darker it felt and the more nightmarish the sounds became. A risked glance at Boss's face indicated that he was still out of it, his head rocking loosely from side to side, but Leon could sense that he was growing more agitated. Leon wondered if the strange sounds were also affecting the thoughts of his only half-conscious mind.

Another turn and it grew darker still. Closer, more immediate sounds replaced the indecipherable background sounds. Machinery. Engines. People grunting and huffing. The group was obviously moving towards the sounds, as they were becoming louder and more frequent. A hysterical laugh burst out from behind Leon, who jumped, dropping Boss face-first onto the ground. The guard behind peeked out from under his blindfold and scrambled over to help pull Boss to his feet. He slung his arm over his shoulders and dragged Boss, almost single-handedly, back in line with the rest of the group. Knowing that even his armed escort was afraid of falling behind frightened Leon more than the laugh.

The voices were all around, now. People running back and forth or in circles, Leon couldn't be too sure, though he knew they were definitely surrounded. Whispers and screeches were echoing past. Leon heard a few words among the noise.

"Leave."

"You don't belong here."

"Get out."

Leon's blindfold was growing hot, and Boss was fidgeting and mumbling even more. The soldier tightened his grip on Boss, and Leon did the same. Something pushed at his chest. Then his side. The people were upon them now, tugging at their clothes and growling in their ears. The soldier couldn't keep it together anymore, and he began running, still dragging Boss along with him. Leon, caught unawares, was dragged to the side and stumbled as his legs crossed beneath him. He landed and slid across the ground, grazing himself on the cobblestone. Without thinking, he jumped almost instantly back to his feet and began running, arms outstretched completely. The odd shadow moved across his blindfold, but as he approached the silhouettes, they seemed to vanish before him. Boss and the other soldiers remained out of his reach. Leon turned and ran again, wondering if maybe he had strayed off course. He was stopped abruptly by a collision with a solid wall.

"Hello?" he yelled, straining his ears for any response over the whispers that still encircled him. He flailed around, trying to keep the voices back as he tried again to yell out to the squad. The fabric across his eyes was blocking out even the faintest hints of movement now. Despite the warnings, he saw no other option than to remove the blindfold and hope there was still enough light that he could see his way out of there. With shaking fingers, he pulled at the fabric, tightening the knot at the back of his head. He struggled for a moment, clawing away at any part of the blindfold, hoping to loosen it from his face. The growling approached quickly now, growing louder with his increasing heartbeat. He let out a whimper and pulled down hard on the fabric. It slid over the ridge of his nose and covered his mouth. It was uncomfortable, but at least his eyes were free. He blinked hard and strained them in the darkness, but it was almost as if the fabric was still blinding him.

The only thing Leon could see was a streak of moonlight ahead, which pushed its way through an uneven stack of buildings and peeked around the clothes strewn across lines above him. The growling dimmed to a faint rumble, leaving Leon with the horrifying sound of his own heart in his ears. He backed up to the wall behind him and shrunk into a ball as he did so. Something was approaching from the moonlight, and he didn't want to know what. He didn't really want to see what, either, but the only thing more terrifying was seeing nothing at all, so he stared forwards at the figure. He took his time to pull the blindfold further down so that it hung loosely around his neck, and he strained his ears for any clues as to what was coming.

Once again, the darkness shrouded him, and he could no longer tell if his eyes were open or closed. He heard the scuffing of footsteps over his beating heart, which sped up again as panic nestled in. The figure took a breath, and Leon clenched his fists, ready to fight blindly against whoever approached.

"Kid?" The voice was raspy but undoubtedly Boss's.

"Put the blindfold back on."

Leon did as Boss asked, pulling it back up over his nose. To his surprise, he could now see the faint outline of Boss. The voices no longer surrounded him, and Leon heard them fade as whoever was responsible fled in all directions.

"What's out here?"

Boss might have shrugged as he grabbed Leon's wrist and pulled him to his feet.

"Did you hear them?"

"No one's there, kid. All in your head. Let's go." He leaned on Leon heavily, still not fully able to support himself.

"You mean you didn't hear those people screeching?"

"All I've heard, up until now, were my own dark thoughts talking to each other. Making plans. The Ville heart messes with your head. You just need to keep moving." He iterated his point with a tug forwards, and Leon increased his pace. The voices and footsteps left each time he or Boss spoke, but they slowly began to return once silence fell between them. Boss could feel the agitation of Leon, who kept saying random words to keep the other voices at bay. He removed his blindfold and tied the second one over Leon's face.

"It may be better that you don't see whatever it is that you're hearing. I can direct us from here."

Boss kept up his pace, seemingly unhindered by anything he was seeing, but Leon could feel the tension as Boss struggled internally with his own thoughts. He had also been mumbling the odd thing to himself, though Leon couldn't make out any specific words. It was probably a good thing that, through the two blindfolds, Leon couldn't see just how terrified Boss really was.

Another minute was all Boss managed before he began to crack under the pressure. With one hand gripped tightly to Leon's sleeve, Boss used his other to cover his ears as best as he could, trying to figure out a way to wrap his one free arm around his head. He settled for pressing one ear into his shoulder while he cupped the other. It meant that he wasn't looking directly ahead as he shuffled along, but it would have to do. The voices in his head were back now, louder than before, but they seemed to be coming from outside of him. It was as if he were listening to a recording of himself from the next room over. He pressed harder against his ears and continued trying to ignore the mimic of his voice as he still dragged Leon onwards. Something else reverberating through the Ville heart stopped him in his tracks—a second voice which answered Boss's mimic. It was Marbles's.

Boss loosened the seal around his ear now, curious about how Marbles had made it to the Ville's heart. As he did so, an image formed from the shadows ahead of him. It was Marbles, bruised and bleeding, asking for help. Boss watched as Marbles stumbled forwards. He opened his mouth to call out to him—tell him to stay close and keep his eyes covered—but the mimic voice spoke instead.

"Stay away, kid. You let me down, and now you can pay the price. This is all that you deserve."

Marbles looked straight up at Boss. Boss reached out, his mouth open again, but as before, the mimic masked his words. Another string of insults flowed at Marbles, who looked down, defeated, and began shuffling back to the shadows. Boss was able to call out now, though his words went unheard. He yelled for Marbles to come back, that he was sorry, that he didn't say the things Marbles had heard, but Marbles just continued to slump away until he vanished. Boss growled in frustration and pulled Leon onwards, trying to increase his pace and catch up to Marbles so he could explain himself. He was still calling out and felt a flood of relief as the figure formed again.

"Marbles, wait up! I can get you out of here!"

"Boss?" It wasn't Marbles's voice. The figure continued to form, and this time, Cookie stepped forwards.

"Chef!" Boss couldn't contain his excitement at seeing an old friend. "You are worthless! Always holding me back while I built the business from the ground up. You should have been put in here a long, long time ago!" Boss's smile dropped suddenly as he heard the mimic's words once again drown out his own. Cookie looked up at Boss with surprise, which quickly turned to hurt. Boss could see the life drain from his face. His eyes sunk deeper, and his shoulders deflated. Cookie looked old now. An old, bitter man who had lost his best friend many years ago. Boss tried to apologise—tried to explain that he hadn't said those words, but the more he spoke, the more the mimic threw insults at Cookie, continuing to put him down until he faded into the dark, just as Marbles did.

Boss roared and continued onwards, feeling just as defeated as Cookie had looked. Ahead of him, walls came into focus. He hoped they were nearing the end of this nightmare. He reached out a hand and touched the alley's wall, then retracted it quickly as it made contact. All at once, horrifying memories flooded back. The alley, despite its appearance, felt more than just familiar. The walls were padded. As he stared at the bricks, they began to shimmer, and the alley before him turned into the cell he had been running from for the past year. The pathway before him was suddenly blocked by a row of federal agents. The middle one he recognised from the van earlier. He turned slightly, ready to run, and saw that behind him the darkness had taken on the shape of the pizza shop. He watched as everything he loved rebuilt itself from the shadows. He wanted nothing more than to step back from the padded cell and go back to his comfortable, lucrative life.

He tried to put rational thought before reflex, though his muscles, clearly not receiving the memo, continued to twitch. His left leg acted without consent and stepped towards the pizza shop, kicking Leon in the shin as it did so. Boss looked down at the disorientated kid before him, double-blindfolded and wholly trusting Boss to get him out of there. He turned towards the padded room once more and watched the feds, who still waited for him patiently. Boss took a deep breath and forced himself towards them. *It's all in your head, It's all in your head…*

The mimic's voice cried out in protest. It was going on about self-preservation and not belonging in jail and several other desperate comments that made Boss realise he was walking back towards the place he hated most. He covered his ears again and kept moving. The feds were close now. A couple more steps and he would be within arm's reach. The pizza shop called behind him, and he glanced once more at the place that had made him rich. His gut wrenched as he realised the mistake he'd made. He stumbled backwards, trying to turn and head back towards his precious shop. The fed dived in and gripped at his shoulder. Boss closed his eyes tight.

The haunting and familiar voice of the fed spoke. "We've got you."

45

THE FOOL

A SPOTLIGHT BURNED ABOVE Marbles, who was chained to a chair in a small metallic room.

"Okay, do you want to tell us why you're here?" asked a uniformed man.

"I don't know."

"Better you come clean than us find out for ourselves. And we *will* find out."

The uniformed man crossed his arms and stepped forwards. The inspector's badge on his chest had been recently polished. He meant business. Marbles's breathing quickened. "I don't do well in confined spaces." His hands were shaking, as he hadn't been able to replace the pizza from earlier and was still hanging out for a fix.

"All the more reason to tell us what we want to know. Sooner you talk, sooner you can leave this room."

"What do you want to know?" Marbles managed to reply, hands subconsciously rubbing the back of his neck.

"What's the matter? Still feeling the sting of a barcode?"

Without any further response from Marbles, the inspector stepped over and studied the patch he had been scratching at. The skin was red and raw. "That looks infected. Have you been trying to remove barcodes yourself?"

When no response came, he changed tactics and opened a file on the table in front of Marbles. A photo of a police sergeant sprawled on the ground, hole in his chest, eyes gazing at nothing, slid from between the covers. Marbles grimaced and looked away. He instinctively tried to push the photo out of sight, despite the tenta-binds restricting his movement. It wasn't quite the reaction the inspector was hoping for, so he discarded the questions he had ready and decided on a less aggressive angle.

"Do you know this man?"

Marbles swallowed hard and shook his head.

"Do you know why he's dead?"

Again, a shake of the head.

"What if I told you that I don't believe you? That I think you know exactly how he died?"

"Well I don't," Marbles choked.

The inspector pretended to consider this as he walked back to the file and flipped the page. Another image. Once again, Marbles didn't react in the way he'd hoped. This picture was from the first-person perspective: two arms holding a large, homemade firearm, nozzle aimed at the centre of the police sergeant's back.

"What if I told you his name was Sergeant Ford, that he was in charge of the organised crime defence unit at the federal PD, that he was investigating the delivery methods of certain narcotics, that those are your arms holding an illegal weaponized concoction, and that these images were ripped from the very barcode that still irritates your neck—the barcode that you somehow got away with handing in before you fled whilst trying to illegally self-remove it? Were you hired to stop Sergeant Ford? Was he close to a discovery?" His voice was growing in volume as he spoke, and once he started, he stopped for nothing until he ran out of breath. Marbles's denials were also growing in volume but remained drowned out by the inspector. By the end, Marbles was yelling nothing more than "no, no, no!" as he shook his head and held his eyes tightly closed.

Keeping his gaze fixed on Marbles, the inspector walked over to a pigeon hole in the room and removed a small screen on which a video had been pre-loaded from the scanner-craft above the station.

A bind from Marbles's shoulders readjusted its grip at the control of the interrogator, angling Marbles towards the screen and holding him tightly in position. Marbles could do nothing but stare unwillingly at the screen, and once the inspector was satisfied that he would not look away, he commanded the video to play. It was a memory on screen—one that Marbles had no recollection of. He was still mumbling to himself out of disbelief as the character, in a very *Marbles* fashion, scaled the wall of a suburban home, broke his way into the skylight, and fiddled with a security alarm before the Gatling gun had reared itself enough to fire at the intruder.

"I don't know how to do that..."

But the inspector wasn't listening to Marbles anymore as he stared, disgusted, at the screen. The arms of the intruder disappeared as they fetched something from out of sight. Then they reappeared, holding a weapon. Marbles watched as one of his fingers flicked the setting to "full power" and the light on the side pulsed.

The intruder systematically searched each room and disposed on the sergeant's wife and two children, then stuffed valuables from each room into a backpack. The perpetrator continued into the hall, where Sergeant Ford stood and fumbled with a switchboard, trying to reactivate the alarms. The video was littered with choppy audio of bangs and screams, and despite the horror that Marbles currently felt, he couldn't help but analyse the different effect that the adrenaline was having on him in this memory capture compared to his previous one. Apart from the audio being a bit out of sync, the picture itself remained quite clear. How was it possible that murdering an entire family generated less adrenaline than the street chase from the warehouse?

Sergeant Ford tackled the intruder with all of his strength. The video ended in a long shot of a carpet as the intruder was held in place and Sergeant Ford burned a barcode into his neck. The whole memory capture was quite clear and precise, with barely anything that Marbles could recognise as a blip or adrenal blur.

Only once the screen was blank did the inspector look back at Marbles, and he instantly spotted the expression so obviously plastered across his face. "Yes? Brought back a memory, has it? So to speak."

Marbles was frowning. "No. Could I watch it back in slow, please?"

"You're sick! Is doing it not enough? You want to make me sit through it again? I will not give you the pleasure."

"I'm looking for a blip."

This caught the inspector off guard. He narrowed his eyes till Marbles could see nothing but black slits. He leaned in close, trying to get a read on Marbles's face. His breath was unpleasant, Marbles noticed, like a forgotten cup of coffee left to go cold, then microwaved, then forgotten again. He cringed, which pushed the inspector to lean closer still.

"How do you know about blips?"

Marbles held his lips tightly together, but his mind was saying a hundred things at once. He powered through his usual techniques for talking his way out of situations, but nothing believable came to mind. The longer he waited, the less believable anything he had to say would sound anyway. With the inspector's hard face so uncomfortably close, his eyes piercing to the back of Marbles's skull, Marbles wasn't even able to think of a simple "dog ate my homework" excuse.

The inspector asked again, and Marbles was once again close to losing control of himself. He could feel the shakes increasing. He didn't want to speak. He just wanted to curl up and wait for it to be over. He didn't care if it would get him in trouble. Could he even be in any more trouble?

He closed his eyes tight, his lips tighter still. He tried to shake his head and felt the tentacle constrict further. The inspector asked Marbles one more time. Tears welled in his eyes as his heart thundered and his breathing neared panic-attack speeds. He could no longer think. For the second time tonight, he had been forced out of options.

Marbles talked. He confessed about the warehouse incident and his trip to the code-crackers hideout—and would be glad that he did.

46

THE BOWELS

BOSS WAS PULLED ASIDE and fell to the ground, slamming hard against the floor. Leon landed somewhere nearby.

"Where is he?" The voice sounded worried. Boss caught a boot to the ribs. "Dammit, where is he?"

The leader stepped in, putting a hand between Boss and the aggravated soldier. "If there was hope, it's gone now. He must have given in to the heart."

The soldier stepped back, shaking. The leader stepped over to the door and swung it closed, leaving the third soldier lost in the heart. He had obviously just been through as hard of a time as everyone else, and it was showing on his face.

Boss rolled over, rubbing at his side, and propped himself against the alley wall. Leon, still terrified by the voices and shadows, only moved once he heard Boss talk.

"Couldn't have walked around, eh?"

The leader shook his head, almost apologetically. "Only a few know of this exit, and this is the only way to it."

Now that natural light was once again fighting through the strung garments above, Leon ripped the blindfolds from Boss's face. Boss climbed to his feet. "You okay, kid?"

Leon nodded and crouched next to Boss. "I guess so."

The leader consoled his one remaining team member before heading off with a beckoning wave of the arm. The journey continued in silence as the odd group wandered obliviously, each coming to terms with whatever the Ville heart had revealed to them.

Ahead, another ex-military man stood watch and saluted as the group approached. Boss recognised him from earlier. He was the one who had told them to go ahead while he helped Dubbs back into his chair, though now he looked very different. His face was grim, and Boss instantly felt sorry for the guy and didn't want to imagine what was on his mind. He too would have passed through the Ville heart ahead of them, and what he saw was obviously still haunting him, too.

The leader gestured to the one-eyed mohawk man. "This is Boss."

"We've met." He nodded at Boss.

"And you remember Leon?" Boss asked.

"Yes. This way. Dubbs is waiting."

The two remaining soldiers looked at each other before one of them spoke up. "Uh… should we come with you, too? Dubbs might need the extra firepower, or maybe we could scout ahead, or…"

The grim guard understood. No one wanted to go back through the Ville heart, which meant that the only other way out was forwards, through the secret exit. He nodded. "Dubbs would appreciate the gesture. Please, this way…"

The soldiers were glad that they weren't forced to beg.

A cave entrance opened up ahead, looking out of place in the city, let alone in the twisting walkways on this side of China-Ville. Around the last bend, by a large crack in the earth, stood a thick, steel-plated box. The box was mounted on tracks much like a tank's, and those tracks were mounted on arms. After examining the box, Boss concluded that the arms could fully rotate so it could continue to drive even if something toppled it. The grim guard spoke. "Something Dubbs threw together in case of emergency. He's pretty much invincible in there, unless they call in a multitude of airstrikes. Not impossible, but also not overly likely."

Boss wasn't so sure. "With all they've been through so far, I wouldn't be surprised if they nuked the whole damn city." He walked over and rapped on the side of the Dubbs carrier, which failed to let off the metallic clangs Boss had anticipated. "Cosy in there?"

The guard stepped forwards. "He can't communicate with the outside. He is completely concealed until we arrive at a safe location."

Boss smiled at this and gave a knowing nod. The guard had confirmed whatever Boss was thinking. "Better get moving then, aye?"

The guard nodded and signalled to the rocks around him. The rest of the militia emerged. A small team encircled Boss and Leon, and another took its place beside Dubbs. The group ahead, who were escorting their "guy," signalled their acknowledgement before continuing on. Leon gave Boss the eyebrows. "I feel like a VIP."

Boss snorted. "The last time I had this much protection, I was being escorted to jail."

47

AMBUSH

THE HALOGENS APPEARED to dim as a new source of light fought its way through the tunnel ahead. A scout jogged back and announced that they were indeed nearing the end of the escape route.

"Jesus, it's about time," mumbled Boss.

Leon turned, chiding remark at the ready, but thought better of it when he saw the look on Boss's face. Something was bothering him—that much was certain—and Leon didn't want to make himself an easy target in case Boss blew up in his traditional style.

They continued on, cave slowly revealing its surface colours through the shadows. They could see the exit ahead, though it was still deceptively far away. The party quietly celebrated and put away their flashlights to mark the milestone.

"Not long now," one of the soldiers felt the need to say to no one in particular. The odd hum or grunt came in response. After walking for what felt like the better part of a day, none of the men were in the mood for talking.

Boss's words pulled Leon from his daydream, catching him off guard, as he had barely spoken for the entire walk.

"What?" Leon asked.

"I said, once we're out of here, I want you to go with Dubbs. He's going to need your help."

Leon looked at the Dubbs-mobile, then back to Boss. "Seems like he's the only one who *doesn't* need any help, actually."

Almost as an afterthought, Boss looked at the vehicle and grunted. "That's not quite what I meant. He's going to need help setting up shop again, and it's important that he's back doing what he does as quickly as possible."

Leon let out a single "hah" and shook his head, smiling. "Already thinking about lost profits, eh?"

"This isn't about that!" Boss snapped, then looked away, taking a deep breath. "I don't expect you to understand, kid, but I trust you, and I need you to help him."

Leon nodded, confused. "And what will you be doing?"

"Doin' my thing." Boss added a wink, trying to make it light-hearted, but Leon wasn't buying it. His smile was too sad, almost too genuine, compared to the usual cheeky grin that Leon was so used to seeing splayed across Boss's face—when he wasn't smashing things.

Leon thought about the Ville heart and what he had seen and what he had felt. It had obviously affected Boss in a way that he was struggling to deal with. He would make sure to ask him about it as soon as they were away from the judgemental ears of the ex-soldiers. Leon knew that, even with Boss's unexpected soft side that sometimes briefly showed itself, he wouldn't want it revealed right here in front of so many manly men. Any kindness, if one could go as far as to call it that, was only ever in small doses and for a select few people. Even then, Boss seemed to regret it, trying to balance it out with displays of wild rage in the hopes that someone wouldn't find him too soft. Leon nodded to himself, agreeing with his own insight. He would wait until they were out of this tunnel. For now, he just said whatever Boss wanted to hear him say and kept placing one foot in front of the other.

The scouting squad returned from their outing and spoke casually with the leader of the other group about their surroundings. They had found roadblocks and a few other unexpected hindrances around the area, but not a single person or officer. From the way that they spoke, Leon gathered that the scouts didn't feel any need for worry, which was reassuring, but that wasn't the information that he was straining to overhear. He knew the tunnel had been long, but from what descriptions the scouts were giving, they had made their way to an almost forgotten part of the map. It didn't at all sound like what he was expecting, because he was not used to seeing empty streets in amongst such a heavily populated city. The leader gave the all clear to the rest of the group.

After passing one last rocky bend, the leader took a few steps forwards so he was directly below a rectangle of light. Then he typed a passcode into a hidden keypad. A portion of the wall hissed smoothly aside, revealing a normal-sized metal door. He swung it open and another burst of sunlight pushed through.

"Oh."

"Yeah, that's more like it."

"Sweet!"

The leader smirked and led the way out of the tunnel. They formed a semicircle around the door once outside, then set up a small secured perimeter while they waited for Dubbs to make his way through. There were fewer ex-soldiers now, partly because the other kingpin's team had exited the tunnel an hour earlier and partly because some of the militia had left Dubbs for their own employer. Despite Dubbs's status, they were only loyal to whoever signed their cheques. The remaining men sat with their backs to parked vehicles or bollards or posts. From this side, the exit of the tunnel was as completely disguised as any of the other warehouses or buildings around here, which made the situation look even more ridiculous as the Dubbs-roller tediously tried, straightened up, and tried again to squeeze through the doorframe.

"You're at least twice as wide as the gap," growled an irritated Boss. He was only prepared to endure a few seconds of this torture, and already his infamously short temper was being tested. Against his orders to wait for Dubbs and secure the area, he set to work on widening the doorway slightly with his forehead. Nothing much remained of the frame now, but Boss continued to vent his frustration on the general area, completely unaware that the soldiers had set to work on a different exit. Only when one of the squad members chuckled did Boss turn and see everyone watching him. Not sure who to take his anger out on first, he turned left to right, flexing his face muscles.

"Didn't want to help open the roller door then, Boss?" the bravest yelled.

There was another wave of cackles, followed by a whirr, as the Dubbs-roller passed through a larger garage door that another soldier had found and opened. Ignoring Dubbs, Boss looked over at Leon and gave him a meaningful nod. Its meaning, for now, went misunderstood.

"There he is, men! Move in!" bellowed a police officer from the rooftops. The officer had been following a red beam across the city over the course of the last day. Through his binocu-lenses he could finally see the man it was emitting from. He tapped his earpiece, activating it.

"Chief, we've got a visual. Moving in now. Numbers approximate seven, sir. Armed. Also, there's a tank."

"My God, did you say tank?"

"Yes, Chief. Some sort of metal box on tracks. I guess you'd call it a tank."

"Are there guns?"

The officer peered back around the billboard, binocu-lenses cranking back up the zoom. "It doesn't appear so, Chief."

"Then why'd you say 'tank'? Bloody hell, I near on shit myself! Will a handful of ground units do the trick?"

"That would be very helpful, Chief."

"I'll book them in."

"Thank you, Chief." There was a click.

The binocu-officer watched as his team moved in below. Already, Dubbs's militia had dispersed and taken cover, unaware of just how many officers were approaching. It didn't take long for the gunfire to start, though, and once it did, it seemed as if it would never stop.

Leon lay on the ground behind a family box car, keeping his legs tucked in and his ears covered. The group of ex-soldiers in charge of protecting Boss, Dubbs, and Leon joined together with the scouts and the leader, who began formulating some sort of plan in code words. Now that the firing had started, this was how it would be. Most of the militiamen were deserters and convicts-in-hiding, and to be caught would mean life imprisonment at best, anyways.

After the militia's quick huddle, they volleyed more bullets in all directions, forcing the newest teams of officers to take cover in this trench-like warfare. Boss dived across a gap and landed next to Leon.

"Think we can hold them off, Boss?"

"No chance, kid. It's a trap. We stay here much longer, we're gonna be Swiss cheese… And it won't be worth the cheddar."

Leon nodded. They too began making their own escape plan.

"The bright side, those guys are a great distraction." Leon risked a finger jerk in the direction of the militia.

Boss laughed, though it was barely audible over another burst of machine-gun fire. "It's 'cos they know they're fucked. They'll keep shooting until they're shot."

"Well let's get moving before that happens." With that, Leon rolled onto his feet and, keeping his head low, slid from car to car. Boss followed behind, leaving a good distance between them so that if one was spotted, it didn't give the other away. Leon had made it to the third street away before a team of officers blocked his path. He squeezed between the two front wheels of a parked van, trying to slow his breathing and hear any footsteps over his own heartbeat. He closed his eyes, as he wouldn't need them in this position, and focused instead on his breathing. A calm came over him much more quickly than he expected. There was something quite relaxing about handing one's life over to an idea of fate. He would either be found or he wouldn't. Nothing to do but wait and find out.

A moment of silence, and then the scuff of a boot on gravel. They were here. Leon took a deep breath and held it, listening. Another scuff. The approach was slow. That was okay; Leon had all the time in the world. Something clicked, and he heard a small charge pulsing through a circuit. Someone had activated tenta-binds. That was it, then. Game over.

"Come out with your hands up!"

Leon exhaled, long and slow. He thought it would feel different to this. He expected that realisation would hit him eventually, maybe on his first night behind bars, but for now, he felt nothing but peace. What will be, will be. He bent his head down to squeeze back out onto the street and into the binds of his captors when a voice froze him solid.

"I'm unarmed. Don't shoot!" It was Boss. Leon opened his eyes now and glanced under the parked cars. He could see Boss's feet walking out into the road. "I'm unarmed!" he repeated as the officers passed the van and headed towards Boss.

Leon began to panic now. He pulled his head back under the wheel arch, breathing increasing as adrenaline pushed through his veins. *Shit! They didn't see me!*

Smiling like a madman, Leon clambered out from under the back end of the van. All he could hear was his heart in his ears. It didn't matter. Fate had spoken; now was not his time. He just needed to keep moving.

Without looking back, he ran.

48

SEND-OFF

"**G**loomier than I remember," Voice said to Dubbs's assistant as they approached the building.

"Let me out!" growled Dubbs from the trunk.

Voice popped the trunk open, and Dubbs cooed as he felt butt cheek and side boob flop from the car. The assistant dove outside and approached where Dubbs lay, unable to exit the vehicle without aid.

The assistant removed a collapsible roller chair from the roof and assembled it on the road beside him. He pulled at Dubbs's clothing, watching parts of him slowly unclog the back of the car as Voice's suspension cried out for mercy. After a couple of long minutes—once a large portion of Dubbs was released—gravity helped the assistant finish the job. The reinforced wheels of the roller chair made some rather unhealthy sounds, but they managed to hold together against the weight. It took another few minutes for Dubbs to readjust the cushions into the right grooves.

Heading off to scout the area, the assistant did a very slow lap of the warehouse that Voice had brought them to. The conveyor belt seemed to be the only way in, but there was no way Dubbs could squeeze through the gap. He tugged pathetically at the chains across the main door, knowing they wouldn't budge, before he headed back to relay his findings. The assistant approached, listening in to the conversation between Dubbs and Voice.

"Obviously I don't like the man, but I do respect him. That, on top of everything he's done for me so far, has got to be worth *something*."

Voice's speakers crackled. "Of course, I understand. If you're my father, then he's practically my brother."

"Well, I'm not your father."

He continued on anyway. "He was in a tough situation and he knew what he needed to say to get out of it. It's what he does. It's all part of the skill set that you needed of him in the first place."

"I suppose that it's the facts that count. It would have been natural to consider turning me in, but he never actually followed through with it. The escape was his plan, you know? Back at C'Ville. He knew that they would still be tracking him, so he led the decoy away while you smuggled me out of the front gate. That sacrifice was his apology to me."

Mixed feelings brewed in the assistant's stomach, and now that he'd heard the full story, he felt his anger fall away. The assistant wanted to share his newly formed opinion. "If he's to be judged on his actions, then I'd say his most recent ones speak the loudest."

Dubbs turned to his assistant, who flinched and expected something resembling a scowl, as that was all he was used to receiving. Instead, Dubbs relaxed his brow, and for a moment, he looked more human than he had looked in years.

"Yes... Yes, you're quite right." He smiled, and nothing else could have made his assistant feel more uncomfortable. Another moment passed.

"Well, it is decided, then. There are three cartons of medication in the back. I will keep two for the zoners here. Be sure that Leon receives the third and supplies Boss whenever he can. It should be enough to keep him going for another few months. By then, I should have a new batch ready, depending on how that blood sample back in the vault proves. It may even be the last batch anyone will need."

The assistant removed two cartons from the back and walked them over to the warehouse, then placed them gently beside the large chained door. He also removed a backpack and placed it on top of the crates. Dubbs watched him carefully as the contents of the backpack rattled about. "Please be careful with that bag. It's the only lab supplies I had time to salvage. Hopefully the zoners have some things I can borrow, but I doubt they've anything this intricate."

The assistant nodded, making sure that it was secure, before he looked up to Dubbs. "Okay, now we just need to figure a way in. I don't think that conveyor belt would be…" He considered his words carefully, not wanting to infuriate Dubbs with any comment that could possibly be taken as a weight-based insult. "I just don't think it looks that safe."

"Lucky I came prepared!" roared Voice as he kicked his engine to life and slammed his doors shut. Without explaining any further, he drove in a semi-circle and backed up to the chained doors.

"Alright yo, hook me up!" A clunk followed Voice's words, and the assistant walked to the back of the car to see an unnecessarily thick chain with a large hook on the end, which extruded from the frame of the vehicle. The assistant pulled out a length and held it up so Dubbs could see what it was.

"Ah, so that's where the extra twenty-five grand went?"

"Most of it, but I also got myself some new speakers. The last ones were a bit fuzzy. They hurt my ears."

"You don't have ears, Voice."

"Don't blame me, Dubbs. You wrote the program."

"No, I never was any good at writing programs. I merely tweaked a few bits so that you would be more useful to me. Obviously I still haven't worked out all of the kinks."

"Speaking of kinks, would you be careful not to twist my chain as you connect it up? I got somewhere I need to be after this and don't want to embarrass myself if I can help it. Thanks, man."

Dubbs struck his palm to his face. He loved seeing his realistic emotion simulators at work, but sometimes they were nothing but a pain in the ass.

The assistant wrapped the chain around the binds on the door and hooked it on tight. He took his time as he waited for Dubbs—too stubborn to ask for help—to tediously wheel himself out from in front of Voice. When the assistant looked up to see that Dubbs was still trying to roll the chair out of the way, inch by inch, he did another few loops of the chain.

"You ready, Dubbs?" Voice asked casually, making the assistant cringe.

"For Christ's sakes, give me a minute!" Dubbs huffed.

One last loop of the chain, and now the assistant had used almost the entire length. There was nothing more he could do to stall for time, but the assistant decided Dubbs was far enough away now anyway. He tapped Voice on the side. "Okay, good to go!"

Giving the assistant barely half a second to get clear, Voice put his accelerator to full and set his chain to retract. There was little in the way of resistance as the entire door bent and ripped from its hinges, followed by a series of screeches and crashes as the rest of the wall caved in. Dust, splinters, and fragments kicked up all around the entrance, forcing Dubbs and his assistant to cover their faces with their shirt sleeves.

Voice whooped and took off down the street, the weight of the door causing him to fishtail in plumes of dust. The remaining two both watched him, shaking their heads, though neither could keep the amused grin off their faces.

"He always did like to do things in style," Dubbs managed through a still covered mouth.

"You think he's coming back?"

"I thought he would at least say goodbye before he took off." Dubbs sighed. "But perhaps not."

Dubbs shrugged and turned back towards the huge entrance. Sunlight ignited the dust in beams, pushing the shadows aside, which now clung ever tighter to the back-most corners. He began wheeling himself forwards and was thankful from the push by the assistant, although he would never acknowledge it.

"We've got a lot of work to get through, Dubbs." The assistant spoke as he looked down at the panel on the ground, remembering what Voice had told him about the hidden tunnel's entrance.

"Sure do, though it's not the first time I've had to start over." Dubbs thought fondly at how strong the signal from the blood was when it first arrived at his other office. He could almost be certain that the vial contained exactly what he needed. "Though I hope it will be the last time, with the help of that sample."

Dubbs must have been smiling again, because shivers ran down the assistant's spine. It happened whenever something wasn't quite right, and Dubbs in a good mood was a rare occurrence even on a good day. "Does something seem out of place to you, Dubbs? Can you feel that?"

Dubbs almost cackled. "Nope. Actually, I'm feeling pretty good about this."

Dubbs felt resistance in his wheels, and he struggled to push himself any further forwards. With great effort, he looked back over his shoulder and just caught a glimpse of his assistant, stood rigid with his hands raised. The crate he was carrying smashed heavily to the ground a moment later.

"Wha—?"

"Don't move. Hands in the air," spoke a muffled voice through a visor.

"Don't move, and also put my hands in the air?" Dubbs huffed.

The voice belonged to a police officer, who stepped forwards and cuffed Dubbs's wrist. Another officer cuffed the assistant. Only once they were both secured did the remaining officers emerge from the shadows, bio-hazard suits fastened, guns raised.

"Sorry, officers. Are we trespassing?"

"Cut the crap, Dubbs." Unlike the others, *this* voice wasn't muffled. It was clear, and Dubbs recognised it immediately. The blood froze in his veins. He felt his heart pause for a moment as it considered just cutting its losses and stopping altogether. Panic took on a physical form as it reached up from the ground and tugged at his shoulders and his lungs and his guts. Dubbs felt like he was going to implode. He thought of Boss's new blood collection method and how, with a few more months, he could immunise the masses from the lethal Bug.

"No. Please, not now. You can't!" Dubbs cried for mercy.

"You've been running a long time, Dubbs. No more hiding in the dark or looking over your shoulder. I'm here to free you; I thought you would thank me." The man who spoke stepped forwards from between the police officers now, and his face shook Dubbs to the core. It was the face that had been hunting Dubbs ever since his desertion from the government's Crowd Control Division. The face that had cut a deal with Boss before unknowingly infecting him with the Bug. The face which had followed Leon to the code-crackers and bribed the boys in charge. The face that had hired prototype Neuro-surrogates years before their development was complete, just to get the edge in the search for Dubbs's hideout. This face belonged to the fed.

"No. Please, it can't end here." Dubbs had, to his assistant's surprise, pulled himself from the chair, and he was grovelling on the concrete at the fed's feet.

The fed turned to the policeman beside him and said aloud, "Officer Kev, your excellent police work has led to the containment of our most wanted criminal and one of his associates. I commend you. Though before the promotion, I need you to do one last thing. The associate is… unnecessary." He followed this with a small hand gesture, and Kev raised his weapon to his eyes. As the fed let his hand drop, Kev let a bullet fly, and the single shot caught Dubbs's assistant square in the forehead, launching him backwards and out of the warehouse. Dubbs squeezed his eyes together, cracking one of his lenses and letting a tear run free.

Dubbs mumbled in self-pity. How close he was to finally ending this was what was killing him the most. So close to being able to make a cure, but also so close to the one man who could stop him from creating it. The fed hissed at the police officers, who grumbled among themselves as they exited the warehouse. Despite the heavy radiation suits, the air was cold. The clouds shifted into a darker grey and, before long, began their process of urinating on everything below. The fed continued, one on one.

"Impressed by the blood sample that I had Boss order, were you? I always did feel that I was the better scientist out of you and me. I couldn't believe you hadn't worked out how to collect such a sample yourself, after God knows how much trial and error. In your defence, though, it must have been hard working with second-rate equipment in some hidey-hole and with so much commuting between tests."

The fed kicked the backpack of lab gear and smiled again when he heard something crack. He leaned close, staring into Dubbs's black-hole eyes and soaking up the pain and sadness he saw there. He was enjoying it too much.

Dubbs closed his eyes and, against his atheism, mumbled a few prayers. The Bug was never meant to kill its host, only emit a traceable DNA signal to the scanner-crafts above. Its purpose was to make it easier to keep track of everyone in the ever-growing population. The citizens' arrest barcode-burners had been introduced a few years prior, but the system was open to too much exploitation. It was a temporary fix to keep the public subdued due to fear of one's neighbour, but it was never destined to survive the long haul. Dubbs's team was assembled in secret to develop signal-emitting bugs and release them into the water supplies. It meant that the police could watch whomever they wished without stirring the public with an increased presence on the streets. There would be less risk to police personnel, less wages, and more capital. The problem was that the Bug began to feed, breed, and grow.

For all the good it would do, Dubbs followed up his prayers with apologies. He apologised to his family, who had been killed in the testing of the first Bug strain in Zone A. He apologised to the zoners for sentencing them all to death. He apologised to the world in general for delivering such a destructive bio-weapon into the hands of the government and the police company.

The fed leaned closer, smelling the fear radiating from Dubbs. "Oh, by the way, I wanted you to know that the sample definitely would have worked. Just in case you still weren't completely sure—not that you have any chance of going back for it now. Its signal is so strong because it contains the Bug itself, not just the excrement or whatever you were only just managing to extract." The fed chuckled at his own wit. "We took a lot of risk allowing it to get to you. Had the patrol Neuro put on quite a show for the news cameras as it chased your wagon. I've enjoyed toying with the Pizza Boss, too; even had one of his men framed to void his probation. I'm going to eradicate everyone involved in this shitstorm of a mess, starting with you."

The fed wiped his eyes clear. His heart raced. He was finally living the moment that he had been planning for years. Excitement pushed itself into a menacing grin. His plan had come together perfectly. "You were meant to be on the side of your country," he snarled. "You were meant to help us keep our little hiccup quiet, not go off playing the hero with your cheap equipment and your mediocre medicines. But it was all for nothing now anyway. You're as good as dead."

He raised his voice. "Officer Kev, get back in here. Come and see what a man who crosses me looks like."

Kev trudged back in, wiping his visor. Both figures before Dubbs looked red-faced, menacing, and horrifically inhuman. Dubbs was staring at the fed, but he wasn't listening to him. He was busy focusing on a little red glow that he could see hitching a ride in a rain droplet on Kev's shoulder. Dubbs managed a smile.

Amusement creased the fed's face. "Something you would like to say, Dubbs? Before I kill you?"

"You're not quite as smart as you think."

The fed cackled loudly. "I really thought, with a brain as powerful as yours, that you could have mustered something a little more interesting. Well, I suppose knowing death is imminent must do some strange things to one's thoughts. I won't hold it against you." The fed's eyes darkened. He raised his arm to gesture as before, but this time, his arm fell, and the rest of him fell with it. He was dead before he hit the ground, for the red glow on Kev's shoulder belonged to the newest evolution of the droplet-hopping Bug, and in taking such enjoyment in tormenting Dubbs, the fed had worked up quite a sweat.

49

DUMBASS

THE INDICATORS OF THE DARK convoy ahead blinked left, and as if they were all on rails, one turned directly after the other, with Voice tailing close behind. The scanner-craft above was controlling the cars remotely, meaning that all five seats in all three cars, minus Boss's seat, of course, were able to hold armed men, all at the ready.

"How long till he breaks out of there, then?" Cookie tried to keep his tone light, as if he knew something would happen; it was more just a matter of when. He smiled, forcing himself to feel better about the situation. Voice didn't respond, and the monotony of silently tailing the convoy was quickly undermining all positivity that Cookie could muster.

"Seriously, though, I've dodged the cops twice so far this week. He's got some catching up to do." Cookie topped this off with a snort and sat back in his chair, hoping not to disturb the jovial air he was trying to create.

A sigh sounded over the speakers as one of Dubbs's human emotion scripts activated in Voice. "I hate to tell you this, man, but he won't be breaking out of there."

Cookie shrugged this off. "Of course he will."

"Dubbs was telling me the other day that Boss didn't get caught, man. He handed himself in."

Cookie's mind stiffened. He felt dazed and tried to shake his head clear. "What?"

"Okay, remember Marbles? Well he's more than likely doing some serious time. *Has* to be to warrant hiring Neuros to go after him. Boss has also done some things that he regrets—he's built his whole life around being a criminal. It's in his DNA. You know that; you know him better than anyone. By turning himself in, he's stayed in control of his own fate, which is all he's ever wanted, and he can look out for Marbles on the inside while he's at it."

Cookie looked dumbfounded. He gawped and flailed around inside the car for a moment before he realised that Voice couldn't see him and his display was going unnoticed. "Marbles?" He choked on the name. "That prick has been up to something from the start! I'm sure that he was tipping off the cops about our—"

"Wrong again, dude."

Cookie stopped suddenly and found himself leaning towards the speakers, waiting for Voice to explain.

"Boss has been trying to hand Dubbs over ever since getting out of jail. He never escaped, man, but was let free in exchange for Dubbs. When Boss finally had Dubbs within reach the other day, though, he found out that the fed who cut this deal had somehow infected Boss with the Bug from the zones. The sneaky bastard had never intended on letting Boss go free. The Bug would have killed him soon after he'd turned Dubbs over. So instead, Boss made a plan and helped Dubbs escape the Ville when it was all going down—his way of making amends about the whole situation."

Cookie sat back in total disbelief, strange gurgles flying from his flapping mouth before any decipherable words emerged. "Does that make him contagious?"

"It wasn't always contagious. Maybe he's got an old strain. I dunno, Dubbs will figure that out once the new lab's up and running."

Voice chirped up now, quite enjoying the irony of this string of events. "Haha, and I suppose Boss must feel like a complete crotch bulge since the only one who can save his ass from the Bug is the guy who he'd almost betrayed. I wish I was there when that conversation went down between them."

"So is Dubbs keeping Boss immunised?"

"Dubbs is a good man, and he stays true to his word."

Cookie hoped that that meant yes.

"Problem is, I still haven't heard from Dubbs since he nuked his labs."

"You know where he is, though, right? We could help him set up."

Voice clicked his digital tongue. "There's no way he would let me expose his new hiding spot."

Cookie was getting frustrated. "If he stays quiet for much longer, I think we should go and visit."

Voice snorted in response and slowed down, keeping his sensors peeled for Leon.

A smooth panther of a car lay resting to the side of the road. Leon emerged and closed its door behind him, then headed for the driverless car that approached. Voice stopped and lowered the window, and Leon waved. "Hey, guys." He peeked through at the interior. "Looking much better than the last time, Voice."

Voice responded casually. Cookie snapped out of his reverie and glanced up, distracted. "Oh, yeah. Nice to meet you. I'm Cookie."

"Ah, so it's you who I need to thank for allowing me to get pulled into this crazy pizza delivery business."

"It used to be a lot easier when we were just delivering drugs, believe me." He poked his hand out of the window. "So you must be this *Leon* I've been hearing about?"

"The one and only."

Cookie cocked an eyebrow. "Well, Boss appreciated your work, so thank you, on his behalf. I know he probably wouldn't have said it himself." Cookie glanced forwards and saw the convoy making a turn further down the street. He pulled his beeper phone out of his pocket and handed it to Leon. "I'd tell ya to hop in, but you probably shouldn't leave that beauty parked along the street around here. Take this and set it to frequency 92.1. It will transmit your comms to Voice's. You can follow us to the detention centre."

Leon took the device and headed back to Boss's petrol car. He tweaked a dial till it displayed the right frequency and spoke to the glowing screen of his comms. "You hear me?"

"Load and clear, pal," Cookie responded. "Now let's close this gap between us and our friends there."

Leon followed Voice closely, his arms shaking as they drew closer to the detention centre. The bleakness of the mood seemed to come in waves, pulsing between rather uncomfortable and almost completely overbearing. He needed to talk, just to hold the eeriness at bay.

"So what do you think is going on in there?" Leon sounded nervous.

Voice's speakers crackled. "Absolutely nothing. Boss is smart enough to know that if he wants this to work out, he needs to cooperate."

Despite Voice's wise words, Leon kept imagining one of the car doors swinging open and the agents being flung from the vehicle. Or maybe a series of muffled gunshots followed by Boss's emergence from the middle car. Leon imagined it so vividly that he could practically see it happening.

But it didn't.

The small convoy pulled into a gated driveway and waited for the multiple fences to close before anything else happened. Voice, unable to follow the cars any longer, pulled alongside the fence with Leon still close behind. The doors popped open and Leon stepped up onto the doorframe, then looked through the fences. Cookie stepped up beside him, and they both watched as the convoy doors all opened at once and the fourteen armed officers surrounded the door that Boss stumbled from. He was struggling with the vast number of shackles and tenta-binds holding him.

Once on his feet, his precious car drew his attention and Boss smiled inwardly as he caught a glimpse of Leon. He noticed that the other car was Voice, too, and had yet again changed chassis, which helped the smile reach his face. It felt strange to no longer care about something that would have infuriated him to no end only a few days before.

The fact that Dubbs had sent Voice was a message in itself, and it wasn't lost on Boss. Dubbs would keep his promise and would get his medication to Boss somehow.

"I owe ya one, fellas," he yelled as loudly as he could, knowing that he wouldn't get a chance to repeat himself. As he did so, the officers closed in, and one fastened a muzzle over his face. It didn't take long before the entire party was secured inside the building. Leon continued to watch, unable to believe what he had just seen. Before, Boss had been indestructible, or so it seemed. Not just an enraged mass of muscles and profanities, but a symbol of resistance, persistence, strength, and whatever else. Leon couldn't think of the exact words, but *he* knew what he meant, and since he was only talking to himself, then that was all that mattered. He thought that Cookie would have probably known what he meant, too, as he had known Boss for what sounded like most of his life.

Leon stepped down to road level and dropped himself back into the seat, sighing heavily and leaning right back against the cushion.

Voice broke the quiet. "He will be fine. You know it."

"Of course he will. He can take care of himself better than anyone. It's just..." Leon sighed again. "I just feel bad that it turned out this way, like I owe him an apology."

Cookie spoke across the comms this time. "It's not your fault."

"No. But I never gave him enough credit."

"But you stuck around, even when you wanted out. He recognised that. Don't worry; some things don't need to be said."

Leon nodded slowly. "I know you're right." And he did, though it didn't help him feel any better. Leon couldn't help but wonder that if Boss had fought back at the tunnel entrance instead of surrendering so quickly, could he have escaped with Leon? Then they could have busted Marbles out of jail somehow, the way he had busted himself out before, closed the shop, and started again somewhere else.

The scenario played on repeat in his mind. "I just wish he had fought back. I got away, and he could have, too. I should have helped him instead of just running off."

Cookie huffed, not really bothered about having this conversation again but understanding how Leon must have felt since he didn't know the facts. "There was nothing you could do, Leon. Boss was planning on handing himself over."

Leon's face mimicked the one that Cookie had pulled at Voice only a few minutes ago.

"Long story short, he's gone in to watch over Marbles." Cookie still held some hostile feelings towards Marbles, though he wasn't too sure why. It was almost like he preferred Marbles when he thought he was a backstabber, because the truth of it was actually worse.

Leon considered this, drifting into a daydream. When the sealed door inside the fences reopened, he didn't notice.

The oiled gates slid silently apart as Leon continued to sit there and stare at the wheel in front of him. He subconsciously reached for a thick cigar that he had brought in Boss's honour, and he lit it up without saying a word.

Something rapped at the window. Leon jumped back to reality and turned to see a confused face staring in at him.

"How did you guys know I was getting out?" the confused face asked.

Leon just kept the stare, not believing his eyes. Leon lowered his window and Marbles leaned in. "You here to give me a ride?"

"What? No, we came to say bye to Boss. He turned himself in."

Marbles's confusion multiplied. "Why?"

"So that you had someone looking out for you on the *inside*. What the hell are you doing *outside*?"

"I told you guys I hadn't done anything. Those assholes at Grey Town switched my barcode with one of theirs and tried to frame me for a cop murder or something. They have caught on to the real murderer now, though, so my name's been cleared. Well, cleared for the murder, at least.

I've still got some community service for cracking into the barcode."

Leon couldn't believe what he was hearing. Boss's entire sacrifice now seemed all but pointless. He should have just shut down the shop and moved on or gone into hiding with Dubbs or started a new business somewhere with Cookie or moved to the zone and lived off of his own pizzas. *Anything* but go to jail for *nothing*. Leon faced the wheel again and took a long draw on the cigar. "Shit," was all he managed to say.

Voice turned up his outbound and pierced the atmosphere with a few words. "Guys, we expecting anyone else?"

"No." Leon lifted the passenger's seat door. "Marbles, get in."

Marbles did as he was told and clambered in beside Leon. At the end of the street, a large black vehicle had emerged, its windows tinted and engine whining. It wasn't the same type as the ones from the convoy. Cookie squinted through the sunlight as it approached, unable to make out the driver. "Who is it, Voice?"

"I'm not too sure."

The group continued to watch as the car kept its speed steady and headed straight towards them along the side of the detention centre. When the car came to within twenty metres, the side window rolled down, and the passenger leaned out, resting on thick arms. He held a large automatic rifle in his hands, a chunky barcode tattoo on his wrist, and one angry snarl on his face. "Fuckin' rat!"

The man opened fire on the parked cars, blowing out all the windows before speeding past in a cloud of steam. Cookie, who had dived flat across the front seats, yelled across the comms. "You guys alright? Anyone hurt?"

A moment passed as Leon and Marbles felt themselves over for bullet holes. "I think we're okay, Cookie."

Leon raised his head first and checked the mirror to see that the mark-cracker's car was coming back, and this time he wasn't the only one. The sound of a distant mosquito tickled at his ears, and behind the approaching car he saw what appeared to be a seething migration of bugs. After a double take, Leon realised that it was a six-wide span of black vans made tiny in the reflection, and all were whirring and buzzing loudly as they approached.

Armed guards stepped from the outpost and the entry gate started to slide open.

"Everyone buckled up?" Voice chirped.

Marbles fumbled with his seat belt clip. He was breathing deep and deliberate, trying to calm himself.

"Running out of time, boys. It looks like there's a scanner-craft inbound, too. I don't want to get stuck in the middle of this thing." Cookie was leaning out of his window, looking up at the large silver disk making its way slowly but surely in their direction. It cast a shadow over the nearby buildings as it moved.

Leon helped Marbles with his seat belt, doing his best to calm the nervous passenger. Voice revved a challenge to the vehicles behind the fast-closing gap of road. "Alright, let's see how far the rest of Boss's gas-go credits can get us. Hold on tight!" With that, his theoretical foot slammed the accelerator and held it to the ground. Leon followed suit. Dust and stones and rubber flew from behind them as bullets chased them down the street. Leon spoke as clearly as he could manage over the thunderous engine and Marbles's wailing. "Once we lose this lot, I think we should hide out with Dubbs. Lie low for a while."

Cookie eagerly agreed. "Exactly. You hear that, Voice?"

Voice didn't respond but set to work on finding a plausible alternative, for Dubbs's sake. He pulled from the side road to a main road, then back onto a highway that led straight to the city's outskirts. He continued to compute the data, but no alternatives presented themselves. A pink splash painted the horizon ahead of them as the buildings became smaller and the sky grew larger. At the speed they were going, Leon felt they could suspend themselves in an eternal sunset as they chased it around the spinning globe, mark-crackers lagging far, far behind.

GUITAR MAN

As I walked the concrete path
of Human presence aftermath —
A sound pulled me from reverie
and teased my ears a peak.
Midst chattered voices, crowded through,
A lonesome bird, a dog or two,
There came a strum of instrument
that slowed my walk to sneak.

While holding breath I stepped anew,
Upon this ground where nothing grew —
Yet no one else had faltered,
Maybe only I had heard?
I closed my eyes and followed sound
now resonating all around,
Which led me to a man who strummed
without a singing word.

Belongings gathered in a pile —
It looked like he'd been there a while,
And planned to stay a while more
where blankets covered street.
Yet still he plucked acoustic string,
So hopeful on what it might bring,
And all the while a sign requested
coins, so he could eat.

His chords reflected in me, true,
As from his strumming, sadness flew —
For in his sound I heard the
weeping sky and Wilting earth.
I asked of that man, quietly,
"How is it that, so clear, you see?"
And in response, his clouded eyes
said he'd been blind since birth.

Jon writes poetry at www.jbestbooks.com

THE AUTHOR

Although originally from England, Jon now lives in a tin shed in the baking wastes of Western Australia. Among other escapades, he does still delivers the occasional pizza… Just to keep an eye on things.

Join the resistance: facebook.com/jonbestauthor
Stay in the loop: twitter.com/jbestbooks
Read poetry and more: jbestbooks.com

Reviews are gold to authors! If you've enjoyed this book, would you please consider rating it on Amazon and Goodreads?